The Liquid Land

THE
LIQUID
LAND

Raphaela Edelbauer

Translated from the German by Jen Calleja

SCRIBE

Melbourne • London

Scribe Publications
2 John St, Clerkenwell, London, WC1N 2ES, United Kingdom
18–20 Edward St, Brunswick, Victoria 3056, Australia
3754 Pleasant Ave, Suite 100, Minneapolis, Minnesota 55409, USA

Published by Scribe 2021

Typeset in Adobe Garamond by the publishers

Printed and bound in the UK by CPI Group (UK) Ltd, Croydon CR0 4YY

Scribe is committed to the sustainable use of natural resources and the use of
paper products made responsibly from those resources.

978 1 913348 07 6 (UK edition)
978 1 925849 96 7 (Australian edition)
978 1 925938 98 2 (ebook)

This publication has been supported by the Austrian Federal Ministry for Art,
Culture, Public service, and Sport.

Catalogue records for this book are available from the National Library of
Australia and the British Library.

scribepublications.co.uk
scribepublications.com.au
scribepublications.com

1

In the small hours of 21 September 2007, I spilled around 200 millilitres of coffee over my insistently ringing mobile phone, which had so abruptly prompted me to pick it up, disturbing me with its withheld number, that I didn't have time to put down my cup. Vexed by the interruption to my work, it took me a few seconds to comprehend who was speaking to me. A policeman was on the line, and, without the verbiage of an elaborate greeting, he told me that my parents had been killed in a car accident that night. 'Killed?' I asked, even though I had understood immediately. While I continued to stare at my talk on vector spaces, and watched the intricate scalar products dance before my eyes, the officer informed me what had happened: the red Audi, the licence plate of which having been used to identify my parents, must have come off the road last night and swerved down a scree in the vicinity of Syhrn Valley like an avalanche. The peculiar thing was, the officer explained to me, that neither of them exhibited any wounds or bruising. There was a dented section on the car resulting from the confrontation with the crash barrier, and yet there was much to suggest that this was not the cause of their deaths.

The vehicle must have slid towards the slope at a rate of infinite slowness after the impact, rolling sluggishly onto its back like a dying insect, before finally slipping, softly grinding as it went, over the ridge into the depths. The descent, which had been completely invisible to other drivers on the Semmering Expressway due to heavy fog, had probably come to its soundless end in a common oak tree, according to the policeman.

I was sitting in bed in pyjama bottoms and a bra, my laptop with the script of my inaugural lecture open on my knees, and suddenly found myself in the middle of a painting with erroneous perspective: the corners of my apartment, the park outside my window, every chair, every shelf began to creak into motion, jamming up against one another. The man on the telephone continued undeterred, keen to bring his diplomatic task to a close: it is, therefore, clear that the impact did not lead to their deaths, nor had (and he stressed this) the road-construction measures been responsible for this tragic accident. The pathologist's report would bring us certainty about the cause of death in a few days, the man told me, and I could tell from his tone, which fluctuated between the style of a traffic officer and a detective, that he was also facing this situation for the first time. But by then we had both mechanically said goodbye and hung up.

For an endless morning I lay silently in my nightwear, alternating between lying on my side, my stomach, and my back. From my bed, I watched the metronomic phases of the traffic lights outside my window until I gradually gave up hope that a change would occur within me. Instead, I was overcome by an intimation from which a certainty slowly emerged: I had evidently long been part of a calculation, a ceremony put in place prior to my birth that was now about to unfold. A cosmic barrel organ had been cranked into motion. All the roles had been allocated, the cogs meshed together, all cylinders in the mechanics were waiting to be called for their mourning duty: I would, of course, organise a funeral.

No sooner had I thought these words than I was able to act. I got dressed: my new tights had a silky sheen as I released them from their packaging. I made coffee and opened an Excel document. Over the next few hours, I itemised requirements, compiled those in need of notification into a mailing list, collected addresses for undertakers and parables for the card of condolence. I got things moving and postponed my work commitments. That meant first cancelling my lecture and postponing a meeting with the supervisor of my postdoctoral thesis.

'That won't be a problem, Ruth, I'll send you confirmation of compassionate leave right away,' the secretary of the institute told me gently. 'We'll inform the students that your class will start a week later.'

It was now twelve o'clock, and because it was a Friday, the students sprang from the New Institute Building across the street and surged into the tram in formation; in their hands, ready for flinging, were suitcases of dirty laundry, which their Upper Austrian or Styrian mothers would transfer into the washing machine in just a few hours. I, on the other hand, felt as constricted as if my silent apartment had tightened itself around me. I forced my breathing into a rhythm, closed my eyes for a few minutes, and waited for my pulse to even out again. Nevertheless, a pressure was released: I cried, loudly but briefly, thinking of my parents, my father's firm hug, my mother's perfume, sitting together at the dining table all those years, singing at Advent, the quarrels — a thousand little moments that rushed at me in complete disarray, while I braced myself on the bed. It only lasted a moment and then vanished again, as if my body couldn't yet contain the pain, and a nothingness wrangled a place in its stead. Complete silence once more: only a ticking sound coming from the gas boiler.

It became imperative to do something. I fetched two Xanax from the bathroom cabinet, then lay on the couch and swaddled myself in a quilt. I was so exhausted from the past few hours that I finally nodded off: the couch seeped murkily into the living room wall, and into the greyish, cloudy mood of the early afternoon.

When I came to, my back was weighed down by a moving load. Hands were rubbing my shoulders, verifying I'd had a shock. Indeed, it was a reminder: I had opened the door for my aunt and two of my cousins, who had received the news shortly after I had. Each of them had her hair firmly clamped to the back of her head in a bun and was dressed in black, so that all three looked identical in every way.

My aunt had put her arm around me and had laid out food she'd brought on the table, knowing that I hadn't partaken of anything all day.

'Ruth, you know we can help with the household and with everything else. That's the least we can do.' My aunt was facing me, and yet her words reached me on a delay. We were soon embroiled in a serious conversation about the arrangements of the funeral when I dropped a glass, which, in my mental absence, someone had filled with orange juice. I watched the liquid run unchecked beneath my sofa and I had no means of stopping it.

The table slipped away beneath my palms, the furniture was unfamiliar to me, even though it was mine. The handkerchiefs drawn by my cousins, the mobile phones vibrating endlessly, the solar disk passing over the firmament, the rhythmically falling tears from my own and other people's ducts keeping time, the bellows of my lungs operating in the empty space. The processes were sundered from their logical interrelationships, I thought. *You've had a shock*, one of my cousins repeated senselessly and pushed my hair against the grain — into my field of vision instead of out from it.

My aunt explained to me between trumpet blasts from her full-to-bursting nose that it had been the unwavering and incontestable will of my parents to be buried in Greater Einland. 'Greater Einland,' I said several times, in order to recall this long-forgotten name. 'Greater Einland, Greater Einland, Greater Einland.'

'Greater Einland,' my aunt proclaimed as a final amen, then I jumped to my feet.

(Greater Einland: I'd last heard this name twenty-five years ago and rediscovered it that evening in a tingling, revitalising déjà-vu. Like many people who had worked their way up from humble circumstances, my parents had taken care their entire lives to hide their rural origins. Of course, they went much further than most other people: as far as I could remember, we had never visited my parents' hometown — and since my aunt, who was my mother's half-sister, had grown up in Graz, and the relations on my father's side had broken away right from the start, I didn't know anyone who had ever been to Greater Einland.)

I had to drive there right now, I explained, and take care of everything else in Greater Einland. I would drive there alone and immediately, about which, I entreated my aunt, there would be no discussion. I wanted to clarify the possibility of acquiring a grave plot in the desired cemetery, otherwise it wouldn't even be possible to arrange the transportation of the bodies. A guesthouse would need to be procured, ground-floor level lodgings for the older generation, no doubt a small brass band and marble cherubim, I concluded, determinedly pushing both cousinly bodies towards the door. I had the urgent need to be alone. I was being firmly grasped by the shoulders, but I twisted free of this hold and uttered appeasements that instantly fizzled out.

'Please get in touch first thing tomorrow, otherwise we'll worry,' I still managed to hear, then saw my aunt and her cohorts disappear into the stairwell. I set about packing for my departure right away, ignoring my mobile, which was ringing almost relentlessly. All these relatives wanting to express their condolences or to extract the details about the exact circumstances of the deaths from me, until, after about the fifth call, I decided to switch it off. The falling night stripped the contours from the slats of the parquet floor, on which I piled my clothes. My luggage comprised the following: five shirts, two blouses, two dresses, four pairs of trousers, one pair of shorts, a coat, seven pairs of socks, five pairs of underwear, four bras, two towels, running shoes, trainers, high heels and ankle boots, a laptop, Xanax, phenobarbital, modafinil, oxycodone, an MP3 player, ten books (Wittgenstein, Serner, Max Brod, Tristan Tzara, six standards works on physics), and a small bag of toiletries. This was all I would have with me for the next three years. At that moment, I wanted to shed my apartment like an old pair of shoes. I took several stairs at once as I hurtled from the fifth floor to the ground floor, and got into my car. *It has to be this way*, I thought feverishly as I started the car; it was my duty to organise a decent burial without delay.

As I was leaving Vienna, I was overcome by an infinite sense of relief: my chest was relieved of a dull pressure. When a valley opened up before me at Alland, it seemed to me to be an act of providence, and I twisted deeper and deeper into the blackening scenery. I fleetingly wondered if I should tell one of my friends about what had happened, but I found the idea repugnant. The roads were empty, and by two in the morning the highway had nestled into the landscape, which I, of course, could only surmise in the prevailing darkness. It was only when the stony screen of the Semmering mountain pass appeared before me that a change took place. A plunge as if under a blanket: needle-like viridescence fumed into my brain; I had cranked down all the windows, and felt my car billowing with autumnal air from the inside. It smelled so good and fresh that the vanilla aroma of the tree-shaped air-freshener suddenly irritated me — I tore it from the mirror and threw it outside.

I took a random exit to the left: I had absolutely no idea where I was going. Yes, I did know: Greater Einland, only I had driven off without any idea of where Greater Einland actually was. As if to protect myself I turned up the radio, from which Janet Jackson was blaring, but she was soon swallowed up by the sound of the wind rushing into the car. The moisture-saturated air whistled in through the windows; I only vaguely comprehended that the treetops were swaying in the fallen blackness. I have never been the best driver, and I was struggling to control the ageing Ford: I must have accidentally found myself on a forest road, because my tyres kept slipping as if I were driving on bare earth, but there wasn't enough room to turn around. And then I came to a tarmacked road, and thought momentarily that I could make out a signpost, which, as I got closer, turned out to be a large piece of branch, and continued on my way without a pause on a slight incline. I felt hot, driven on by the landmasses that sloshed around one another. Then the route snaked up a hill on winding roads. For the first time I realised the significance: both dead, both died at the same time, and on some accursed road in the middle of nowhere.

The more alpine my surroundings became, the more graceful the undulations in the rugged rocks, the steeper the roads, the gnarlier the forest. I saw rippling ridges appear all over the meadows, break, then disappear again. The wind seemed to be pushing against the forest, the forest against the fog, and the fog against the grasslands, which piled up towards the clouds, distressing them. And I was no less moved by it than nature itself was: something that had kept me in the world up to now had become unhinged. The whole countryside rose up beneath me; I was sailing upon the wavetrains of a liquid mass. My hands trembled in their grip on the steering wheel, and the contractions of my tense body made the car lurch dangerously. I had to evade the land's grasp, and that a sign for a rest stop appeared at this very moment was a signal from heaven.

As soon as I drove onto the concreted area, these imposing impressions came to an end. This comfort station for drivers — the most banal of all places — brought me back to reality. Behind the still virtually opaque wall of rain I made out a fix-mounted set of chairs, littered with used serviettes and plastic plates. The manmade structure, no matter how disgusting it was (half-eaten sausages, spent porno mags, and tampons had been discarded on the hedged pathways, trampled for the sake of nature's call), released me in that moment. The ground had stopped shaking.

The engine hadn't been off for even a minute and I began to freeze, and because I assumed that the toilets would be heated, I grabbed my sleeping bag and waded through the sodden meadow to the little cabin. No feelings of disgust, alienation, displacement: all that was left for me to do was to wedge myself in while sitting on the toilet pan and sink into sleep.

When I powered up the following morning it seemed like only a moment had passed, but someone was thundering their shoes against the partition, causing the whole structure to tremble. It took a minute before I could feel my legs again, another to mobilise my wound-tight lower back, and one more to finally venture in the direction of the door, from where several voices were cursing me. I finally unlocked it. A corpulent man in blue overalls pushed into the cabin so aggressively I was thrown off course and, without further ado, left the toilet on the spot. The queue was massive:

furthermore, I had spent the night in the men's bathroom. I reached my car amidst whistling and hollering — my neck stiff, yesterday evening nothing more than a strange memory.

Still, the air was mild, and as I wondered about the sudden surge of warmth that mingled with the scent of the freshly drenched meadows, I realised I was in the forest. Surrounding the toilet cabin where I had spent the night, in the midst of an otherwise heathlike landscape, small clusters of trees could be seen merging together on the horizon to form an ocean. It hit me, the Wechsel mountain range; and indeed, when I finally retraced yesterday's odyssey on the map, I discovered that I must have alighted in a gorge near Feistritz. The car was modestly damaged, that is, the exhaust and bumper were noticeably battered and being held just off the ground by two thin wires. I took out the road atlas from the side door to determine where I actually had to go. Greater Einland — this name could not be found in the glossary, and apparently, I was already too high up to have internet reception. With attentive care I once more reviewed each of the sub-maps that comprised the Wechsel area, but that, too, was unsuccessful. A phone call, then: the directory provided me with the number for the Provincial Government of Lower Austria, which in turn gave me the number for the local authority: 'Good morning,' I said, 'I'm looking for a town by the name of Greater Einland in the Wechsel region.'

'Greater Einland?' the lady asked, hammering the letters into her machine. 'No, there's nowhere by that name in Lower Austria.'

'That can't be.'

'But Wechsel also borders Styria — perhaps it's in their territory. I'll give you the number,' the lady offered; ergo, I called the Austrian Federal Administration to ask the same question, but no, there wasn't, the Federal lady said this time, a place by that name in her listings. 'A merger, an incorporation maybe?' I asked hopefully.

A pause. 'No. There's never been a Greater Einland in Austria.'

I hung up without saying anything, and sat silently on the bonnet for a while. Only now, when I had to find it for the funeral, did I realise how little I actually knew about Greater Einland: just that it had to be somewhere in the Wechsel region, because that's what I'd heard my parents say when others asked. But I hadn't broached the subject with them for a number of years. Not because I had found it uncomfortable or had considered it taboo: the past just seemed to be irrelevant. Holidays were the opportunity to rush away, to flee the continent with closed eyes, on an aeroplane if possible — but never to dive deeper into our so-called origins or even go skiing like everyone else, whom we secretly despised for it.

It was what was shared between the lines that came back to me most strikingly: I remembered my mother telling me that in Greater Einland you could climb underground with a ladder. 'In a damp cavern, ten or fifteen metres high at least, there were old aeroplane parts that we used to build dens with as children. Sheet metal doors, armoured glass, and then there were wing parts we would see-saw on,' she'd said.

Or the no less thrilling story my father would tell: during my primary school days, curled up together in front of the woodstove's eerily crackling fire in our living room, he spoke of someone called Hans the Woodcutter, who had bought a shed next to his childhood house. It was winter, and whenever my father brought his cup to his mouth in the middle of telling the story, he spilled a little black tea into his beard, which would drip onto my legs as if from a stalactite.

Hans the Woodcutter locked himself away in his shed every evening bang on ten o'clock. This was where, my father whispered into my ear, he had collected the hearts of every mammal, one placed next to the other in glass jars filled with formaldehyde, and among them: a human heart, but no one knew exactly where he had got it from. 'And as boys,' he said, 'we threw stones at the window pane, in silent dread and urgent anticipation that Hans might appear, clutching one of his preservation jars.'

It was the first of those rare moments when I heard him talk a little about his own childhood, but what does a horror story like this tell me? I was lost.

2

I spent the second night kneeling on the floor of a guesthouse in Kirchberg am Wechsel. Bed and nightstand were encased in heavy, dark-wood panelling, a Bible in the armoire and an event calendar from the tourist association from the year 1998 on the wall. The landlady had brought me goulash and a bottle of beer; I was the sole guest. It slowly got dark, and I could hardly make out the work of the elapsed hours that lay before me on the floor: a carpet comprised of countless pieces of paper, from which annotated notes branched out all sides. *A memory map*, I had said to myself, and had started with a sketch on an A4 sheet. It was supposed to connect all the things my parents had ever told me about Greater Einland. Soon, however, the drawing had proliferated out the sides of the much too small sheet, become too voluminous, so that I attached another one to it with tape without foreseeing that the boundless expansion of my thoughts would soon lead into the dozens. But one recollection simply led me to the next, and I couldn't write down an event without it throwing up three more. This was how I suddenly realised that six hours had passed; space-time buckled by the gravitation of my thoughts.

13

Earlier that afternoon, it had suddenly felt like autumn; the air was damp and cool. When I set off from the toilet in which I'd slept, in the first direction I headed, the hoarfrost was already hanging from the branches on the highlands and dripping on the still-warm earth.

The Wechsel fans out before a traveller coming from Vienna wanting to cross the mountain pass to Styria — a lunarscape furrowed by lower peaks. Sloping rock surfaces rise up and fall back into gorges, in which alpine streams have cut deep into the landscape over the course of millions of years. Pyrite stockpiles, gleaming strangely, lead into soft alpine pastures. The Wechsel would have looked like the surface of a remote planet, if there hadn't also been a hotel complex on every protrusion of this pre-alpine mountain, to which German tourists flock in both winter and summer: groups of pensioners decked out as if intending to climb K2, spending the day shuttling from one ice cream parlour to the next. New money and old money, dressed in polo shirts, lie on the levelled surfaces a foreign entrepreneur had chiselled out of the stone, then concreted over, then given the name 'Nature Hotel'. I had stopped at one of these places to take out some money, afraid, as I always was, that nothing would come out of the machine in the last week of the month, I still had just under two hundred euros.

At lunchtime, hunger had forced me into one of the hotel cafés: a dining room reminiscent of service station, crammed with Japanese tourists, who were unloaded from the buses every hour and driven back in good time — a few locals among them, who had arranged themselves optimally in this showcase. Stiff from the night before, none of this mattered to me for a moment: I had submitted, passively, to these streams of people and was swept inside with them. We were led past the glass fronts of the confectionary shop in miserably slow-moving columns, only to end up run aground on one of the benches. I was particularly horrified that they were selling punch cakes with Ludwig Wittgenstein's face on them.

'What'll it be, young lady?'

The waitress wore the white, double-breasted imperial-and-royal confectioners' garb, like the ones in old illustrations. Caught off-guard by the speed with which I had been addressed, I ordered a typical Viennese breakfast and, discombobulated, one of the Wittgenstein cakes, which, when it was brought over, I left untouched like a devotional object.

I clung bleary-eyed to my large white coffee and pieced together yesterday's route in my road atlas. Essentially, I had driven parallel to Semmeringstrasse, then over it, then back in the other direction and so on, so that I ultimately delineated a circle right over Ramsattel, Steiersberg, and Liesling. Amid the incessant shrieks of the children at the neighbouring table, who were pelting one other with scrunched-up paper napkins, I threw everything back into my handbag and headed for my car. The wind pressure thundered over the mountain ridges in strong, erratic thrusts — every tree trunk swayed and passed on its swaying to a thousand branches, which, in their quirky choreography, passed on their interference to the individual leaf surfaces, which surely couldn't have known anything of the initial tremoring. There was that strange tension in the world that appears shortly before a rupture; fields of clouds rubbing up against one another, from which something threatens to fall at any moment —

With my legs wet up to my knees, I had decided that I had to seek out proper lodgings. In the next town over, Trattenbach, I found what I was looking for: a sign on the main road had directed me to a taciturn landlady, who handed me the keys for a so-called guestroom. Alone in the dreary, claustrophobically narrow chamber in the middle of nowhere, I once again re-evaluated what could give me useful information regarding Greater Einland, but at some point, I inevitably came back to the fact that all I had left were my parents' stories. From then until late into the night I was occupied with creating a kind of mind map that soon covered the entire floor of the room and laid bare everything my parents had ever mentioned about their origins. I linked story with story to form a ganglionic network, through which blood finally began to flow in the late hours of the night. The fact that neither of them had had to leave the town in order to attend high school provided information about the dimensions of the place. I also vaguely remembered my mother telling me that she had been looked after by nuns in kindergarten, but my father hadn't been — in which case it was likely that there were two kindergartens. Then there was the fact I'd heard my father tell how as a boy he had been caught setting off firecrackers on the steps of the evangelical church. The evangelical church — one could only imagine what that meant in rural Austria. I began to estimate Greater Einland to have around 10,000 inhabitants. But then I realised how hasty this conclusion was, for which counterarguments could easily have been made. It was too little — too little proof of everything.

I had to start working from other, more personal nodes, where there was hardly any room for interpretation: it was Easter '93 or '94, and I was at the height of adolescent dismissiveness, but still lured outside by the egg hunt, which never lost its charm. I had come across *Legend of Zelda: Link's Awakening* hanging in the apple tree, and my father and I were sitting on the garden chairs underneath the oak in our garden, which we called an English garden, simply so we didn't have to mow the lawn every week.

I was bent over my game, Dad over some molecular-biology literature; silent harmony in the garden with the scent of spring. At some point a light drizzle set in, and we huddled under the tree. My father heroically held his book over my Gameboy while I tried to save my score.

'Do you know why I planted this tree?'

I closed my eyes on the floor of the guesthouse and thought I could still recall the exact wording. 'When I was a child, we went to the Thousand-Year-Old Oak Tavern every other evening. They had an ancient tree, at least ten times as thick as this one, which the tavern had to be built around at some point, because it kept growing for years. An oak that ran right through the middle of the building.'

'An oak can't be a thousand,' I had said.

'Behind the tavern there were silos, vineyards, concrete pipes that led heaven knows where. And Haflinger horses. The oak was one of the few things that I missed in Vienna, and that's why I planted this one.'

So there was a perennial wine garden (a Heuriger), not a seasonal wine shop and inn (a Buschenschank), which meant that Greater Einland was on the Lower Austrian side of the Wechsel. The mere fact that the tree had grown so well there narrowed my search even further, as flicking through a nature guide in the guesthouse revealed that oaks didn't thrive at altitudes of over seven hundred metres above sea level. But those vineyards — how could there be vineyards in the Wechsel, where there are no winegrowers, where the slopes shoot straight down? Or was I remembering it incorrectly? Had it actually been cider?

I had been kneeling on the floor so long that my legs had gone to sleep, and I used that as an excuse to get myself another bottle of beer from downstairs. The goulash on the side table had long gone cold. I lay on my stomach and continued to spin the threads of my memory.

I had been told dozens of times how the two of them met, and I had absentmindedly heard the story whizz by, its provincial romance halting it, giving it the sluggishness of a slow-moving train. My father, Erich Schwarz, grew up in the parental home of my mother, Elisabeth Schalla, from the age of two. The exact reason for this had been fiercely suppressed because in the broadest sense it had to do with the fact my single paternal grandmother was unable to keep him after a series of so-called hysterical breakdowns. This must have been around 1944 or '45 — in any case it was a time when those living with mental illness weren't helped by medical professionals, and orphaned boys were not given the security of a state-mediated foster family. In order to spare little Erich the fate of growing up in an orphanage in the now crumbling German Reich, my mother's family, neighbours of the family Schwarz, took him in. This is what I always found strangest: growing up as siblings; later, the adoption revoked before the family court to circumvent the ban on incest. There was something inappropriate about it, even though there was no blood relation.

The now father of two, the woodcutter Joseph Schalla, had integrated the child so completely and without question into the family that the preparation for the take-up of the mantle began immediately. This, too, was still fresh in my mind because my father had repeated it on every hike, but above all because it was always very special for me to hear something about his childhood: Joseph, he said, had carried him as a small child into the forest on his shoulders, on steep, damp slopes that in spring exhaled all of the mustiness of the winter. He had trained his eye for the strength of one stock and the weakness of another. The weak had to be ignored, but if a tree had grown straight, it would bring him a mischievous pleasure. He would then lean back against the bark, his head tilted so the wood scratched his scalp, look up into the sky, and say: *This is good growth*.

While my father told me this, he had often lifted me up onto his own shoulders and leaned back against a tree, but mostly against crooked ones, I now remembered. I drew small, branchlike lines of thought leading off from the main story: while my grandfather had tried to hammer home the criteria of the value of wood as a commodity for the boy, he was instead interested in the taxonomy, relation, and internal functioning of those plants, whose international shipping ought to have become his main concern. Since he was a child, my mother always told me, it was impossible to go down a tree-lined road, or take a city trip, without factoring in a couple of extra hours each way, because he lingered over all the branches and buds of the local flora with a classification guide. I struck out these details. They had nothing to do with the point in hand.

I drew a line away from the main story and added four more notes: my mother had inherited the entrepreneurial spirit — had already put on a show at every flea market by the age of ten or twelve, seized every opportunity to mow someone's lawn. My polyglot mother, who would lie in bed all day with language textbooks, who had carved out her perfect French, and learned Norwegian — everything to prepare for the export.

On top of this I could think of a myriad of situations where I wished I'd listened more carefully. A barbeque, for instance, at which I'm fifteen, and all around us in the little Viennese garden are all my parents' old friends, who were always at the door on summer evenings: somehow the conversation turned to first loves, and everyone began to tell their story in turn. I can still clearly remember the urgent flight reflex that seized me. I had always avoided conversations that had anything to do with this subject, had attempted to steer the conversation to other areas or had withdrawn to my room on a flimsy pretext, in the hope that no one would notice how on edge I was. But on this day, it had been impossible. We were, after all, in the middle of eating dinner, and I felt captive by the idea that someone could quiz me. Then it was my parents' turn to tell; my hands were wet with sweat.

They must have been seventeen or eighteen, around the time the two of them decided to move to Vienna, in any case, when they discovered their interest in one another. I knew that during their studies — my mother economics, my father biology, of course — they lived together in a maisonette of around twenty-five square metres: toilet and bathroom in the hallway, one room with a bed, two desks, and a so-called armchair, which my father still hadn't parted with even decades later. My parents financed this apartment, with its hanging scraps of wallpaper and stain-studded carpet, by working nightshifts in a sausage shop. That must have been 1965–1970, years in which people declared solidarity with all sorts of things and hid dissidents in their houses, demonised nuclear power, and occupied what was in danger of being demolished, all in all just playing at revolution, while secretly working towards a conventionally successful life, because babies were already on the way everywhere. Including me, of course. I crossed out this branch, as it was a one-way street: everything was about Vienna, nothing about Greater Einland.

A dense network of lines, cross-references, and streams of thought had unfurled. Each node led, via a nerve cord of small, anecdotal digressions, to another story, so that soon a web of scraps of the past had formed. I had never really thought about it, but now that I could survey all the pieces, I realised that a rupture must have happened, that in all these stories of excess and exuberance and multiculturalism there had at the same time been something deeply tragic. Wherever there was nothing of Greater Einland, it had been there after all, as a lack, an absent hometown. But why?

I was dazed from the effort of remembering, from all these details: that there had been a hill behind my parents' house you could ski down in winter. Or a scar on my mother's neck that I'd felt while learning to swim and that supposedly came from a kick by a horse whose hooves she had scratched out. How my parents had learned to interpret constellations in their childhood bedroom, because a large window was built into the sloping ceiling through which they could see the night sky.

The worst thing was the small, the tender, the intimate: the fleeting touches and the hands laid on my head. I recalled eccentric character traits that I'd found embarrassing about my parents, but now longed for. Events that had taken place so very much between the lines that I would never be able to formulate them adequately, and that were inextricably linked to every memory. Open days aiming towards a future, lipstick marks on my bicycle helmet, favourite muesli bars that found their way into my backpack. And finally, as if a valve had broken, I was able to cry.

Long after three in the morning I folded up my map. I did a recap of the leads I had in order to decide where I had to head the next morning after breakfast. There were a few ideas of regions, a rough idea of how large the town might be, along with a few anecdotes. Nothing that could have revealed anything.

If there is no time, there must be another principle — independent of the automatic continuation of things — that sews the course of the world together. According to Barbour (Oxford, 2008), this consists of so-called time capsules — content-substantive signposts that signal to our minds which path to take through a landscape where everything exists simultaneously. These time capsules are solitary in our world — the only elements that refer to a past. Certificates, photos, history books are part of this — objects of personal memory that seem to prove something that doesn't really exist: the causal past. In addition, there are the time-pointers that are arranged within the brain structures of organic beings; miniature versions of the universe that are, as it were, frozen, implying a sense of origin to humans. Time-pointers simulate continuity, when in truth they are merely logical connections, not causal ones. Because our world consists of nothing but the present — and while the mind is still clinging to the time capsules, everything stands still.

It was the fourth day of my journey in the Alpine foothills, and I'd sat down with neatly split bread rolls in order to plan my trip for the day. As if this inconsequential rhythm of stopping off at inns, contemplation, dinner, sleep, and breakfast buffets were leading me to utter lethargy, I decided every morning to uphold it. I hadn't yet been able to let go of the hope of finding Greater Einland. I loved the simplicity of the conditions. An inn with guestrooms was just like another inn with guestrooms: identically proportioned chambers with the same floral duvet covers and Bibles in the desk drawer; liver dumpling soup and the same overcooked parsley stalks boiled to tatters, in dishes depicting a rural scene in blue. Sitting next to the same red-faced inebriates who thundered their sausage-fingered fists on the wooden table tops while drinking the completely consistent wine, Zweigelt or Veltliner, from identical curved wine glasses, followed by the schnapps bottles tipped low over the glasses in a synchronised ballet. At last you lie in a wood-panelled room with sloping ceilings, on a double bed with the same gap in the middle, and carry out the same rural sleep, before the landlady, always around forty, always stout, appears rattling the breakfast things at seven. And always the same hostelry all the way to Salzburg and over the border towards Bavaria, where the current of hospitality ebbed away at some point.

That day I drove far out, past Mariensee and down into the Kamp Valley, to a quarry, a furrow in the land, where the tectonic plate had broken away from itself in shock. Here, at last, seemed to be the right place. The autumn was steaming from the gently rotting ground, yet it was still warm enough that I could leave the car window open. The ground was damp; I had to slow down. The fact that my mobile phone had been going off constantly had tormented me for days, as if the messages were waiting at my door like irksome unexpected guests. I would have to take a more radical step, and so here I was: at the cleft in the stone that led into the depths, adjacent to the main road.

Into this abyss I threw my phone. I watched with excitement as it tumbled a hundred metres into the valley, as if I had shaken off an intrusive tracker. I thought I heard it burst against the jagged stone walls and finally come to a stop. Feeling euphoric from this sound, I looked a moment longer into the depths, but was already moving backwards towards the car.

3

Although I was shivering, I adamantly drove the stretch I'd planned that morning to the end. I now regretted not having considered that without my mobile phone I would also be without my navigation device. I was cutting through a place called Puchsberg, when a signpost caught my eye. I braked reflexively, parked the car on the side of the road, and walked closer to a hand-carved sign hanging from a tree to confirm my first impression: THE THOUSAND-YEAR-OLD OAK TAVERN.

The building was on a hill less than five minutes from the town. I had to make four attempts at getting into a parking space, the last available one out front of the inn. I could already see from the outside that the oak had split the building, as if it had been struck by wooden lightning. I stood for a moment in the rain, wondering why the building wasn't completely overflowing with water, as the tree's crown protruded unshielded from the hammer-beam roof. It was exactly as my father had described it.

Perhaps on account of the wet weather, the guesthouse was full inside. I could see that from the reception area: every table was fully occupied, and there were another two or three fold-out chairs at each. Entire extended families were sitting on and at sturdy wooden furniture, shouting things to each other across the tables, and, just when you believed that there wasn't any space left whatsoever, there were a few infants distributed on laps. A Swedish stove crackled in the corner — a buzzing, hot room of animated people.

I briefly worried whether any rooms would be available at all. But of course, said the woman on the reception when I put my question to her, one would be prepared in a few hours, and I ought to order something to eat in the meantime. I was led by a waitress who, like a small child, had taken me by the hand on my entering the dining room and now weaved through the groups with remarkable agility. I couldn't with the best will in the world imagine how even one more person could be accommodated here. She finally put me at a tiny table with a man who was deeply absorbed in his coleslaw.

As little as I could endure the intimacy of an arbitrary merger, my counterpart looked interesting: he must have been in his forties and was dressed in an extremely strange robe — a kind of violet Coptic tunic that was so different from the clothes of the other patrons that I wondered why no one was staring at him. He wrote in a notebook positioned beyond his coleslaw — and it was in a script I'd never seen before. It resembled Korean, but little hats and tails grew out from the letters in a way that made one consider they might be related to the Slavic family. I ordered bread with a selection of spreads, drank the first quarter of my wine, and wondered how I could hide my indiscreet glances at the man. He was just slipping the most unappetising of all dishes — a so-called jellied brunch — out of its tin onto his plate and began, I assumed, to look for the fish in the yellow mass of egg foam.

Our eyes met for a snip of a second.

'Fate has not been kind to you,' he suddenly said, almost to himself, but when I looked up again, he had his finger pointed at my chest as if in accusation.

'They mixed up your order,' he said, and I finally noticed that someone had set down a slice of caraway roast pork in front of me.

'This is your first time here,' he began, for a third time, and this time, I felt that I had to react despite strong feelings of reluctance.

'Yes, it is. And only by chance and just passing through. I'm waiting for a room to become free — I'm exhausted from the long drive and would like nothing more than to go lie down, but the inn is terribly overcrowded.' My answer had got away from me, as was always the case when I was actually trying to break off an interaction. While he was listening, the man had shoved the sardine he had finally discovered into his mouth, the tail of which was poking out from between his lips.

'You want to go to bed already? At this time?' he asked, puzzled, and spat out the rear fin. He had a point: it was still broad daylight.

'Travelling', I said evasively, as if the word offered an explanation, and, as if out of embarrassment, added: 'Do you come here a lot? It's a very nice inn.'

'Perpetually crusty,' the man said, drawing out a stained handkerchief from his bell-bottom trousers. 'The fish, I mean.' And he coughed hideously into the rag, making the table shake.

No sooner had he composed himself than he placed his elbows imperatively on the table. 'And you're travelling for business, too?

I'm a travelling salesman — have you ever heard of the Flying Mask Dealer?'

'No,' I replied, not knowing which question I was answering. 'I'm a physicist and I'm here on personal business.'

'Physicist, how nice. And which field are you devoted to? Theoretical, practical? Mechanics, thermodynamic, the theory of relativity?' The man, who still had his face turned towards me, moved disturbingly little.

'I work in research on block universe theory. I'm currently writing my postdoc, well — at least that was my plan a few years ago. I've had a recent setback.'

Even though he didn't ask anything further, I kept talking.

'Yeah, I know, what does setback even mean,' I said, now blushing with shame, as if I had been yelled at to provide a justification. 'I tripped myself up, to some extent. When I began my work on Eternalism years ago, I actually thought it would be liberating. Sure, I was rebelling against my professors, who hardly knew anything about it at the time. But the more I immersed myself in it, the more — how should I put it? Let's just say that my research expanded into my life, that, like a tumour, it began to displace other tissue.'

Time and time again he nodded while I spoke these words, and the heavy jewellery that lay on his chest clattered each time, as if he wanted to goad on an anxious herd of cows.

'There wasn't anything else anymore, you know? Twelve hours of work seemed too few to me, fourteen, sixteen was my average in July. Of course it can't be done without medication. Hardly any contact with anyone, for four years, not even at the institute.

I didn't go to any Christmas parties, nothing.' And as a form of explanation I clumsily added: 'I hadn't been to my parents' house in ages. I didn't want to see anyone at all.'

I was shocked by the haemorrhaging of this monologue, which had run unstoppably from my lips.

'Let me ask you something,' the man said politely, and began to dig between his front teeth with a toothpick. 'What exactly is block universe theory?'

'I beg your pardon, of course.' I cleared my throat, even though I didn't need to. 'It's an alternative theory of time. Picture the following: if time is unreal, as we know it to be today, then the past, present, and future are actually taking place at the same time. Similar to a three-dimensional block, supposedly consecutive moments can be read as being closer to one another. This means time becomes more a direction in space than something that would ever change things. It's complicated.'

I folded a serviette into an improvised cube.

'You see, this cube contains all the situations that have ever happened or will ever happen. The walls here,' I pointed to the sides of the serviette, 'are the limits of physical possibility. Now time is measured as distance — but everything happens at the same time, you see? So we can take any path through the cube without consciousness. We call them paths because when viewed from above there is a kind of landscape, through which our brain seeks out paths with the greatest possible probability — but it's not important for you to understand it right now,' I added hastily, as I feared that he'd mentally checked out a long time ago. 'The decisive thing happened away from my thesis. In those moments when, for example, I went to the institute or sat in the cafeteria with my colleagues, I noticed that a state of mental disorder, which at first was not entirely tangible, was becoming stronger. It was this realisation that shone through from my calculations down in the office with the same unalterable luminosity: *There is no such thing as time.'*

In the middle of this sentence I dropped my cutlery on the floor. I had to dive under the table to retrieve it.

'There is no such thing as time,' I repeated, and stabbed my dusty fork into the roasted meat. 'At first it was only a mild feeling of alienation, as if these streets, which I knew so very well, were fakes. As if I were walking in sets a Hollywood producer had crafted to deceive me. Because I knew there could be no such thing as time. But why did everyone act as if there actually was?' I blushed again while I said these words.

'It was a torturous feeling, a constant state of derealisation. And the longer I remained within it, the more I lost my biorhythm — day and night were one and the same thing, I was never tired. Not ever. Instead I was constantly anxious during the day, like before an ever-nearing exam. You see, I had completely lost the passing of time — I had the unmistakable feeling of a static universe: one day identical to another, one hour just the same as the next. Of course, the first thing I did was go to a psychiatrist, but there was no diagnosis. At least, none that could have helped me. So I resorted to self-medicating. At the time, doctoral students were handing out Ritalin on the sly, and I found that it freed me of my swirling thoughts. So I broadened my repertoire, if you can put it that way.' I gulped down another mouthful.

'Anyway, I started taking modafinil about five years ago to calm my nerves, two tablets every evening. Yet I was often so spaced out at nine in the morning that I went to sleep in the university toilets. Or I got dressed, ran out of the door, and only then realised that it was still pitch-black outside. And through it all I kept my composure, attended office hours, gave my lectures. That's how you make your experiences.'

I had tried my best to be brief, but I didn't succeed. Perhaps because I hadn't spoken with anyone for four days it all flowed out of me uninhibitedly — but I'd probably not spoken with someone in this way for years. For a brief moment there was a horrendous silence. Then he addressed me as fixedly as he had the first time.

'Did you know that, in my role as a mask dealer, I spent a long time in Arnhem Land?'

'Mask dealer,' I repeated absurdly.

'I lived there with Aboriginal Australians. I was there because of the masks, of course, but no one wanted to sell me any for a long time on account of their ancestors.' He coughed several times. 'Anyway, even though I, of course, wasn't permitted to take part in rituals, I learned a lot about their Dreaming. I presume that Dreaming means something to you? Well, then you know what I'm talking about,' he said, even though I had shaken my head in response to his question.

'Spiritual and physical world are connected in an eternally created present, the Dreaming, a place where we can come into contact with our ancestors. The ancestors influence our world through their actions, and we in turn can alter the Dreaming through what we do.'

'But how?' I asked, my voice breaking.

'And indeed,' he said, leaning conspiratorially over the table, 'it takes place via the landscape. What the ancestors — but this includes the metaphorical as much as our actual relatives — do in the Dreaming shapes our landscape, raises them up into mountains and creates rivers. The joke is that we change with them, too. And at such a pace, almost retrospectively, that we believe that the landscape has always had this form. We become incapable of even noticing the change. Is that not a remarkable thought?'

'I see what you're getting at,' I said, but it didn't mean anything anymore. I wanted to be alone all of a sudden, estranged from the intimate details I had told him moments before.

'So, very similar to your theory, there's a cosmic web that binds a topography to time, except that for Aboriginal Australians it is the actual landscape that performs it.'

'Do keep talking. I'm going to pay my bill in the meantime, as my room could be ready at any moment,' I said.

'But what most people don't want to understand about Dreamtime is that the physical world is already the connection between the spiritual and the physical. That the landscape flows around us just like our perception of things — everything from one single source. So the whole world becomes a metaphor. You are a metaphor, as am I, in all our embodiment —'

'Excuse me, I have to go,' I started again. I urgently wanted to bring the conversation to an end, but didn't know how. The mask dealer did not respond to what I'd said. He gave his monologue as sternly as I had mine to him.

I gestured to the waitress that I wanted to pay, but he caught her as soon as she was near us. 'We'll share half a litre of red,' he said before I could act, and even grasped my hand for a split second, as if he had to prevent me from fleeing. 'What you said earlier struck me as familiar on account of the fact that Aboriginal Australians also define time as a path — taking a path through a landscape, that becomes transformed in the act of taking a path. Just in constant contact with one's own ancestors. We cannot take a single step without colliding with our own past. The only option would be not taking one more step, a complete denial of time itself.' I looked on in desperation as my glass was once more filled to the brim.

'Would you look at that, I've lost my appetite,' he said suddenly to a passing waitress and threw his hands up from the table; but instead of pushing the plate away or handing it to her, as I had expected him to do, he reached for another piece of bread, which he shoved whole into his mouth. I briefly drew hope that he would, in that moment, not be alert enough to prevent me from leaving, but I immediately lost my courage again, because despite his mouth now being spread wide, he continued speaking with unaltered fervour.

'I want to be honest with you,' he said. 'It seems to me that we didn't meet by chance. The purpose with which you sat down with me at the table.' He made a sweeping motion of his hand as if he was conducting an orchestra.

'No, that we've met one another here is of a downright fateful quality. Augustine also said that time as such does not exist, rather that the past and the future are only projections from the present.

Everything comes back, so to speak, to this conversation we are having right now, and arises from it. It stands for something.' He once more took my hand, and although this disgusted me, I lacked the resolve to pull back. 'A metaphor is successful when it shines forwards and backwards. It has to change the past because it gives it a different meaning, and even more so the future, because it directs our expectations towards what is to come. In this respect, of course, the ancestors are nothing more than metaphors, or much rather, we are metaphors for our ancestors. Think of it in genetic terms.'

I could have easily got up and left, but I just didn't. 'Within a suitably charged context such as this one,' the mask dealer said with increasing intensity, 'everything becomes a metaphor. You, me, the people in this inn, and everything that goes on in it.' This made me shake, as if I were standing exposed in the autumn air. 'You can see for yourself that you are here for a reason and that you intended to do something when you told me about your life before. But what? Perhaps you don't yet know yourself. Which is why I would like to offer you something. And it is,' he bowed forward deeply as if to ask for forgiveness, and brought something out, 'some wonderful masks from my range.'

Suddenly the tension was broken. The entire philosophical promise was nothing more than a prelude to a sales pitch. In a few seconds the table was covered with masks.

'Here, for instance, we have a wonderful piece, a so-called Bremen mask, made in Bamberg by a family of carvers that have lived there for a hundred years. Ideal for a masquerade ball.' He pointed to a stylised bird's head that would come down as far as one's nose, an abomination.

'Fine, I'll buy it,' I said.

'And perhaps this, too. A particularly magnificent piece from Mali, the eye of truth. It's made of bronze and brass, for ritual purposes naturally, but there's no need to fear it. For over the fireplace, perhaps?'

'Okay, I'll get this one to complement the first one,' I replied, without even looking at the mask.

'Gladly,' the mask dealer said hastily. 'That will be one hundred euros.'

I was glad that I had the sum with me in cash, and, even though it would have seemed like a ridiculously high amount under normal circumstances, I couldn't put it down on the table fast enough.

'Thank you, and I'll now excuse myself for the evening,' the mask dealer said, already getting up from the table.

'It was a pleasant discussion,' I replied, but he was already in such a hurry to put away his masks that he only replied with a hand gesture that was most probably intended to be a wave, but which appeared far more like he wanted to dispel an unpleasant odour. Then he went to the bar and briefly debated with the landlady in a manner that made me assume that he owed her money. In fact, she took a large part of the money I'd just paid him. He left the inn without looking back.

Shortly afterwards, the waitress came to my table and told me that my room was ready.

I awoke from a night of deep, undisturbed sleep and saw the past week for what it was for the first time: a delusion lasting several days. It is one of the strangest facets of life, how that which previously appeared to be the most natural of all actions shifts in an invisible, sudden drift. Idiocy now pervaded the last few days, just like when you realise in sobriety that you had danced on the table while drunk the night before. More importantly: I felt the strength to admit and correct my own mistake. After breakfast I would gather my things, telephone my relatives, and return to Vienna to carry out the funeral preparations. That was the only sensible thing to do. While I was putting on my socks, I worked everything out — I would eat eggs, bacon, and muesli, wash it all down with several glasses of water to get rid of the oppressive hangover, and rush to the nearest telephone as soon as possible to convey my decision to my relatives. I jumped into my trousers; I suddenly couldn't be in enough of a hurry. There was something deeply comforting about the idea of being in Vienna before lunch — sleeping in my bed, finally talking to my friends about what had happened. I threw my things into my suitcase without arranging them, as one does when they know they are going home, and sprang down the steps into the breakfast room. But when I entered it, everything had already been cleared away.

There was only one waitress standing in front of the sideboard, who, as in a Hans Moser film, was rhythmically rattling the glasses and building them up into a huge pyramid-like monument for the next morning.

'Why is there no more breakfast?'

'No,' she replied, bypassing my question, but with a friendly smile.

'What time is it? I should have been woken at seven.'

'It's half past eleven,' the waitress replied and, as if she were thinking of some great piece of bad news, she turned away from her glass tesseract. 'Oh dear. Frau Rosenthaler went to the hospital last night with her husband. He had a heart attack.' I vaguely remembered that Frau Rosenthaler was the landlady to which I had given my urgent request to be awoken punctually. I expressed my sympathies to the waitress, and she promised to at least bring me a cup of coffee — unfortunately, there was nothing left to eat.

While I was sipping the milk foam, I felt a strange stirring within me: the powerful images of my journey home, of my early arrival in Vienna that I had imagined since waking, and the whole momentum attached to them, had faded. An ineffable effort towered up before the task of now getting behind the wheel. It didn't matter, though — I had to get it over with. I looked at my watch — if I set off right now, at least I would be back home that afternoon.

No sooner had I started the engine and was driving down the first autobahn than I heard the piercing warning alarm of my petrol tank: I remembered that I had been near empty when I'd arrived at the inn yesterday. I tried to remember how to drive in a way that would conserve fuel, and let the car roll on the downhill roads — even leaning forwards to use my negligible body weight to gain a few metres. I turned off at the next junction, passed through a town, and managed to reach what appeared to be a small, old-fashioned service station.

The petrol station was a model of desolation: a little single-storey hut with East German character, and directly behind it was a coffee kiosk with yellowed, tin Coke advertisements. The petrol station attendant, a young man in a Ducati jacket who was smoking confidently in front of the pumps, was responsible for fulfilling all needs, and was just bringing two other customers cups of espresso, which he set down on their car roof.

I breathed a sigh of relief as I clicked the nozzle into place at this most old and miserable model of petrol station. This was the end of my odyssey, the last abidance of this parallel dimension of the Austrian wasteland. In a few hours I would be back in my apartment, in my orderly everyday; I would sit at my desk and plan the funeral in peace. While I was waiting for my tank to fill up, the two figures at the neighbouring pump caught my eye. They tore me from my daydream. One of them was a stocky man with a pointy beard, who filled a colossal double-breasted suit and had a monocle in his eye. He was offering the other man, who was unscrewing the petrol cap, a cigar from a kind of portable humidor, which the latter refused with a wave of his hand. He, too, caught my interest: he was a direct opposite to the first, a gaunt, you could almost say dwarfish, little man, who busily tinkered with the car, polishing the windows, checking the oil level, and finally lighting the fat man's cigar. He was wearing silk trousers and a dirty shirt, with which he cleaned his glasses from time to time.

'So if we can pull it off — and there is no doubt that we can do it' — began the fat man — 'we should lay a foundation within a week, put up three of the walls — the last thing, the facade, ought to be made of marble, you understand — so, if we pull it off, I say to Blumenkranz, putting in the arcade hall, orchestra pit, thirty-seven dressing rooms, two thousand seats and so on at that speed, I also want something from you!' He tapped the ash from his cigar onto the ground before continuing.

'In short: if we keep that promise to build your opera house on the Glatzalm by October, two hundred parking spaces within twelve hundred metres, then you will have to pay me and Master-Builder Keinermüller in pure gold.' He laughed uproariously; his companion's shirt sprang upwards as he tried to put the car antenna back up. I delayed refuelling as long as I could in order to follow the conversation for longer. While the one who was apparently a business man — who, incidentally, was wearing a wide-brimmed hat — looked freshly polished to a high shine, the car cleaner had something dull about him; even his trouser buttons were tarnished.

'*We still have the gold standard*, I told him, and that's when he fell right over, not literally, of course, but he fell back into his chair. Cat's out of the bag! I told him we wouldn't do it for less than three million. Otherwise I'd be pauperised!' With these words he slapped his hand down on the windscreen, leaving a grease mark, which the other man had to wipe off.

'Did Huber quote the estimate?' he asked jubilantly, rag in hand.

'*Schlaf, I don't have three million, please, the inflation, the economy, I'm still feeling the effects of the schilling,*' mimicked the fat man. 'Fine, I say, then a hundred thousand. Handshake! Suits him. There'll be a made-to-measure hat and two boxes of nail clippers on top.'

'Brilliant,' the little one said. 'Are you going to build a funicular that goes up there?'

Even though my car wasn't particularly dirty, I now began to wash the windows, so very fascinated was I with this strange set-up. A moss-scented wind slammed my car door shut. For a moment both of the men looked at me. I averted my gaze.

'I'll take care of everything,' pontificated the other man, who had his expensive cigar burning in his right hand as if it were nothing more than an accessory. 'There are very few people nowadays that do everything, Fredi. People think you need knowledge about something in order to get started. I'll tell you something: knowledge is absolutely useless! Thinking is a beginner's error. Everything consists of transactions — trade is the root of world affairs, especially Austrian retail.'

'You're a genius, you'd even make it in America,' came Fredi's muffled reply, his head under the open car bonnet.

'This is how we have always grown rich in the town. The Countess paved the way, and we follow her lead,' the big guy said and tossed away the cigar. 'Look, I'm just a man, unlike you.'

In spite of this obvious insult, Fredi very carefully closed the doors and bonnet, shook the other's hand, and they exchanged envelopes. I had assumed that the small guy was a kind of broker or servant for the first man; I couldn't figure out what else could have brought the two of them together. But that didn't seem to be the case: 'It's always wonderful doing business with you,' Fredi said casually. Their interaction was a mystery fraught with tension, but to my chagrin they both started making a move to leave.

'Ditto. Shall I take you home?' the small man asked.

'No, I have to go back to Greater Einland,' the other replied.

'Fine by me — I'll take you there, got nothing else to do.'

'Well, there you go.' And the two of them left the petrol station.

Greater Einland.

I had heard it clearly and yet it took a moment for me to realise I hadn't imagined it. I threw the attendant fifty euros and ran after them to the carpark. I wasn't able to catch up with them before they reached their car, and as I was about to jump into mine, I noticed that I hadn't removed the pump. I had to awkwardly pull it out, hands shaking, before I could get in and start the engine, panicking that both men had already turned out of the exit. I accelerated without paying attention to the speed limit, and yet I'd lost them by the first intersection. We were in the middle of the village, and the houses were too close to be able to see very far. I caught sight of them again as they turned down a forest road far off in the distance. I had to reverse to be able to follow them, but then they were already gone again, and I stopped, without a clue to go on, on the dirt lane that had led me through a field and to a hill. There weren't any turnings, so the car could have only gone in one direction, but the uphill path was anything but suitable to get around quickly. The road ended at a steep forest. The only option to get down the other side of the slope was an even smaller trail that couldn't even be described as a road. And even this trail, probably intended for hikers, soon ended. The only way left to proceed was through a gap that led steeply through the trees.

4

I clearly remember driving along the bumpy path, which swayed in my rear-view mirror as if suspended between the trees. The improvised access road seemed anything but an authorised road-construction measure: the spruce trees had been sawed through with a chainsaw so close to the ground that larger cars could have gone straight over them. Even though the trunks had been trued up in this way, new branches were already pushing up from the ground. I immediately lost my bumper, even though I was only moving at a walking pace. My progress was combined with substantial difficulties because the topsoil — on which I was driving — shifted in all three spatial directions. As I was attempting to go downhill, a moment of momentum sent my car sideways against a tree trunk. While driving out of the ditch I'd been forced into, I carved into a bush, which ripped off my left side mirror. Even though it was only 3pm, the forest had become so dense that the light was weak. My car became stuck between two fir trees. I had to get out and push it from behind through the bottleneck, before rolling a bit further forward as soon as I was sitting in it again. An hour had gone by, and I had barely moved.

The forest finally ended in a meadow, but better than that: I could see another surfaced road beginning in the distance, leading into a town. I let my car, which was already creaking from all axles like an insect fallen on its back, roll for the last hundred metres out of the forest. Branches were wedged all over the bonnet, and dents in the doors made me question whether I'd be able to get out at all. When I was finally driving on asphalt again, I saw a sign looming before me as if it had just been erected: GREATER EINLAND.

In the timeless universe, all possible worlds lie next to each other in perfect simultaneity. Wherever our mind wanders within this infinite space of possibility and what it experiences as the present is influenced by a fog-like quality that lies above the configuration space. This fog, also called 'mist' in literature, is, of course, only to be understood metaphorically: what is meant is a distribution of probability that something will be experienced as the present — the capricious wave function that in quantum physics predicts the occurrence of an event. The crucial question is what ensures that this is concentrated in some areas but thins out in others — why does such a seamless plausibility seem to prevail in the succession of thoughts? Herach and Tocker suspect that the mist mainly collects where a particularly large number of time capsules can be found: The configurations are joined to one another because they contain a large number of reciprocal links. So the preferred whereabouts of consciousness is therefore where it and others have already remembered many things.

I was never more aware of what an Austrian town looks like than in the moment I let my shameful vehicle roll through the openwork town wall. About a hundred metres after a small settlement, I crossed over a stone bridge and arrived in the town centre. In the well-ordered manner that only a medieval market can achieve, the epicentre of the everyday goings-on came into view right at the town gate. A rectangular main square framed by picturesque buildings; a dollhouse-like primary school; a post office painted red with a golden horn insignia; a bakery with a shiny pretzel bobbing outside its doors; an inviting, cosily lit tavern; and a milk bar, gloomy in the already sparse light. Because I hadn't visited any busy urban areas for a week, the sight of the buildings, the cobblestones, the lanterns seemingly lit by hand, made me feel overblown happiness. Small, winding streets advanced in every direction and mysteriously disappeared behind cornerstones. Everything was incredibly clean and intact — a perfection such as I'd never seen in any square metre of Vienna. To the right, far behind the town on a rugged cliff, a four-turreted, brightly lit castle could be seen proudly towering upwards.

In the middle of registering these impressions I heard a gentle knocking on my side window. From inside the car I saw nothing but an erratic flickering beside me. When I rolled down the window, I saw a figure wearing strangely old-fashioned garments. He was a short, compact man with a moustache and wiry hair, dressed head to toe in a black uniform and, befitting of his cape and hat, carrying an antiquated gas lantern in his left hand. In his right, he was holding a halberd.

'Are there driving restrictions here, officer?' I asked, assuming that a costumed policeman officer had been installed as a tourist attraction.

'I am the night watchman,' he replied. 'And there are no restrictions.' The man was obviously not in the mood to joke, because he was already jotting down my number plate on a notepad.

'Where are you going?' he asked me brusquely. 'You won't get very far as an outsider.' He kicked the curb with the tip of his shoe, making a metallic clang, and I saw that he had steel toecaps on his boots.

'I'm looking for a place to stay tonight,' I replied. The night watchman turned away from my car and blew his nose incredibly thoroughly; for a full fifteen seconds neither of us said a word. 'Do you know where I can find somewhere? A guesthouse maybe? As you can probably see, my car is practically ready for scrap, I must have lost my way in the forest …'

'I can see that, but you won't get a room here.'

'And why is that?'

The night watchman laughed and shook his head, then shrugged four times in a row, shook his head again, and rocked back and forth several times.

'Because you're not a resident — you're not registered in Greater Einland.'

'Well, that's quite true,' I said quietly, ' but if I were a resident, why would I need a room in a guesthouse?'

That seemed to be too much for the night watchman: he writhed like a man attacked from all sides.

'Look, it is simply a requirement that you need a registration form to get a room in a guesthouse as a tourist. You can try, but they'll tell you the same thing that I have. It's a question of regulations.'

'But that can't be a law. Who stipulated that?'

This question made my interlocutor break out in a sweat.

'The Countess,' he said at last.

'The Countess?' I asked, sure that I'd misheard.

'Obviously the Countess. Well, listen. I see that you are in dire straits, and I don't want to be a monster. Go to the inn called the Jolly Pumpkin, and tell them that the night watchman sent you and that you will fetch your registration and your special pass tomorrow. For this one night.'

'My special pass?'

'A document that allows official papers to be backdated a day. Then they are already valid before the date of issue.' Greater Einland was already one of the strangest places that I'd ever been to, but I accepted this explanation. And his good will seemed more than fair when I got out and saw the extent of the damage to my car: two of the tires burst; the bonnet, with perforations on the sides, hanging on only by a hinge; three of the four side windows cracked; the exhaust dangling at an angle over the cobblestones.

I parked the car and walked in the direction the man had indicated. The way to the guesthouse led down a colossal stairway, along which little shops interlocked with one another like chain links. As I passed under an arcade into a no less picturesque part of the Old Town, I imagined how my parents had walked through these streets as children. This was Greater Einland — I had found it. But the imaginings met no emotions, and I had difficulty recalling their youthful faces, which remained abstract and distant.

The placid impression continued: a hairdressing salon with an iron statue of a pair of scissors on display; an optician's in whose window bespectacled bears were taking tea together; a butcher's with wooden stairs that led to a lovingly carved balcony. Among them, however, as if thrown in at random, were strange shopfronts: 'Shooting Gallery' was the first establishment whose name I tripped up on, a shop with a rather makeshift facade and bars over the door, through which one could make out targets. 'Midnight Shop' I read on another; 'Open 24.00 till 24.59 weekdays; film and audio recordings are permitted.' I didn't find it remarkable for long, however, seeing as even the tidiest of towns have their mavericks. What *had* grabbed my attention, on the other hand, was something else: that beside all these shops, next to this apparently flourishing retail trade, in a barely visible street, the asphalt was missing. Steps, invisible in the blackness, led down at this point, making it appear as if a huge mouth had sucked up the paving of the entire street from underground.

At the end of the subsequent row of houses I alighted upon the Jolly Pumpkin, which was, as I could already establish from outside it, actually more a tavern than a place to stay the night. An overwhelming soup steam hit me on entering the bar, as if an ox had been chopped into pieces and boiled complete with its skeleton, as if the whole animal hung in the air in vapour form among the people. Even breathing was filling. A waitress walked by carrying two dozen beer tankards on a tray — an uncannily cliched sight. I was glad that the reception desk was in a dead corner of the inn, as there was a palpable sense of exclusivity among the patrons of such the like I'd never encountered in any inn before. An unbelievable volume betrayed that everyone was conversing with everyone else at the same time, throughout the entire establishment.

I rang the bell on the desk as gently as possible, so as not to draw the other guests' attention towards me. Perhaps I had neglected to draw attention to myself at all, because for ten minutes no one came, and I was getting more and more timid about having to enter the bar. Through the fogged-up window I could make out the shapes of cheerfully huddled human flesh — limbs that hung over the plates like bloated sausages. There were collisions of bodies: handshakes, stumbling into one another, claps on the shoulder.

'Mayor!' someone shouted from across the room. 'You've still not renovated the entrance to the motorway — are that lot in Wastl von der Hoh breathing down your neck again?' Everyone laughed uproariously at this question.

'Schlaf the Hat-Maker should take care of it, he knows how to run a business,' someone else shouted, and a fat man in a suit with an imposing top hat started talking loudly.

'I'll do it soon,' the mayor said, barely audibly. The clothes of the men, which I could vaguely make out around the corner, were indistinct: I thought I recognised traditional Janker jackets made from loden fabric, but with bourgeois silk shirts underneath and shiny gold cufflinks. Only the beer was beyond question, and the empty tankards piled up beside the gnawed gristle of the grouse. Everything about the scene repelled me. For a moment I considered spending the night in my car, but that would be in the workshop until tomorrow at least. Fortunately the receptionist showed up behind the desk at that moment — a spritely woman in her fifties, who, as was to be expected, was wearing a green-and-red-patterned blouse with 'Frau Erna' embroidered on the chest in Kurrent cursive script. Nothing that I hadn't seen in a dozen variations in the last few days, except that she only looked at my face once and then resolutely lowered her gaze. I don't know whether the conversations on this first day only struck me as odd because I didn't yet know the way people spoke in Greater Einland — and whether that's the reason I'm hopelessly exaggerating their idiosyncrasies. But at the time, it seemed incredibly strange to me:

'Do you have any rooms available?' I asked.

'All booked up,' Frau Erna said without looking up.

'The night watchman recommended this inn to me.'

'Of course we have rooms free. Your name?' the woman said with as much ease as if she hadn't just said the opposite. Her closed countenance flipped into a servile expression, like an ambiguous image.

'Ruth Schwarz. But I only have cash. And not an infinite amount at that,' I said, embarrassed.

'No problem, you don't pay till checkout. My name is Dorothee — if you need anything, just let me know.'

I pointed to her chest. 'But it says Frau Erna?'

'No, no, that's the name of the inn.'

'Isn't this the Jolly Pumpkin?'

'Yes, of course, that's right.'

Although I had not become any the wiser, I took the towels presented to me, after which my key was finally handed over.

On the stairs to the first floor I regained control and confronted myself for the first time with the thought that I was *actually in* Greater Einland. Other than a rustic double bed, a few manned crucifixes, a table for one's morning ablutions, and a bathroom with floral tiles there wasn't anything else to discover — no Bible, strangely enough, no printed matter at all. The windows were comedically small when compared with the rest of the room. I could hardly imagine that I would be able to escape in case of a fire, but I didn't care in my present state of fatigue. I longed for a hot shower, got undressed, and turned on the water: this was the moment I saw the stale white water for the first time. When the colour didn't change after five minutes, and because it didn't smell strange, I got into the cubicle anyway.

I went to bed just after 8pm. The muffled voices of tavern patrons rose up from below, putting me in a sleepy mood. Before I could form one more clear thought, I stripped naked and wrapped myself in the sheets. When I had closed my eyes and was already almost asleep, I suddenly saw the black cavity in the asphalt once more, gaping in front of me, and thought for a moment that I was falling, before I finally drifted off.

> The hole was of unknown depths, bifurcations, and dampness. It ran like an underground mycelium under the mountaintops and settlements, broke to the surface in the form of ducts and webs, and, like a continental drift, pushed the unstrung soil together into gritty, respiring heaps, beneath which the putrid, fungus-like process of decay had nested.

The crust of the soil had become softer and softer over the decades: squishy sediments, carried away beneath the houses and streets, surrendered to liquefaction, which was accomplished through the meticulous work of dew and drizzle, damp autumn evenings and garden hoses. It wasn't rainfall that, like a spontaneous haemorrhage, almost burst this aneurysm, simmering beneath the town.

The hole was basically unmanageable. It was an endless exhalation of land, the chest of which sank as far as the ribs, breached them, and displaced the organs. The only blessing was that it had all happened so infinitely slowly that generation after generation had distributed the concern about it — and for the sake of an alibi you could pour concrete into manholes every week and have enough time to swap out the shattering window sills that gave way to the subsidence before the kids got out of school.

The main chasm, an abyss no less than fifty metres wide and two hundred metres deep, gaped under the Market Square and endangered the equilibrium of the entire city centre, which had its foundations on porous froth like the top of a chocolate-coated marshmallow. This shaft, which was not created by chance, but had rather been driven into the heart of the city through centuries of mismanagement, had a main entrance, now boarded-up and secured, directly behind the church — but also seven or eight side entrances, the ones in the school, in the park, the castle ruins, which were proof that it had been drilled and plundered deeper, century after century. Every side and parallel activity of the exploitative mining, the privately organised explorations, and the glut of commercial access points over the centuries, had made the cave so thin-walled that it was easy for nature to close its fist around the structure. Underground, however, none of these changes were noticed: in absolute tectonic standstill, and in complete darkness, all aliveness found its end. The horses that had dragged the slaked lime out of the rock two hundred years ago had first had their eyes gouged out — a seeing horse would never have willingly descended into the blackness. The animals had to endure these conditions for twenty years or more — that is, the entire life of a horse — in order to serve as transporters for the minerals.

That I later discovered the history of over-exploitation was not difficult. People would say: it's all out in the open.

In 1890 an industrial magnate named Winfried Kneiss began to mine the limestone deposits known of since the Middle Ages, whereby a rumoured legend of gold strikes hung over the entire enterprise. He had equipped himself with a legion of daywage men from Burgenland and western Hungary, who were transported by train to Gloggnitz every Monday, after which the group would cover the twenty-three kilometres to Greater Einland on foot between four and nine in the morning. The streets swelled at this time, and apartment buildings divided into small parcels were bloated from the inside with human material, until the pressure was released again at 9pm on Fridays, and the village turned into a ghost town for the weekend. The lime was removed from the mountain in tons and tons, and pumped into the aortas of the Austro-Hungarian Empire's nervous systems, as it was needed in Prague, Krakow, and Lemberg for the flourishing iron industry.

Nothing happened between the wars — that is, of course, everything happened: after the mine officially came to a standstill due to a spontaneous sale, the population who'd been standing patiently at attention now began to enter unauthorised with improvised materials. The hole exerted a mesmerising force, a collective desire that sought to break through the economic membrane that had separated the country from its people. In a very short time, an underground amusement saloon was set up, and a casino, and, a year later, a brothel.

But its depths eroticised individuals, too. Groups of young men climbed into the side shafts as a test of courage; impoverished families followed the long-held hunch that gold could be found at the bottom of the stone belly; somnambulistic old people were seen near the tunnel at dawn and disappeared without a trace.

In 1939 the shafts, which in some places were digging forty metres deep into the mountain, were taken over by the Wehrmacht: an invisible, bomb-proof location for ammunition production. A branch of the Mauthausen concentration camp was established, and now, like fifty years earlier with the Hungarian workers, it was the most normal sight of all to see the malnourished men and women walking through the city centre, moved overland from their barracks behind the woods and into the tunnels.

All of this had been reviewed and reappraised, framed and consolidated to form information boards, planted into the ground. There was a memorial that allocated remembrance within a precisely circled radius, and in its orbit about two dozen gladioli could be planted. So the hole had a clearly defined biography that nobody shied away from stirring — it was simply that the entire porous, honeycomb-like land threatened to crumble under such contact.

5

It took less than ten minutes of expert examination the next morning before the mechanic informed me that a quick repair wouldn't be possible. Due to the delivery time of specific parts, along with the evaluation of processes that were incomprehensible to me, I had to stay for a further week in the Jolly Pumpkin, which I was actually pleased about. I immediately bought a hairdryer, notepads and pens, a dressing gown, and other household items that could suggest I had just settled in for an entire year. Something about Greater Einland urged me to stay — after the almost superhuman effort it had taken to find the town, I felt the irresistible desire to stay a few more days. I could still take my meals in the tavern; that way I would save myself the need of buying a hotplate and also have the opportunity to get to know some of the locals, a prospect that brought joy for the first time in my life.

As soon as I had left the garage, I sat down in a coffee house that was a little way from the main square, next to a small church. 'One-Pot Café' was the slightly odd-sounding name mounted over the premises. The church's facade was easily visible from the window: cascades of ivy leaves tumbled over one another and condensed to a chiselled frame, so that the uninformed observer would have to long puzzle over placing the church; it could have been in Cluny or in Oxford. Against this backdrop, I immersed myself in the local newspapers.

On this very first day I met Ferdinand, who would later become one of my best friends in this place — and who came through the door at that very moment. Gasping under the weight of his considerable gut, he climbed up a ladder to put up posters, before returning to the floor, drenched in sweat. All the tables in the place were occupied, and after he had looked around for a good while, he finally approached me. I hadn't got five pages into the newspaper when, a bundle of wetness, flesh, and rhythmic puffs of air, he sat down at my table without so much as a greeting.

'Tomorrow's the day,' he said, as if we had recently broken off a conversation. 'Unfortunately I can't lift that much, what with the umbilical hernia —' and with these words he pointed at his stomach, on which there was a ball-shaped bulge, which was probably poking through a bandage.

'We have to pour five thousands kilos in the hole this week, otherwise the market place will be hanging a metre lower by March. After the rain last week everything's sunk about thirty centimetres.'

'I see,' I said quietly. 'Well, then you better not lift too much.'

Even though I had tried to not let it show, when he mentioned the hole I felt a spontaneous excitement — an unconditional desire to find out more on the subject.

'Do people help with this or is it a council matter?' I asked.

'Well, actually no one's really done anything so far,' he

replied, shrugging his massive shoulders, making his vest bulge above his navel.

He was a man of about forty with a blue flat cap on his head, who so roundly filled out his clothing that I dared not imagine how organs other than his stomach and intestine could fit inside his body. It wasn't really a surprise that he ordered beer at ten in the morning, but the speed with which he drank it down truly was. Like a hurdler, he picked up the glasses without stopping. What amazed me most was that I immediately liked him.

'How can a market place hang?' I asked carefully.

'The hole,' he repeated with complete naturalness. 'It's growing. At first, we thought it was only really bad in the spot between the church and the Cultural Association, I mean, twenty years ago. But now the town hall has cracks, too, all over the place — in the plaster, in the parquet, all the renovations are now purely cosmetic really.' He picked up a pile of three or four coasters and carefully ripped them in two. 'And now we've poured a good hundred tonnes of concrete in it, but the entire hill under Greater Einland is hollow, can you imagine that? I've always said that that thing is bottomless. Someday Pergerhannes himself will climb out of it.'

'Who's Pergerhannes?'

'No one,' Ferdinand said quickly. 'In any case, the pit is getting bigger every day.'

'A pit underneath the town,' I repeated softly, so as not to interrupt the flow of information.

'We've been throwing rubble in it for years anyway. It has to all be done by hand, and it's horribly dusty like nobody's business.

I've got back problems from it, you know, chronic obstructive pulmonary disease for five years. The insurance won't pay for the treatments, but as long as I do my daily rounds through the town and write a report, the Countess will pay me for it.'

'Which countess?'

'Which countess! Which indeed. The only one. Our Countess.' He had to cough vigorously from laughing. 'Personally I have my own rituals with the hole, like almost everyone here does. If something is bothering me, I write it on a piece of paper, put a drop of blood on it, and throw the note into it. Brings you luck,' he said, winking.

I soon found out that Ferdinand was actually a truck driver. 'Trained and got stuck up to my knees,' as he put it — however, due to the bad roads, he hadn't driven a truck for nine years. As I had correctly ascertained yesterday, there were no intact roads out of the town and only a single carriageway, which, due to a construction error, went in a circle — that is, led from the exit directly back into the entrance.

Instead of driving trucks, after he'd had to move back in with his mother, he'd opened a shaving salon, which was 'also and especially for women,' he told me. 'I'm there shaving everyone by my own fair hand from 2pm till 5pm for four euros. Four! Two people for eight. Three for twelve, and so on.'

Alongside his rounds, this ensured him a livelihood and his COPD treatments, to which he went twice a year. However, I refrained from promising him a visit, even though that was obviously what he had in mind. He had the shakes so badly that someone would surely fear for their life while he was shaving them.

'Of course, people can shave themselves, but it's something a lot of people resent when you can actually outsource it. People absolutely want to give up certain responsibilities, that is very clear, we live in an age in which we want to transcend our bodies.

For a confused proletarian with a football scarf tucked into his leather jacket and a corroded bunch of keys hanging from his neck, Ferdinand expressed himself in a remarkably sophisticated way. I felt an irrepressible desire to see the hole, and the more time that passed, the less I could defend myself against this urge, so I soon paid my bill and prepared to leave.

'Do you know where I could go on a short walk today?' I asked, trying to seem casual.

'Over there is the edge of the town boundary,' Ferdinand said. 'You can happily walk ten or twenty kilometres inland. Maybe we'll see each other at the salon soon!' I thanked him and left him with his third beer.

I decided that before I betook myself into nature, as Ferdinand had advised, I would pace every corner of the walled town centre. It was broken up into four quadrants like a spliced cake, separated from one another by walls — North Town, South Town, East Town, West Town. So there were four quarters, which were visually very distinct from one another, and which I now explored in a clockwise fashion. Greater Einland was incredibly beautiful, similar to the scenery of a film set in the Middle Ages, in which the highpoint of handcraft was evident along its immaculate facades. Everywhere people were sitting happily chatting on the cobblestones drinking their white wine spritzers, even though it was already autumnally cool. You couldn't get away from the idyll. Of course, I found the conservatism disquieting, as I always did — many of the social formations resembled election campaign material: families sitting, having lunch, with a bowl of water under the table for their dog; young couples whose body language seemed to be relentlessly expressing: *Don't worry, we're already engaged.* But then I arrived at the main square.

In the light of day I finally noticed what I hadn't been able to see yesterday evening: the whole market had sunk elliptically a good metre, reaching its lowest point, concavely, in the centre. Worse still, behind the town walls you could see the church spire, which had tilted to the right at a dangerous angle. *The hole*, I thought excitedly.

The mosaic that I was now looking at, however, was still undamaged. One immediately understood that there wasn't any danger from the statics, that a decades-long process was at work here, but the caution that prevented me from even carelessly stepping on a glass bridge was a powerful deterrent that kept me away from this pit. I didn't want to cross the square; it appalled me — something subterranean seemed to have pulled the square into the depths with its earthy lips, which rasped sphincter-like on the insides of the houses. In fact, none of the passers-by walked in the middle of the square; everyone intuitively made their way around the edges. I read an information board that had been installed in the corner of the square, but the letters suddenly began to swim in front of my eyes:

> The floor mosaic to be admired here reveals, when
> viewed from the air, a picture of the Archangel

Michael falling into hell — how he chokes the serpent Satan and dashes it into purgatory with his sword. It is a reproduction of the motif on the former Market Square, which was restored in 1946, based on drawings, in the wake of it being filled in. Since the paver and restorer of the original mosaic, Georg Springinsfeld, had fallen in the war, his apprentice, Karl Weigand, created the new version, which was much less artistically executed than the original and, due to cheaper materials, did not defy the weather conditions as well; which is why the serpent Satan is often interpreted by non-residents as a dark-brown dachshund, and the archangel, with his green breastplate, as a woman in a bustier.

A feeling of uncanniness crept over me in broad daylight; the few characters who were on the move, housewives and newspaper delivery men, cast deep shadows that didn't seem to fit the position of the sun. My gaze was drawn towards the castle, which tapered into a grey vortex. And yet I found more and more details that caught my eye: at the top, on one of the three gables, someone had begun attaching figures. A Napoleonic sinewy horse in the middle, and two putti to the left and right, enthroned on the roof. A tower looming up in the middle glinted as if a battle believed lost had been won.

In a moment of lucidity I realised that I was two hours late to take my medication; I jogged the way back on the waxy ground, and, inside the inn, crushed up the last half tablet of oxycontin that I had, and snorted it deeply. The table creaked at right angles with a groan, my spine straightened itself back out, the world became smoothed out, and I lay sweating on the flor.

I looked in my bag of toiletries from where I'd taken the tablet; after a week on this trip I had nearly reached the end of my supplies and had no idea where I would be able to procure more. I dragged myself to bed until I was sure my ancestral brain metabolism had been restored, then I stood up, went downstairs, and greeted the landlady as if nothing had happened.

I set off on my walk much more soberly. As I passed the South Gate, I saw a sign announcing that the cemetery was in this direction, and I followed it, suddenly driven by rationality. I would have to visit the cemetery anyway, see the grave, prepare everything for the funeral. This part of the town corresponded far more to the general image of a middle-class residential neighbourhood. The street was lined with carefully pruned chestnut trees, and from the detached houses parked behind picket fences, a harmless family idyll issued forth from all sides. It was barely a five-minute walk: to reach the cemetery, a steep footpath led to a walled plateau, which squatted like a fortress in the hollowed-out quarry. There was, of course, a small chapel with mandala-like stained-glass windows. The obligatory florist cowering on the left, a few shamefaced grace metres away for the sake of decency, so that the business of mourning wouldn't be exposed at first glance.

I vaguely surmised that now I was fighting for my life, I would have to come face to face with death, that it would come to a confrontation between me and my feelings, which I hadn't yet encountered in the town. Nevertheless I stood utterly business-like between the tombstones, infinitely far away from connecting the thousands of dead that lay here with my parents.

I walked along the rows of graves in search of my grandparents' resting place, but this turned out to be more difficult than I thought, because there were at least ten names on every stone. As a general rule, the deceased carried the same last names and were carefully laid out in family groups — but they were sometimes also mixed up and separated from one another by hyphens, as if randomly stacked according to the date of their departure. Up to twenty of them fitted on the upright rectangular stones in question, and from these it could be read that the only thing that united these dead was their death, which had occurred shortly after one another. I imagined these graves stretching twenty metres deep into the ground; how the slab of land was pierced through by towering cavities, where those who had been strangers in life were now resting cheek to cheek.

Their names were soon dancing before my eyes — the sun was already going down, and it wasn't easy keeping my concentration. Schwarz or Schalla, Schwarz or Schalla; I searched obsessively, but the later it got, the more impossible it became. I had to crouch in front of the gravestones to be able to read the tiny engraved letters. I was finding it all unpleasant when I heard someone coming down the gravel path and I made a backwards jump away, but the man spoke to me from afar.

'Who are you looking for?'

'Our family grave. My grandparents, or rather, Petra and Joseph Schalla.' I scraped the tips of my shoes in the stones, as if to pretend I hadn't been standing on the grave.

'Come with me!' he called. I brushed the earth from my knees. Even close up I couldn't make out the man's age; the sun was as if swallowed by the nearby mountains.

'I'm from the gardening shop over there, and work on the side as a gravedigger, too. What's your name?'

'Gravedigger on the side? Ruth Schwarz,' I said distractedly. 'And yourself?'

'It doesn't matter,' he replied, and I wasn't surprised at this statement for even a second, because it really didn't matter at all. He led me to a beautifully tended grave complete with a black monolith. From its centre rose an iron bar with two fat cherubs dancing around a butterfly: repulsiveness without parallel.

'Here, that's it, isn't it? Leopold Schwarz. Petra and Joseph Schalla. Heinz Schalla, Reinhard Markovic, Peter and Liese Schwarz. Richard Schalla, Ernst Schalla,' he said.

'Yes, that's it,' I confirmed, even though seven of those names didn't mean anything to me.

'Then you're the granddaughter? Good that you're here. I've already told your parents that we'll have to remove the ivy soon.'

'No, I think you have me confused with someone else; my parents haven't been here for years. My parents are — were, sorry — Elisabeth and Erich Schwarz.'

'What do you mean, were?'

'They passed away. That's why I'm here,' I began, as if hoping to clear up an unpleasant misunderstanding.

'No, that's ghastly. What happened? They were tip-top when they were here last week doing the grave.' Now the man pulled his cap from his head and sloped his eyebrows together to form a pointed roof, which I only saw because he suddenly came uncomfortably close to my face. (Ridiculous, I thought, how he'd perfected this rehearsed gesture; he probably received news like this on a daily basis.)

'What do you mean, last week?' I was stunned, but the shudder for what I'd learned only reached me as if I were insulated in cotton wool, as if there was an eternity lying between me and the realisation. Now wasn't the time for this, I thought, and pushed these thoughts away.

'And you're sure that they were here?'

'Almost always on Thursdays, as long as I've worked here. They were only flying visits, but that grave was always lovely, freshly cared for all year round. That's how you can know they're stand-up people. Respect for the dead. Incidentally, my condolences. Did your parents not tell you about their visits?'

'We didn't see each other very often,' I said.

'Shame. Do you live far away then?'

'No,' I said absentmindedly, 'we just had our differences.'

'Maybe there just wasn't an opportunity to mention their visits.'

'Maybe,' I said.

'I knew your grandparents; I was two years below your grandfathers at primary school. They were inseparable for a lifetime. They always used to say they were baptised together when they were two weeks old, and were best friends from then on. And then Joseph raised your father like his own son, when Leo disappeared. Oh well, old stories. If you need help with the funeral, I'm practically always here.'

'I do,' I said, and suddenly saw in the light of the chapel that the man was geriatric. 'I'll come by again tomorrow,' I said slowly, pulling up the hood of my coat. 'Good night.'

The earth squelched beneath my steps; whether I was walking over graves or paths, was impossible to say. The ground pressed against my soles, under which I noticed a slight movement and suddenly thought I had caught trails of ants, earthworms, beetles feasting on the freshly sunken corpses. I stumbled once or twice and only caught myself at the last moment, before I would have plunged in the fresh earth like into a black, velvety swimming pool.

6

From day one in Greater Einland my productivity exploded. On the second morning, after a hearty breakfast, I sat at my desk and noticed how everything that I had tried to get on track to no avail over the last few years flowed of its own accord onto the paper. I worked ten or twelve hours, forgetting to count the chimes of the bell in the nearby church tower, until the sun went down.

Long before I had a clear idea of how I could get the funeral preparations underway, I had found a modus operandi in which I could function like clockwork. A system I had been seeking all of my life up to that point: I got up every morning at six after a heavenly and always undisturbed night, found my way to the always already lit and warm dining room where the landlady Erna, who soon had a soft spot for me, put down a bowl of steaming porridge with nuts, pieces of apple, and raisins. After eating, I jogged to Kastelburg — exactly four kilometres away — and back in around forty-five minutes, often cooling myself in dry weather in a secluded reservoir. At eight I sat at my desk, alert and invigorated by the cold, working on drafts in which I thought I could already discern the final characteristics of my postdoctoral thesis. I occupied myself, completely entranced among the piles of papers, my laptop, and the physics books I'd brought with me, until 1pm, when I had arranged for Erna to knock at my door and bring me lunch. I didn't have to interrupt my work for even a minute, as they'd had someone bring a drip-filter coffee machine to my room, from which I now brewed cup after cup, and which transformed the cloudy, whitish mixture that flowed from the pipes due to the limestone content of the soil into aromatic coffee. Complete privacy, blissful simplicity. So I put off the funeral and all of its requirements for a few more days, even though I knew my meagre savings would soon run out.

I always finished working around six, and, wrung out but happy, went for a walk in the forest, which I fell in love with more and more every day. I sat on fallen tree trunks and looked out with an empty mind at the misty valleys; I pulled up the moss with my hands and inspected the black earth's crust for scents and concealed creatures. The force with which the formation of the landscape in these mountains had advanced captivated me. Up to that point I had only known it from textbooks: the birth of a mountain was preceded by the massive subsidence of sediment in the oceans, and billions of tonnes of soft, liquid organic material was pressed and conglomerated into plates in the depths. The sea took hold of me for the first time: a long time ago the mountains had been just an unified flux, and it took aeons before the concentrated layers began to rise again through the collision of the continental blocks. I contemplated the force it took for the earth's layers to unfold, like a stocking pulled up over a knee, and what a microorganism I was in comparison to them, alone on my walk through the forest. Over time, mountain ridges had collided with other mountains, creating an interference pattern, as if someone had thrown a pebble into a lake. Stony waterfalls formed in those places where the earth's crust hurtled down in free fall. In the blink of an eye of a planet, this undulating lake had become an unchanging stone monument. Every evening I came home, breathless with happiness.

This sequence of activities seemed to me, even though I had only carried it out for a few days, as if it had always been this way or as if its strength had always been within my basic nature and had only been waiting for this place in order to burgeon. At the time, I still thought that it would be a kind of holiday and that my stay in this freedom would be temporary. Returning promptly for dinner at eight in the tavern was the only compulsion that I submitted to each time — and only there did it become inevitable every evening to encounter the characters of the town.

I understood the rules immediately: either one had the reputation for appearing in a certain inn every day, or one didn't — in the first case, one showed up at the same table with almost nomological dependability, so as not to be a cause of concern for those persons already waiting for you. In the latter case, one probably never frequented these places. Nobody made a change for change's sake. There were, in individual inns, villages-within-a-village, microcosms, in which veritable parallel societies formed.

At eight, the locals were lined up like figures in a large music box on which cardboard cut-outs were pulled along a steel rail to the tune of their little melodies. I was on the scene punctually, too, as if it were a sacred duty. I studied their social interactions with the utmost concentration, in the beginning I even noted down the relationships: people became objects of observation, whose interactions with one another I learned to appreciate after only a few days. Although the dynamics of this system were formidable, each of its elements served a specific purpose.

The mixing of these people in these places was incomprehensible to me at first, though: proletariats sat at the same table as the self-evident aristocratic excellencies who appeared in tails and ascot ties to discuss their land over the cheapest set menu or to nonchalantly describe themselves as 'men of independent means'. Others were wrapped from head to toe in the colours of their local football team, TSV Einland, every day without exception. Among them, however, were individuals who apparently embodied cliched types — the priest, the town-hall clerk, the nurse, the professor, etc. — that rationally I knew had to exist, but who added something of the commedia dell'Arte for the townspeople gathered together. What almost everyone had in common was the habit of being tremendous drinkers. More or less every table was conducted as a regulars' table, and even I as an immigrant was assigned one on the third day.

In one corner was Hat-Maker Schlaf, whom I immediately recognised as the man from the petrol station. He was an old-fashioned industrialist with modern means, who had retained the Austro-Hungarian variant of Manchester capitalism. His age was difficult to determine — though he spoke enthusiastically of the fifties, he looked barely older than forty when he shaved. He shipped everything possible and impossible to China, always had his own crystal glass with him, which he had the landlady fill with hundred-year-old madeira wine, and reported to an ever-growing gaggle of polo-wearing young conservatives about tax breaks. He glorified the old currency, from the schilling right up to the krone, yet in the same breath, he extolled the creation of gigantic online retailers.

Near the bar sat the entourage of the Master-Builder Keinermüller, who was the coarsest, most uncultivated person I'd ever seen, barely able to read the daily menu, so that one of his girlfriends had to spell it out for him.

He himself was an ardent admirer of the construction worker Larry Fortensky, the seventh husband of Liz Taylor, and was obsessed with the idea of having a musical written about his life — an endeavour for which he intended to use all of his profits.

At my own table was Sister Elfriede, who reminded me of the Widow Bolte from *Max and Moritz*, but who possessed quite sophisticated tendencies and who asked me every few days for an interpretation of Maxwell's equations or something similar. She was a passionate amateur in the field of science, which was remarkable in light of the fact that she ran a soup kitchen on wheels during the day, and was mainly occupied with dicing carrots and celery. She misunderstood each and every one of the derivatives I wrote for her on serviettes between place settings, and mostly brought along her own miracle formulas the subsequent evening: jackalopes of the theory of relativity and the uncertainty principle, which said, for instance, that with the help of a silver coil and a little chlorine solution, one could travel forwards in time.

I was quickly accepted in the circles of locals, as I, too, had had to make an appearance at dinner every day due to the lack of cooking provisions in my study. The pleasant thing was that people neither ignored me, nor perceived me as a foreign body, but instead treated me as if I had left a few years ago and had now returned.

Ferdinand in particular, whom I'd only known for a few days, took me under his wing during this initial period.

'Come with me, mathematician,' he said every evening, as soon as I'd eaten the last bite of my dessert — and completely indifferent to the fact that I was a physicist — and led me from table to table, where constantly new wreaths of people stretched out their hands to me. The more time that passed, the more courageous I became in further investigating the structure of the town. Once after dinner, when I didn't have any cash on me and I apologised to Erna, she answered cryptically. 'Oh, that's no skin off my nose, you have to sort that out with the Countess.'

'But the Pumpkin belongs to you,' I said, confused.

'Yes and no,' Schlaf, who was sitting nearby, replied, because Erna had disappeared behind the servery in embarrassment. 'Erna owes the Pumpkin to the Countess. That was a scandal last year, when it came out that Erna's mother hadn't done any labour in lieu of tax on the building for twenty years. The lazy sow,' he whispered. 'It's now been put back on the inn as credit.'

'Put back?' I asked, aghast.

'Hereditary debt. Now Erna has to be open three hundred and sixty-five days a year,' Schlaf said, and slurped the soup of the day. 'Better for us in any case.'

'But no one talks about it outside of here,' Ferdinand said, putting his arm around my shoulder. 'What happens in the Pumpkin stays in the Pumpkin.' And as if he had quoted a secret motto, everyone said it in unison: 'What happens in the Pumpkin stays in the Pumpkin.'

The fact that some attempts were made to explain didn't mean that the really essential things had become clear to me; there were secrets that I could not further penetrate, subtexts, whisperings that I perceived crackling in the air as clearly as I knew that asking about them would be pointless. In the beginning, the most prominent topic and, at the same time, the one that presented the greatest mystery to navigate, was, of course: the hole.

On the following Tuesday I realised that I'd spent a whole week in Greater Einland. I only noticed when my medication was running low, though I could have sworn that I'd only arrived two nights ago, everything had proceeded so marvellously gooeyly. Only now did I realise the urgency with which I needed to attend to the funeral.

I called the funeral parlour right away and made an appointment for that evening to finish what I had come to do. After I hung up, I needed a moment to regain my composure. I once again had a sinking and constricting feeling; a scratching at the back wall of the throat that led to a vision: how the coffins, lowered down by a crank, would merge with the earth. Once my heart had settled down, all that remained was a sense of obligation — the imperative will to organise the best of all funerals for my parents, full of sentiment and dignity, even if I had no idea what that was supposed to be. I would need to find out more about their roots in the town, something that would be the key to their entire lives. Intoxicated by this great sense of duty, I headed for the town hall, as I'd actually been planning to do for days. It was an eclectic white building — Greek columns, but extremely small Greek columns, as if someone had wanted to build the kind of structure one would find on the Vienna Ring Road and had decided at the last minute that they couldn't stretch to those kinds of proportions.

'Which way to the town archive?'

'To the library? And your name?' asked the woman at the entrance.

'Exactly. I'm looking for documents about the town history. Schwarz.'

'Elisabeth?'

I paused for a moment. 'No, Ruth. Elisabeth is my mother,' I accidentally replied in the present tense.

'Oh, I beg your pardon. It's just that she seems to come very regularly according to the system, a proper local historian. Sorry, I've only had this job a week,' she said, while I just smiled and nodded. I was led to an underground section, with shelves filled with uniform blue-bound tomes set in one wall. It was lit by neon tubes, which lent the greenish room the aesthetic of an air raid bunker.

I looked around for a moment: here were hundreds and hundreds of books about Greater Einland — local chronicles in endless mutations, but also historical works, the contents of which stretched back to the Middle Ages. Thick volumes of historical land registers, entire atlases that named every piece of woodland, and comprehensive plans for every single house that had ever been built in the town. While I skimmed through the magnificent editions, I asked myself who could have written all this in a town with a population of a thousand. There were elaborate copperplate engravings in the encyclopaedias, and an ex libris stamped on the flyleaf in which I recognised the castle. Heritage cultivation must be a kind of popular sport here.

The most obvious thing to do was look for my mother's parental home: in the map index for 1946, her birth year, there was actually an alphabetical glossary of family names. However, this referred, via a critical apparatus, to another quadrant, which could be found in another volume — just as if it was intentional that the simplest information could only be obtained with great difficulty. The authors weren't listed alphabetically either, but rather listed according to the number of letters in their last name, so I first spent an hour counting over and over.

I had in mind a poignant ceremony at which I would weave details of my parents' origins and their later passions into a consistent narrative. Instead I found myself in the folios, amidst trivial details that were absolutely not necessary to know. For example, when I thought I'd found a folder with class lists from the primary school, it broke off half-way through, and only listed the caretakers of the institution, their family relationships, and a log of any renovations they had carried out. Such a quantity of data, this flood of arbitrariness, had exactly the same effect as the inaccessibility of information: it was impossible to deduce anything concrete from it.

'Excuse me,' I finally said to the woman at the entrance, who was herself hanging over a book. 'Is there perhaps a more compact local chronicle than those metres of shelves downstairs? The material is far too extensive.'

'I'm sorry,' she replied. 'You only get access to them once you've registered as a resident, madam — it's not desired for non-residents to read them.'

'Seriously? Why?' I asked.

'There's no specific reason for it, I guess, apart from the inconvenience of the customary local practices. But you can find enough on all topics, even beyond the chronicles.'

The woman had to have been about my age and bore the insignia of the young, left-wing academic — the first person I'd met here to do so: fashionable glasses, a bag made from truck tarpaulin, and a mug from a refugee aid organisation. She interested me as a person, because she didn't seem to fit into the image of the town but still somehow harmonised with it in a completely unique way.

'I wonder — no, of course you can't make any exceptions. I couldn't ask that of you. What's your name, by the way?'

'Anita,' she said, and held out her hand.

'Anita — we can, I think, dispense with the formalities.' A tentative nod. 'So you mean it won't be possible to take a very quick look at the local history to see what was happening in Greater Einland between 1944 and 1962? I would bring it right back. It's urgent.'

'It really won't be possible,' she said, but this time with a clearly guiltier conscience towards me; I sensed that she really wanted to grant my wish, but couldn't. Now every piece of personal information, every trigger of empathy, would move her closer in my direction.

'The thing is,' I said, 'my parents died recently. Both of them.' And I left it at that for the time being — because Anita was already melting under the pressure of sentimentality.

'Dear God — my condolences.'

'And now it's a matter of preparing them a dignified farewell. It was all so very sudden, I wasn't able to say goodbye.'

'That's terrible,' she said, and, as if to show her care, she let the book that she had been holding slip from her hand. It was *The New York Trilogy* by Paul Auster. 'I also lost my father recently.'

'Awful,' I said, then added: 'You keep thinking about the last thing you said. It was just a week ago. I don't have any siblings and I have to organise everything on my own.'

I watched her features closely — it was easy to overdo things like this. But I had judged it exactly right: her eyebrows were drawn down by an invisible weight. She wrestled with it.

'And now I need the local chronicles because I don't have much research time left in order to find out, well — I basically don't know much about it. I've never actually been here before, and in my current emotional state it would be very difficult to sift through all this material.'

Anita was in a conflict that seemed to rock her body back and forth.

'Are you an informant?' she suddenly asked quietly.

'An informant for who? No, of course not.'

She blushed and looked around. 'The Countess sometimes checks that we're keeping to the rules. And I've already taken a book without issuing a borrowing slip.' Now she leaned across the table towards me, her mouth to my ear, so close that I could tell that my plan had worked. I felt guilty all of a sudden. 'You can never tell anyone about it, okay? If the Countess finds out, I'll be fired and out on the street.'

I took the book down to the basement and put it on a table, on which I had now gathered the most important volumes for my objective: I wanted to know more about where and how my parents had spent their childhood. With help from this new local chronicle, I ought to be able to find out where the street my mother's parents' house had stood on was today. Instead, I came across a section on the subject of estate names.

In Greater Einland, as well as in most of the rural regions of the German-speaking territory, the name of the estate or common name has always been understood as a designation of the place of residence in addition to the surname, which is given to all residents of a estate, even married couples, servants, obligated persons, children, godchildren, and yes, from time to time, animals. In spoken usage, the estate name usually overlays the family name after a certain time. One would say:

'Hofer, commonly known as The Oakery' or 'The Jewry is on the Stocker Estate' or 'Lukas Hirtner lives up on Pig Hill Farm, so Pig Hill Lukas'.

One peculiarity of this mentality calls for an explanation. In many communities, people are understood as being part of a landscape. One cannot say that the environment would ever adapt to the residents — rather, the residents must grow into the landscape, adapt to it, belong to it.

In this sense, ownership seems to likewise be the other way around, as the place names suggest: the people work for the farm — the farm is what remains, the people who manage it cease to be.

But it also means: only those who know the name can take possession of the land, and only those who have a specific name can belong to the surrounding area. On the other hand, if you have a name that does not belong to it, you have to remain a foreign body. Only those who know what has happened in the landscape can grow into it; those who are not connected to its past cannot allow themselves any hope of a future in it. It is known that after the death of the so-called 'owner' of a farm, people sometimes inherited not only his property, but also his staff and his relatives .

If the traditional appellations were the warp threads, the names newly laid over them are simply the weft threads that weave everything into a tight fabric. Fabric was to be understood mythically here: This has been well-documented at the current Oakery, formerly also known as The Burners, because two different versions of its history were in circulation: that in times of yore a clay burner is said to have sintered the most exquisite goods, is the first. Second, however, that in 1656 a peddler-woman from the

village by the name of Anna Halfer was found guilty
of witchcraft and was burned with her ten and three-
year-old daughters, locked in the hayloft, a few days
before the trial. Both explanations could be correct;
however, an oak tree was planted on the property
around 1860 to end the debate.

I finally understood why it was so difficult to find individual
houses or to orientate oneself in the general material. A register
of every single house was attached, infinitely extensive and rich
with detail, with illustrations of window sills and the most precise
calculations for the construction of the roof trusses. The house
descriptions weren't an isolated case; the entire chronicle had a
peculiar structure. After the long part about the estate names,
there was an account of the history of public buildings with the
same thoroughness. This was made considerably more difficult
by one factor: on 22 April 1945, the town had been smashed into
a heap of ruins. Apparently, the enemy had known that aircraft
parts, essential for the war, were being manufactured in the mine,
and had reacted promptly:

This wrecked form dragged on for about three hundred
and forty days. When the Russians finally allowed it,
everyone comprehended the impossibility of clearing
the set pieces of the former buildings, although
everyone from primary school children to pensioners
would have been willing to tackle it. But Greater
Einland only had around nine hundred citizens who

were even capable of movement — after all, all young men had been sent to the front. So it was collectively decided to pour a total of sixteen thousand cubic metres of concrete and small stones over everything that had once been Greater Einland, and thus the heap of rubble and all the possessions, corpses, parts of buildings, furniture, canals, destroyed vehicles, and buried weapons within it were to be poured into a hardened foundation for the future. After that, the entire town, as it was before the bombing, was rebuilt a few metres higher, and based on historical photos. A true-scale replica. However, no pictures were taken of a few of the buildings and they were simply forgotten during the reconstruction, which is why the grid has slipped imperceptibly. One map had been laid over the other, and this had displaced the first — in some places only by a few centimetres, in others by a few metres. Greater Einland had shifted.

The last chapter was the longest: the historical narration of the town's history in the Middle Ages. It began with a brief summary of the founding of the high market, the plague epidemic, and so on — but after that I found a strange fable, which took up most of the book, about someone called Pergerhannes. He was — as I gathered from the first sentence — a wealthy craftsman in the seventeenth century, who had surrendered himself to a fanatical goldrush and built an underground tunnel system beneath the town. Just as I was delving deeper, I heard footsteps on the stairs and turned around, hoping it would only be Anita. Sure enough, she appeared in the basement. But something didn't feel right at all. Wearing a grave expression, she rushed over to the table, and took the local chronicle, which she immediately slipped into the pocket of her dress, out of my hands.

'The Countess wants to see you,' she said.

7

In front of the steps that led to the town hall, a woman and a man were waiting who weren't, as I had first thought, Count and Countess, but who informed me that they were supposed to escort me to the castle.

'We have come to take you to your appointment,' the woman said after we had gone out into the street. I watched with amusement as they flanked me to the left and right, like I was a criminal being transferred from one prison to another — the situation was so ridiculous that I didn't know what to say and instead cooperated in silence. Even my escorts didn't break the silence as they led me through the less-frequented side streets past the main square to the beginning of the hill, on whose peak the castle stood. Apart from its two towers, the windows of which rose up illuminated from the negative space of the treetops, it was concealed by thick woodland. As we left the asphalt road behind the town wall, we were in complete darkness. The dirt path led into a tangle of roots; stones protruded from the forest track, which I tripped on while walking. In these moments one of my two companions, who incidentally found their way around like cats, would always grab me under the arm and pull me on. Their silence had suddenly become eerie to me: no information, no reassurance, no end, no time, no orientation — and worse still: my own silence in response.

But then we were stepping back out of the forest and standing before the castle, which now presented itself to its full scope. The mood had immediately turned into benign baroque: a so-called French garden, in which the bushes had been trimmed into the form of Platonic solids (cylinder, sphere, cone), and at the centre of which was a fountain, home to half a dozen water-spraying putti. The lawn looked as if it had been cut with nail scissors, and as a final flourish someone had, in this perfect lawn, as if in mockery, hammered in a sign that read 'Keep Off the Grass'. We walked along a white gravel path to an entrance door, which was immediately opened by an incredibly old little man, a person whom I instantly identified from his clothes as a butler. His upper body must have been bent in servitude for so long that scoliosis and age had now cemented him into this position, seeing as he didn't abandon the right-angle when leading me into the building. But his golden buttons sparkled, and his shoes were freshly polished.

'Good evening,' he said. 'Please take off your boots.'

There was something terribly feudal about everything. Up to that point nothing would have come to my mind if I considered the concept of a 'hunting lodge', but I recognised an inkling of this term in this building. An entrance with a huge staircase, decorative mouldings on the coats of arms — but on the wall between them were deer antlers and carved wood panelling, which reverted the overall effect from pompous to provincial. Portraits of countless ancestors, all of whom had put on their jackets to show their connection to the countryside — but in among them, marble busts of the most popular poets and thinkers adorned the knobs of the bannisters.

I was, of course, repulsed.

'Lovely,' I said. 'Where should I go?'

'The Countess is waiting for you upstairs in the orange salon. Go left 'till the end of the corridor, then second door on the right you're stopping,' the servant answered, with faulty grammar. I climbed the impressive stairs and came to a corridor that led deep into the building. Everything was soundproofed: thick carpets were rolled down the two-hundred-metre-long corridor, and swallowed so utterly every sound in its shag fabric it was as if it wanted to oppose the laws of acoustics. I snapped my fingers several times and struggled to hear the sound at all. Every few steps along the corridor there was a door to the left and right; the entire flock-wallpapered passage was windowless and weakly lit. I was briefly surprised that after my escort to the castle I had now been left completely unsupervised. I looked around and ran my fingers over the wallcovering to uncover the secret of its light absorption, but nothing: it was normal paper. At the end of the corridor a door was open on the right. I knocked for decency's sake, even though I had been standing under the huge, carved door frame for a long time already. When no one said anything, I entered the room.

As the name had quite rightly suggested, it was a room of massive proportions, painted orange, furnished like a cross between a library and a study. In front of the farthest wall of books was a large desk that seemed to be overflowing with documents;

behind it, an imperial armchair capped off with two lion heads on the backrest. But before that, on the other side, was the most fragile of folding chairs I'd ever seen. I walked over and looked at the bundles of papers that were hanging over the edge of the table — looked around furtively and picked up a piece of paper: they were all begging letters. The first one read, for instance: 'To your excellency, the Countess von Greater Einland, gracious Ulrike Knapp-Korb-Weidenheim: I humbly request that the tax payments for the calendar year 2006 be deferred for reasons of a personal nature. A hospital bed needed to be purchased for the in-home care of my mother for 1300 EUR, which is why we ask your Countship for your tolerance for a few months.' Other requests concerned the harvest of the fruit fields or planning permission for the building of a window ledge. In short: every official matter that one could imagine converged here on a bureaucratic rummage table. To have people pay court this way seemed absurd to me, a farce, but I couldn't stop reading.

'Good afternoon,' I heard a voice say from the corner of the room, after I'd been standing in front of the table for a few minutes. I turned around. It was only at this moment that I noticed the Countess, who had been sitting up in a recess above the library wall that was barely visible from the other side of the room, wordlessly observing my grubbing around in the shallows of her paperwork.

'Do not nose around in confidential papers. I was already irritated that you pawed my wallpaper. Do you always do that?' she said, and climbed down from her strange gallery. 'But let's put this aside for now. I have more important matters that I have to discuss with you. Since you're already standing at my desk, we can take a seat right away.'

My mind raced with the question of how she could have seen my assault on the wall, and I felt ashamed. We sat down on the available chairs — she on the regal armchair, I on the folding chair — so that, now I could see her for the first time from the front, she seemed to float half a metre above me. I had to tilt my head back in order to look her in the eye. It became clear to me that up to this moment I had believed that whoever had thought up this ludicrous request for me had to themselves be a laughing stock; yet as I was sitting opposite her, we found ourselves in a realm of absolute seriousness.

The Countess, though she was significantly shorter than me, radiated something innately domineering. She had to be in her mid-sixties and wore a bun that was pulled tightly behind her head, which forged her grey hair against her delicate scalp like nylon thread. She was wearing a floor-length blue skirt and a matching jacket, which was stretched tightly across her chest like canvas. Now that she leaned over the endlessly wide table, I saw that her delicate fingers were covered with rings, at least three of which bore different coats of arms.

'Knapp-Korb von Weidenheim is my name. You have probably heard of me,' she said.

'Ruth Schwarz,' I said.

'Yes, I've known that for a long time.' The Countess kept a serious face, as if I had broken into her house at this hour and now had to answer for it. An unbearable tension arose around us as we fell silent.

'Well.' I urged myself to speak. 'What a beautiful building.'

'This castle has belonged to my family for over five hundred years, you know. Castle Weidenheim, seat of the margraviate, formerly used as an organ of high jurisdiction.'

There was really nothing to say about that. We fell once more into thirty horrific seconds of silence. The Countess was above me at such an unfortunate angle that my neck ached from keeping her in view.

'May I ask why you wanted to speak to me?' I finally dared to ask.

'Well, may I not?' she said snappily. 'I know everyone in this town and it ought to remain that way. We ought to get to know one another?'

'Absolutely,' I said, intimidated by her vehemence. 'I'm actually very pleased to meet you.'

'Well, if you don't want to, you can always just leave!' she shouted, as if she hadn't heard what I'd said.

'Of course I want to stay. Are you really a Countess?' I asked mollifyingly, pointing at the stucco moulded ceiling, as if proof of her nobility might be found there. For a moment I thought I had gone too far with this question, because the Countess stood up, frozen and with a far-off gaze like the Statue of Liberty, only to then, with her hand behind her back, step out from behind the desk as if it concerned a subject of utmost depth.

'There is a certain type of character in our town that has persisted over the last few hundred years. You'll notice it soon enough. In any case, in the first instance I was the mayor, elected and re-elected in four legislative periods, democratically and according to protocol, until the office became too much trouble for me. Secondly, as you have probably already heard, my husband and I are the owners of the town.'

She sat back down again, fastidiously positioning her lower back into a ramrod straight position. 'Now, most people would take that to be a contradiction,' she said curtly, and as if to test my reaction. 'That someone can be elected and own the land. Do you also find it grotesque?'

I tried to be diplomatic. 'I don't altogether understand how someone can own a town. When I was looking for Greater Einland, it wasn't even in the municipal directory; it's extremely troublesome to find.' My words were drowned by loud, disjointed piano chords that could be heard from below.

'I beg your pardon — my husband is a great art lover. We're not in the directory. Most of us haven't been registered for our entire lives. Of course, that has to do with Austria as a whole, but also with the fact that certain structures have remained that one cannot remove as such. Do you understand? As if one were trying to pull a skeleton out of a body, something gets forced asunder.'

The non-answer to my question had thus been supplemented by further ambiguities. The Countess had long since got up again and had gone to a shelf on the back wall of the drawing room, from which she took out a large book. It was an ostentatious atlas, on which I read 'Franziscean Cadastre', and which she dropped onto the table with dust-swirling force.

'Please don't touch the horse. I am highly sensitive and pick up colds very easily,' she said with a flare of temper. She pointed to a marble statue of a horse that protruded from the paper in the middle of the desk, which I hadn't shown even the slightest intention of touching.

'I'll tell you how it is — I have a job for you. Look, this is the Franziscean Cadastre, which our dear Emperor commissioned in 1810 in order to survey all Austrian real estate. Here is Greater Einland.'

'What sort of job?' I asked over the book.

'Well, it concerns all sorts of things: calculations, fundamental physical work on the subject of deterioration and erosion, especially of the natural landscape. You must in any case be present at my salons, and then always be working on small tasks in between, maybe also giving presentations to my guests to brief them. Do you understand?' The Countess had sprung up again. She rummaged through a drawer for a moment, but then gave up and switched on a golden desk lamp.

'I don't quite understand. Briefings on what topic?'

'Oh, quite distinct things. You may have heard that we have certain problems with erosion. But if I have to keep explaining it to you, I can just do it myself.' Only now, in the electric light, did I see that, under the violent parting, her high forehead was wet with sweat. 'Someone has to take a look at it in a concrete sense, but above all I have some structural tasks for you, that must be addressed with some urgency. The amount of remuneration is immaterial. You can also pick out a little house, we would take care of that. Come now, I'm proposing something to you.'

'I don't plan to stay very long,' I said.

'Very well, you've persuaded me. We'll do it like this: you work half the day for me, the other half you can use for your postdoctoral thesis. I would make sure that you get all the materials you need, get all the literature that you require, and not only pay you a full salary but double for all I care. Do with it what you like.'

When she mentioned my thesis, panic shot through me. There was no way for her to have known about it. Had she called the university?

'Regarding the salons — of course, you don't even know my salons — one could say that you would act as my right hand, so to speak. The second obligation would be, however, that you would always work here, next to my study, where I conduct my administrative work. In other words, to put it briefly, I would like to regularly look over your shoulder while you work. You can —'

'Sorry, I have to decline,' I interrupted her finally. 'First, because I will be leaving after my parents' funeral, and second, because I'm unable to help you with geological problems. I'm a theoretical physicist, not a practical one.'

'But that won't be a problem. We have some very fundamental questions to clarify first.'

'No, it's not going to work, completely impossible,' I said again. For a moment, however, doubt entered my mind: *finishing my thesis*, I thought, briefly infatuated, but then rejected the idea.

'We have a lot of important people here locally who would help you with every eventuality. We all have something on our minds from time to time.'

No, it was absurd: having to lecture at a Countess's salon on issues I had no interest in, and tolerating people who belonged to so-called higher society. (This displeasure against pearl necklaces and golf trousers, against honourable titles and cufflinks, however, only floated on the surface like a stubborn oil spill above a much vaster shoal. Only much later would I comprehend that something conflicting also lay beneath it: fear. A fear of the Countess, which I tried to mitigate with contempt, a fear of becoming condemned and expelled by her, a vague fear of the discipline that expressed itself in her tense demeanour, but especially a fear of not being liked by her, in spite of the fact I didn't especially like her myself.)

'I would reconsider if I were you. You want to be untethered, I understand that. You remind me a lot of myself at your age, I see a lot of me in you,' said the Countess. 'We've heard a lot about you. One again, my condolences on the unexpected death of Elisabeth and Erich. Two very wonderful people.'

'Yes, sadly,' I said, irritated at how casually she had mixed her condolences among the rest of her agenda, and all the more so because she pretended to have known my parents.

'We were well acquainted with each other. I don't know if your father told you, but we were in the same class, eight years of secondary school. He was an unruly boy — already at seventeen he was a true proto-'68er, if you know what I mean.'

The Countess had a way of looking at me between sentences that made me forget to be quick on the comeback. But now she was silent for a moment, as if she really had to think.

'Tell me, did your parents ever say anything about me? Or anything about Greater Einland?' It was the first question she asked as if she actually wanted to know something from me. I almost could have sworn she looked concerned.

'No, I didn't even know if Greater Einland really existed, to tell the truth. I didn't know that you existed.'

'Yes, your parents and I were intimately acquainted. Anyway,' she said tersely, and brushed the topic away with the wave of her hand. 'Very well, you don't want to work for me just yet,' she changed the subject again. 'You will change your mind at the right time, I can feel it, but very well, you want to make it exciting. Now tell me a little more about yourself. You're a physicist? Where did you study?'

'In Vienna and Zurich, semesters abroad in Shanghai and Dublin,' I recited mechanically.

'Fine. And you've been working on a postdoctoral thesis on the philosophy of time for the last six years. An interesting subject. But why is it taking so long to complete it? You made such quick progress at first.'

'Personal events,' I said, feeling as if I'd been caught out.

'You are unmarried, why? Oh, I see!' Her attempt at smiling was even more unnerving than her austerity, as if she had practised it for a long time, but still hadn't mastered it. 'Of course, you are new and don't know who informs me of all these things. Come over here.' We went to the rear window, and the Countess pulled a kitschy golden tassel, which made the curtains move to the side, revealing a view of the town far below.

'The town is a sensitive nervous system, on whose pathways information is constantly being transported back and forth. The castle is the centre from which corridors, streets, and hidden paths lead into all the cells of the town. Everything that comes out of the town passes through the castle and vice versa, as if we were metaphors for one another, you understand? A kind of spiritual feudal law, from which each of the two parties can benefit.'

The idea disgusted me. So she had been told everything. But who could I accuse? At least there was nothing to hide; it couldn't be said that the people with whom I'd spoken in the town had breached my trust.

'I'd like to go home now,' I said.

'Soon,' said the Countess, as if it were a matter of her own discretion. 'First of all, I'd like to know a few more things from you. If you really want to leave so soon, how long do you intend on staying in Greater Einland, and what form will your contribution to our community take?'

Now I was angry. 'Only until after my parents' funeral. I'm waiting for a grave plot to be assigned. I have no intention of settling here for a long time, and therefore I see no reason to actively contribute to the community. I don't see why a cross-examination such as this is suitable — after all, I'm on public property.'

'You see, that's where you're wrong. We just discussed that Greater Einland is on my private property. You ought to listen better. And that's why I'm requesting information. Well, if you don't have any ideas, I'll offer it to you again: you will come to one of my Tuesday salons without obligation. It would be a shame if I didn't at least introduce you to some of my acquaintances.'

'I'll think about it,' I said, despite the fact that I wouldn't consider it for even a second. I just wanted to get away from this castle. It was Thursday, and surely I would be given the go-ahead for the grave before there even *was* a salon.

'You can go now, I have to be in bed by 10pm. Do you need someone to accompany you back to the guesthouse?'

'I'll find my own way back, thank you,' I said.

She sat back down at her desk and watched me put on my coat. 'Oh yes, one more thing,' the Countess said. 'You can, of course, consider the grave plot approved.'

'And a tap water on the house.' Frau Erna placed a glass of whitish liquid next to my dinner. I thanked her and took the bottle of mineral water I'd brought with me out of my rucksack.

After more than a week I was still not used to it: every time I turned on the tap in Greater Einland, sly, turbid liquid, which only bore a passing resemblance to water, flowed from the pipes. Heavy with lime, it passed, via a glass, directly into the digestive tract of whoever drank it, and in doing so, it was reassured, one wouldn't come to any harm, because it was from an organic origin. This lime, which turned the water in the ground white like fresh milk running from a cow's udder, seeped into the organs and lime washed — I imagined — a body's fluids until they forfeited their deep red in favour of the white colour of the Greater Einland soil. To cleanse yourself of it was an illusion: one sat in opaque baths, drank naturally cloudy tap water, and washed the lime into your hair until the pale dulling of the tips became the norm, because everyone boasted them. One cleaned their room with thick, viscous rags, and cooked pasta stiffer than it was when it came out of the packet.

'Boo, only the best is good enough for the Professor,' Ferdinand said, flicking the glass bottle before throwing his deck of cards on the table. Now that I had been socially accepted after my first official visit to the castle, I often sat long after midnight, drinking and playing skat, while I listened to stories about the town. The mythical world around the hole, especially, electrified me. On one of these evenings, after we'd ordered the fifth round of pear schnapps, Master-Builder Keinermüller paused in the middle of one of his obscene toasts and stared enraptured at the wall.

'Ah, he's seeing martyrs again,' Ferdinand said, poking him in the ribs and laughing.

'Martyrs?' I asked. Everyone apart from Ferdinand seemed a little embarrassed.

'Saint Thomas, the patron saint of room carpenters and builders, appeared before my blessed grandfather in the mine,' Keinermüller said at last with a husky voice, and then was silent for a long time before he continued speaking. 'Saint Thomas was very muscular and his eyes shimmered turquoise, my grandfather told me. He was barefoot and only wore a thin tunic, and yet he wasn't cold.'

'Maybe that was because of his holiness. You don't freeze so quickly,' Sister Elfriede interjected.

'My grandfather took a vow the very next morning. Every house that springs loose from the subsidence, should in days to come be renovated by his business, and only with the limestone from the hole itself at that.'

I watched, with disgust, the thick water in my glass swaying back and forth. Then Sister Elfriede spoke up. 'I remember the

Master-Builder from my childhood, may he rest in peace. He had a serene aura, with his soft eyes and wavy hair. Like in an Italian fresco.'

'And back then he already knew that it was ne'er long now that the hole once more belongs to us,' Kainermüller finished, and Sister Elfriede nodded vigorously.

'What do you mean, that the hole belongs to us again?' I asked.

'And we've had important traditions on St Thomas's Day ever since. The young men go to the old entrance to the mine and hammer a nail into the locked wooden gate blindfolded. With a rock they must have found themselves. And the nail is forged from pewter.'

'Pewter from the region,' Sister Elfriede added.

'Sorry, but who was the hole taken over from?' I asked again.

'Well, from the ones back then, that specific time,' Keinermüller said. 'Where we'd been occupied to a certain extent. It was an expropriation.'

'Only if the victim sacrifices something themselves will they be free again,' Sister Elfriede said.

These stories amazed me: the priest in Greater Einland was a respected man, and some people took pride in appearing at mass on Sundays, but it seemed more of a habit, a long-held custom rather than true piety. I'd never seen anyone in the Pumpkin pray. 'I had no idea Greater Einland was so religious,' I said.

'Come off it, religious! This goes far beyond religion. It's about sacrifice, because we hold certain things in very high esteem here. Indeed, man is wedded to where they come from, with the ground from which we all come.'

'What things do you hold in high esteem?' I asked, but suddenly everyone went silent and couldn't turn back to the skat quickly enough. I had to ask something innocuous to bring the conversation to an amicable end.

'So, is that why you became a Master-Builder?'

'Spades trump,' Keinermüller murmured, and I played.

8

It wasn't until a few days after the strange encounter with the Countess that it occurred to me that I'd had missed my appointment for the funeral arrangements. I hurriedly called the company's office from the reception and invented a tall tale about a psychological breakdown. The lady in the secretary's office gave me a new appointment for the following day without complaint, and asked me whether I happened to already know when my parents would be transferred.

I said that I didn't, and promised to be in touch again soon. Too restless to work, I listened, lying on the floor back in my room, to a couple of Chet Baker albums I'd bought in a second-hand shop, which fused with the autumn weather. It had been damp for the last few days, and, from sunrise to sunset, twilight had covered everything — there was the perpetual sneaking feeling that rot had already set in beneath the autumn leaves.

Heavy-limbed I went back downstairs to do my duty — there was no Internet, so I had to consult the telephone book in discussion with Frau Erna.

I dialled my aunt's number, slowly and almost fearful of the final last digit, which my index finger swiped into the rotary dial

— but as soon as the second ring tone sounded, I hung up the receiver and went outside.

On all of the ten days that I'd spent in Greater Einland up to that point, I had roamed the landscape like a restless animal. I, who had always been a passionate city dweller, now became anxious if I spent more than three or four hours in an enclosed space. I would begin to get up every five minutes and look at the nature outside of my window, which hid itself like a ghost behind the house fronts. Everything seemed to take place in this landscape. Storms and downpours, clouds of fog, but especially thunder gave off an irresistible allure that in a few minutes could compel me into my boots and out onto the rounded, wooded mountain top — in the forest, on the heath, and near the entry points to the hole. There were three or four of them — former exits for the miners who had still been driving into the mountains a few decades previously.

I never tired of exploring the extensive topographies here, for several hours a day. I often didn't notice that I had been walking through clotted mud and that hard clumps of dirt had trickled into my waistband. I had a particularly intense relationship with moss: a soft field was hard to resist. Lying on the foothills of the rocks, I breathed in its earthy scent. It was an endless enticement that changed with the seasons and never lost its charm. Every blade of grass, a sensitive extension of my own nerves — as if everything were made from the same thoughts, and as if that which had covered the meadows with dew after a cool night was now bedewing me, too. On some days, the harshness of nature affected me far too much to resist, and I dropped my work to rush outside. On others, I felt this desire as an analytical thirst for knowledge, borrowed a nature guide from the library, and categorised the plants and beetles until it got dark or my dose of codeine wore off. Even the pine cones seemed to me to be an innate expression of a deep truth that had to be understood from the soil in a hard, knotty language. I didn't have anything in common with the people of Greater Einland — on the contrary — instead, I began to melt into the nature around the town. After just a few days I found my way around intuitively; later, after weeks, the forest had become an extension of my own body. In short, this was a long sought-after sense of belonging, an identification that connected me to the landscape. I would almost say: I'd found a home.

When I came home one evening from one of my sprawling walks, I was stopped by Frau Erna.

'Ruth,' she called, 'someone phoned you back, I wrote it down. Your aunt, can that be right? She said she had a missed call from you, and has tried to call four or five times since then. It sounded urgent.'

'Thank you very much, but I can't call her back till tomorrow. I'll be with the Countess tonight,' I said as a form of deflection, which I immediately regretted when I saw the effect it had on Erna.

'In the salon? You? Ruth, that's incredible, after barely two weeks — Ruth Schwarz has been invited to a salon!' she called into the parlour, and, to my horror, everyone turned in my direction and exuberantly raised a glass to me. Erna was downright beside herself. 'I don't know if you know how exclusive it is, most of us will never get to be at a salon. Our Philipp is sometimes invited, too, he's a geologist.'

The whole scene put me in a tight spot, as I'd only wanted an excuse to delay calling back.

'Philipp will certainly accompany you, if you like. Philipp, when are you going?'

'That's not necessary, I'd like to go on my own,' I said quickly.

'I'll be on my way in ten minutes,' a young man called from the bar, loudly zipping up his jacket. He looked to be around my age, and had the kind of haircut that would go with a band shirt just as well as it would with a polo shirt.

'Together it is,' Erna said. 'And tomorrow at breakfast you can tell everyone what was discussed. We're always curious about what's going on up there.'

Up there, they said when they talked about the castle — a phrase that embodied both awe and admiration simultaneously, because 'up there' referred to a place of longing that was, as long as one still longed for it, as a precaution, always also subliminally despised. Otherwise you would have had to despise yourself for not having yet been there. The whole room trembled gleefully with envy, like a sulky block of aspic. Nothing more could be done; I would have to make an appearance at the salon. Appallingly, Philipp now appeared, the so-called geologist, hat ready to put onto his head. I could tell from his facial expression that he was psyching himself up to flirt, while Frau Erna had clenched both her hands over her pressed thumbs in an ominous good-luck gesture right in front of my face. No sooner had we closed the door behind us and turned onto the main square than I remembered that I was still wearing jeans, which were rigid with mud.

One of the most enigmatic facets of human existence is the speed with which we are able to adapt and take what had seemed so bizarre as a given. When I saw the castle for the second time in my life, it seemed to me the most normal thing in the world that the staff took the coats of the guests being loaded out of expensive cars. I was relieved to be able to part from the geologist, who, as expected, tried to hit on me several times on the way. First, probably to prolong the conversation, he led us unnecessarily through countless cumbersome suburban plots. The highpoint of the conversation was an invitation to his thirty-fifth birthday, which was to be celebrated with a big party in a remote hall in Oberschenkelbach next weekend. '*Bad Taste Party. Motto: Bad, worse, worst, worstest. You should be ashamed of yourself.* That's the theme,' he had begun abruptly and huddled close to me, claiming that he couldn't see anything in the dark. Then he went a step further. 'I was so sorry to hear about Erich and Elisabeth. I had got so used to their visits up at the castle.'

'At the castle?' I asked. 'Why were they at the castle? And when?'

'Well, every week, with the Countess. After all, that's why they were — you know, they'd even spent the night there on the day of the accident. But maybe I'm remembering it wrongly. See you shortly.'

We had turned onto the castle grounds and were, weirdly, separated according to gender at the cloakrooms.

'I may ask you to come to the tables,' said a young woman in an apron, her phrasing as awkward as the old man's had been a few days previously. The reception hall was lavishly decorated. It looked as if Jay Gatsby and Austrian country aesthetics had celebrated their nuptials: abundant arrangements of gentian flowers were placed among the deer antlers, and pumpkin kitsch (floral arrangements, wreaths, macramé), presumably meant to create an autumnal atmosphere, lay inelegantly about the room while people peeled off their winter coats.

The other guests evidently knew one another, and flung themselves about each other with embraces, cheek kisses, low bows, and handshakes. I was a foreign body in this tightly woven network of acquaintances, and considered fleeing one last time. Instead I sloshed upstairs, driven by the crowd, and into the right wing of the building — the one I hadn't yet been in. No one apart from me had transgressed the evident formal dress code. I tried unsuccessfully, as we entered the splendidly decorated salon, to hide my now brown jeans and the coarse-knitted jumper under my coat. The glances were unavoidable, though; I looked like a vagrant.

Name cards for each guest were set out on a long ornate table, but while everyone else found their seats with magnetic assuredness, I was like an aimlessly fluttering insect while searching for mine. It was only when the last person was seated that I could determine my place as a gap between the others. As soon as I sat down, an oppressive silence fell over the company at the table, which lasted almost a minute before the melodramatic clacking of steps could be heard. In a floor-length skirt and matching jacket, the Countess entered the salon and sat at the head of the table.

'Welcome to the tenth salon of this year,' she said. 'Please, be at ease.' An exhalation went through the group, as if they had collectively emerged from the water. Only then did I realise that I, too, had been holding my breath and now, breathing heavily, gripped the table.

'We have a new guest in our midst, the young physicist Ruth Schwarz, who in the future may act as my advisor. In matters of stability, in relation to our great indisposition.'

I protested weakly, but still couldn't catch my breath — I briefly raised my hand, which was only taken by the others as an indication that I wanted to make myself known as the person being referred to. The Countess continued with her introduction: 'Frau Schwarz, here at this table are the most significant personalities in our wonderful town. I will skip an explicit round of introductions, but you will get to know everyone in time. Honoured friends, I plan to initiate Frau Schwarz in all of our projects. She is a native,' the Countess explained.

'Only my parents are from here,' I finally interjected.

'So native,' the Countess cut off. 'Frau Schwarz, this is the town council. If you wish, you may feel extremely ennobled to be present here.'

I raised my hand again. 'Shouldn't we wait for the mayor?'

Everyone except the Countess laughed, as if a child had asked something adorable and dumb.

'Frau Schwarz, the mayor is not part of our business,' the Countess said calmly. 'You see, in this town, as in our country as a whole, there are two bodies that operate separately. There is the old order as we practise it here, and then the new one, which at a certain point was simply spread over the first, without considering the grown, organic structures. These now grind up against one another, which creates a number of problems.' At this point she waved in the waiters, and the topic was over. 'The appetisers and today's agenda, Engineer Heinzelmann.'

Four young women now carried in tray after tray, heavily laden with antipasti, truffle salami, French speciality cheeses, olives, vol-au-vents, pieces of roast duck in cranberry sauce, and dozens of bread baskets full of baked goods. In addition, fine red wines were served. Everything was exquisitely delicious. I was only vaguely aware that an elderly gentleman with a rattling voice had begun to voice the day's agenda. 'Preliminary meeting one, prolegomena for a trade regulation. Main point one, art actions to make use of the collapses; point two, discussions on the allocation of properties on the Wastl-Hohe —'

The rest became a blur to me while I enjoyed a scallop, which, with its orange and garlic sauce and roasted rosemary, triggered an ecstatic response within me. I would just sit in silence at this table, get intoxicated from the culinary delights, and before anyone could infiltrate me, start walking home again. Engineer Heinzelmann was like a debutante, responsible for every curtsy and opening of the floor for every plan point, but was time and time again reprimanded by the Countess, who took the lead on his little dances.

'We have received complaints that people would like to have one of the large supermarket chains that are prevalent in the rest of Austria represented in town, instead of our tried and tested system of grocers,' he said. 'But that's nothing new.'

'Absolutely not, that's out of the question. The discussion is open,' the Countess said with the finality of a judge's verdict.

'Of course, we have no interest in the products of globalisation,' a man in an old military uniform began. I could read the name on his chest: Colonel General Heidenthal. But the longer I studied his regalia, the more unsure I was whether it was a made-up uniform, as there were subtle differences that distinguished it from the normal army uniform. 'So the question can be reduced to how we convey the impression that they are nevertheless there. So far, we have been able to replicate around fifty per cent of the products in demand.'

'Lilly, what do the salespeople say?' the Countess asked an old woman wearing a dirndl and apron.

'We are still working on Coca-Cola. People keep complaining about a liquorice smell. The cream cheese often clumps together, and sometimes we have to write up new lids with different best-before dates on a daily basis. So it's a bit inconvenient,' she said.

'From my point of view, we have to desensitise people and, through public intervention, persuade them that we shouldn't be so sensitive when it comes to tastes. This kind of conversation must be stopped,' the Countess said.

The matter was structured like so: because local products were promoted as part of an almost gigantic initiative, but the population longed for international brands, they had begun to

Raphaela Edelbauer

have the latter reproduced by local companies and passed off as originals using self-printed labels. It seemed, however, to have led to a problem not thought through in advance: people wondered why the gummy bears from the adverts were already available, but other sweets of the same brand weren't, and now a legion of food technicians and grocers were constantly working on copies of a variety of offerings that never quite matched the original.

The supermarkets were, in fact, Potemkin villages, with counterfeit Coca-Cola brewed in pharmacies, locally produced toilet paper in mass-produced packaging, and salamis that according to the label were from Hungary, but in reality came from the butcher around the corner. This reversal of proportions amused me for a while, and I wondered where the oysters on my plate, which had been carried in on great platters, were really from. Puddles in the hole?

'We could task our town council with creating a campaign that blames the cold chain for the slightly different taste. But the message must always be conveyed that the products are still palatable, that it only affects the taste, not the quality, maybe even that the quality increases because of it,' the dirndl-wearing woman said, anxiously watching the Countess's reaction.

I neither understood many of the personal references that were made, nor the measures or resolutions, which always depended on the Countess's opinion. Nothing had progressed by the time the next item was called.

'The art action,' called out Engineer Heinzelmann, in the middle of the discussion already underway. Everyone fell silent.

'The art action will be taking place, that's it, the end,' was the Countess's decree. 'Now everything's settled, I can let Frau Schwarz in on our intentions. You're already up to speed about the hole. And that we've been struggling with certain issues since the beginning of the year,' she said, and pointed incongruously at the parquet floor.

'I've seen the main square,' I said, to show my lack of clarity on the matter. A certain embarrassment spread around the room, which only the Countess herself seemed to confidently command.

'For many centuries we had an extremely lucrative mine in our town, which, over a long period of time, has unfortunately softened the soil a little. The thing is, at the moment the subsidence is happening faster than expected. At times certain properties on the top lip of the main funnel show subsidence of about a centimetre a day. Centuries-old marble floors breaking asunder, and people sitting in their living rooms on the stone foundations, which is admittedly an unpleasant situation,' she explained. 'Of course it doesn't look nice when buildings warp, and visitors notice it, too. Not long ago a tractor was swallowed up, luckily without the farmer, who was in the pigsty at the time. In the last few decades we have tried everything possible to stop the subsidence, but pouring concrete into the hole was futile. We're talking about tens of millions of cubic metres. Herr Loipold, our geologist, can perhaps explain further.'

It was the previously so very intrusive Philipp who now stood up with a plan in his hand, which he laid out on the table for all to see. It showed a lateral view of Greater Einland: the urban area that lay flat like a large birthmark on the muscular shoulder of the

Hochwechsel, the mountain range's highest summit, and sloped profoundly to the left and right. The diagram revealed a gigantic hollow space beneath the town, which, airily underpinned like a gothic cathedral, was only held up by thin stalactite columns. The most calamitous thing about it, which I immediately recognised, even as a layperson, were the water reservoirs spread out over multiple levels — underneath the cavity was another one, and even a third underneath that. As thin as layers of dough, only spongy crusts, on which water was resting, separated the levels from one another.

'The hole is of unknown depths, bifurcations and dampness,' Philipp explained. 'The layers of earth surrounding it have become so wet from the seepage that the walls of the shafts are wet all year round. This ensures that the water trickling down from the reservoirs on the upper levels quickly leads to further breaches. You can imagine the slow slackening of a sand castle that has been built too close to the waterline, and is therefore borne away from below. We also have high concentrations of methane here and here.' He pointed at zones that had been flecked with ochre. A smouldering core of inflammation seemed to extend into the rock like a deep boil — beneath the market, in particular.

'We examined the mountain like a precious body — as minimally invasive as possible.' Philipp winked at me. 'That means endoscopically: We put cameras and other probes into its guts and, interestingly enough, we have found time and time again what would be found in human intestines.'

'Bacteria,' I elaborated.

'Precisely. Due to the ongoing geological activity, fine bifurcations are tearing into the rock — these layers are chemically very active and lead to new cultures. The upper layers of earth, here, as well as directly below the leakages of water are downright teeming with life. The metabolic waste products of these little animalcules — completely harmless in normal forest floors, and even important for the biosphere — lead to stability problems in the slag left behind by mining.' The salon attendees were scratching their heads furtively or eagerly refilling each other's water glasses.

'We have to support the main shaft first, otherwise the most valuable real estate, the historic buildings, will collapse. The subsidence goes back to the sixties,' Philipp said.

'To the fifties, if you must know,' interrupted the Countess. 'And we will support everything, it's about eliminating the overall syndrome.'

I was struck by the way the Countess would always let her counterpart speak first, only to then strike at all the weak points in their speech like a viper.

'You also know, of course, that our beautiful town was badly damaged in the turmoil of the Second World War, and that after the bombing, two-metre-high mounds of earth were added so buildings could be placed on top in their original positions.'

She gave a dramatic pause. 'Unfortunately, in the course of the subsidence, sections of buildings keep breaking through, which is also regrettable for the appearance of the town. Summa summarum, we have decided' — the Countess stood up — 'that our erosion ought to become one of the greatest art actions in the world.'

Now the previously bored listeners broke out into a frenetic applause, which the Countess calmed with royal nonchalance: 'We will declare the subsidence as Actionism and bring together tourists on a grand scale. This is primarily about relevant, lasting art, but earning a little from it would not be undesirable to us. Of course, Frau Schwarz, as you can imagine, a comprehensive concept such as this needs time to be developed. Great art also takes a great amount of effort — and it will take a few months, if not years, until the ideas we have in mind are market-ready. It's for precisely this reason that we need you.'

The idea was absurd. How would mass tourism fit into such a sleepy hollow? There wasn't even a road into the town.

'I have to disappoint you — I'm not artistically talented,' I said.

'No, you stupid girl. You will, of course, find a way of slowing down the subsidence and buying us some time until we have more concrete ideas for the art action. We need a physicist who can develop a filling agent for us that can be injected, and in such a way that brings effective publicity.'

'Frau — Countess, I cannot do that. Again: I am not a biophysicist, but rather concern myself with theoretical physics. With time. Up to now I've never even done a single experiment, I only work on paper.'

'Wonderful, with time. Then you can slow down the time it takes for the Market Square to sink. It's a matter of giving people hope, do you understand?'

Stunned by the conviction the Countess displayed, I was no longer able to insist.

'I'll read up on it and see if I can contribute,' I said. This was a relief to everyone — the group broke out into applause again, and I myself was relieved not to feel all expectations on me anymore. A communality had developed around us — that is, I had wandered from an outside to an inside, as if petals had closed over us. In my promise to the Countess I had already become one of her own, and, shockingly, I liked it for a moment, before I really considered what I had just announced. It didn't matter; after I'd organised the funeral I would just disappear anyway.

'As already discussed, we're planning a major exhibition that is designed for several hundred thousand visitors,' said a young woman, whom I now recognised as the librarian, Anita. 'We're thinking two to three times the capacity of Dokumenta. The first step will be to have the hole declared as a UNESCO World Heritage Site, inclusive of the subsidence, of course.'

I rummaged in my handbag, my fingers stiff, found my tablets, and swallowed a Xanax. I impatiently waited for the drug to kick in, to feel its cushioning effect, the non-appearance of which unsettled me even more. I would excuse myself, I thought, but already didn't know what for. I had washed down the sedative with a copious amount of alcohol. Someone grabbed my shoulder and asked if everything was alright. I saw statistics being daubed on a flipchart. Freshly served goose cuts were flying into mouths, making me feel very numb. I could barely keep up with the pace.

The talk became more and more fragmentary and incoherent, as if it were a piece of equipment in need of assembly: 'The goal we are aiming for is to be able to celebrate the grand opening in around twenty months. To do this, we need to replenish the brass band, and we don't have enough personnel in the volunteer fire department to provide security. In the underground chamber of the town there'll be a real Chagall, which our Countess is allowing us to use' — more applause — 'and the necessary struts have already been ordered from China. The local population will be initiated bit by bit, there will possibly be a referendum. The working title is, as you know: Project Underground.'

In the middle of the lecture I stood up with such gusto that the plates I'd loaded over and over again with food fell to the floor. 'I don't feel well. I'll be leaving early today,' I said, as if I'd been going to the salons for years. I raised my hand to wave, but recognised in the middle of the movement how inadequate the gesture was, and left my hand hanging in the air until I'd finally found the resolve to remove myself from the table. No one came after me, and I flew down the stairs, where I got away through the mercifully unattended entrance hall. The fresh air sobered me up. But the relief of being by myself again was accompanied by the feeling that it had been wrong to leave — as if I would now miss something that I would forevermore be deprived of. An icy, ghostly quiet night still needed to be traversed, and as I turned back again, the tenderly illuminated window seemed enticing once more. Only then did it hit me again: barely two weeks ago, my parents had been sitting up there.

On one of my very first days in Greater Einland I had discovered the so-called memorial while running an errand. It was in close proximity to the supermarket, and yet so inconspicuous that someone could walk by the hedge their whole life without seeing it. I climbed the four steps to the grassy plateau on which a few gladioli were growing around a marble rectangle.

'In Memory of the Incidents' it said on the stone, and for several minutes I wondered which incidents it could be referring to. As I crouched down and touched the plate with my fingertips, I noticed that another sentence had been engraved underneath it, so eroded that I could hardly decipher it: 'In this place some perished who ought not to be forgotten,' I read, and found everything even more cryptic.

A little chapel stood nearby, seemingly independent from it, with a crying Mary in the window. This in turn read: *Thirty-four bodies rest here.*

Since I hadn't let go of the matter even after my return to the tavern, I decided to speak to Frau Erna about it directly. In reply she pressed a folder into my hands and cheerfully asked me how the Countess's salon had gone. I looked at the slips of paper inside the folder, which, in their aloofness, had something disarmingly open about them: no graphic elements, no typographical emphasis adorned the block of text. To this day I am amazed that the information was given as easily at first glance as it had been forgotten by the public consciousness.

I read the history over lunch. It was a sober report with a few isolated contemporary citations mixed in. It was fashioned like this:

On Easter Monday, 2 April 1945, all two thousand prisoners of the annex camp III / Mauthausen / Gau

Greater Vienna were removed from the shallow mine, where they had been tasked with screwing together airplane parts for the last thirteen months. When they had been grouped in squares of a hundred on the meadow in front of the barracks near the main descent, it was decided, since the sheer number of them could not be contained, to send one thousand two hundred of them on a death march towards Burgenland. While the bells were ringing for a second time for mass, and the children were screeching with pleasure looking for the colourful Easter eggs in the nearby gardens, the column filed out as quietly and wordlessly as it had come. The villagers who were on their way to church later irregularly reported having seen this exodus, but most of them claimed to have still been sleeping on the day in question.

It was a cold morning, with temperatures barely above freezing, and the remaining eight hundred men stood barefoot in the grey snow. The camp guards that had been left behind — ten men, six of whom were barely of age — trembled agitatedly. They blocked out the sense of being overwhelmed, the sheer quantity, but not least the cutting cold. The order was given; the utterly exhausted and emaciated prisoners were locked back in the barracks around eight o'clock so that they could be processed in small groups of forty people. They were told to lie on their backs, in the hoarfrost, with their arms stretched out at their sides. Then their striped, soiled uniform was unbuttoned and a petrol injection was administered just under the breastbone.

The inexperienced security guards had orders to save money for the inevitable defence of Vienna. They were slapdash and not up to the task, so that the injections completely missed in a third of the cases. If the heart is punctured precisely with an injection of petrol, death occurs within a few minutes, but if the lungs are punctured, a process of cramps, paralysis, and finally suffocation, which lasts for many hours, sets in.

By that afternoon the ten guards — of which two groups of five took turns digging a pit and giving the injections — had killed two hundred people, of whom at least seventy were still in the throes of mortal agony. Now, since digging a mass grave presented a considerable effort, the men started to get nervous. So it was decided to bury the remaining prisoners alive as quickly as possible.

The bodies were rolled into the pits forty at a time, and the loose earth was tipped over them while the next forty were being fetched from the barracks. It would take more men to dig; it would take the next forty to prepare the ground for the next forty. The guards were frozen and tired when they heard strange noises as they came out of their quarters. In the increasingly blacker scenery it was hardly noticeable at first, when suddenly bodies from below, that is, out of the already filled pit, began to squirm, the last ones still alive, who had worked their way out of the graves, gasping for air. Then shots.

But what I didn't understand was this: if around eight hundred people remained in Greater Einland, and only thirty-four were at rest in the memorial, as had been written, what had happened to the other seven hundred and sixty-six?

9

It was a biting cold morning as I walked into the suburbs. I found the funeral parlour only after some delay, and I even considered allowing the appointment to fall through again to avoid the inevitable. After leaving the guesthouse I had still hoped for something fortuitous, something unforeseen. Something that could keep me from getting there.

The route led past staggered semi-detached houses, each painted in two different colours in order to pretend that they were separate buildings that did not belong together. But the rooms were cheek to cheek, garage to garage — like mirrors facing each other, stretching down the street into infinity. The atmosphere called for rain, and the bourgeois asphalt frayed into puddles at the edges, which, on days like these, the very damp earth of Greater Einland pushed to the surface.

Like every funeral parlour, the name of the company was a composition that was supposed to have a calming effect, and which I can no longer remember because it was so interchangeable: Heavenward or Pale Blue, Chiming Teardrop, Dreamwater, Music from the Heart, Pain Fire, Ever Earth, Life's Drum, Springsummer, Rushing Wind, Autumn Feeling, Swaying Eyes, Green Thought, Fruit of Love, Flight of Air, Eternal Sun, or something similar. Soundless fully automatic doors inhaled me. The employee who received me had evidently been instructed in trauma work and reassured me with verbal cotton balls. Soft swirls of colour hung on canvasses everywhere, and the staff was dressed in pastel, from the cleaner to the receptionist.

I was shown into a meeting room, where I discussed the details of the funeral with a funeral director. After only a few minutes I was exhausted from the list of invitees I'd drawn up in my head, while the woman presented me with a selection of pieces of music: I nodded at everything immediately, my body suddenly bereft of all strength. It had been a long time since I'd thought about the extraordinary ceremony I'd initially decided upon, and I put little crosses under the first coffin, the first flower arrangement and priest's speeches that were brought to me. Everything began to add up to a stately sum, which I eventually signed off on. It wasn't overly expensive — maybe even a bargain for a funeral — but certainly enough that I had to pay for it with my credit card, and immediately suppress the consequences of this payment.

'Good,' the woman said gently. 'When can we expect them, your parents?' Even though I'd anticipated this question, I was caught off guard. It was an irrevocable sign that I would now have to make the call I'd been putting off for so long.

'I have to clarify that quickly,' I said. 'May I use your phone?'

'Yes, of course,' she replied, visibly surprised that I didn't have any exact dates, but not wanting to disturb the general piety. With quiet professionalism, she turned the telephone on her desk towards me. I called the directory assistance to request my aunt's phone number. Every digit was a torture that could no longer be avoided.

When my aunt answered, I was suddenly struck by shame. Before she could say a word, I drowned her in a monologue that broke out of me uncontrollably: 'I'm calling about the funeral. It took a long time to prepare everything due to unforeseen issues. It was so difficult even finding Greater Einland, and then it was almost impossible to get a grave plot here.' As I lifted my bowed head, my face was wet with tears.

'Ruth?' my aunt asked hesitantly. 'Ruth, is that you? Are you alright? We reported you missing a week ago, we thought you had done something to yourself.'

'Yes, I'm fine. I'm doing very well, I have a job here. You see, I'm searching for clues, so I can say something about Mum and Dad at their funeral. About their hometown,' I said, sobbing.

'Ruth, Ruth, calm down, what's the matter? Are you really alright? Listen, we didn't know where you were, and the coroner released the both of them. I'm so sorry, we had to make a decision, and when you weren't here — well, how shall I tell you? Your parents were buried in Vienna three days ago.'

The surface I was standing on folded together, the room compressed, the dimensions retreated, everything shifted away from me.

'You buried them in Vienna?' I asked.

'There's no such place as Greater Einland — according to the telephone book, the guesthouse I called you at is in Kirchberg am Wechsel. The municipal offices don't know any Greater Einland,' my aunt was now almost shouting. 'You have to come back.'

'You ignored their wishes and didn't have them buried in Greater Einland?' I repeated again, clutching the receiver tightly as my hand was wet, my shirt, my cheeks, my lips, all wet.

'I have no idea where you are, Ruth, but come home. I understand that you're upset, who wouldn't be, but … please come to us, we're all so worried. Come home, and we'll talk.' I hung up. My grief had been replaced with bewilderment. Now the situation had become infinitely awkward for me, as the funeral director had followed the whole scene with growing unease.

'My parents have unfortunately already been buried in Vienna,' I explained straightforwardly, as if that was a completely normal turn of events. The woman looked at me with a raised eyebrow.

'But you've already signed, madam,' she said, holding out the slip of paper with my signature as proof.

'Fine, I will keep the funeral for another time,' I replied politely.

'Perfect, let's do that,' she said, now much friendlier again and not in the least bit disconcerted by the suggestion I'd made. 'Please transfer the two thousand euros to me and I'll give you a voucher.'

A two-thousand-euro funeral voucher, I thought. *Two larchwood coffins; who will I ever use them for?* On top of that, I was now on the verge of bankruptcy. But I wrote my credit card number in an old-fashioned chequebook, once more shook the hand of the funeral director, accepted heartfelt condolences from the secretary, and made my way back to the guesthouse.

A week later I had a vague idea for a memorial. Even if the funeral itself had already taken place, I wanted to hold a ceremony, in spite of my relatives, in Greater Einland, and for which this destination would be absolutely essential. I would get hold of the information — poignant truths that the first funeral couldn't have been capable of — and perhaps plan a transfer of the coffins, that is, finally, rectify a deeply felt injustice, which could ultimately restore my self-image, at least. But I lost sight of this goal as soon as the real reason for staying came out.

In Greater Einland everything moved at a different speed, an ambrosia-like timelessness that cast the events outside of this little world in an unthinkable light. Every resident had a precisely quantified significance in this social structure that one could grasp with one's hands, because it was hierarchical and was mostly disclosed according to its terms. The simplest of tasks had something magical about them. Nobody used the Internet, and I tacitly assumed that there simply wasn't any here in the mountains. It would take me two full years to figure out that state-of-the-art fibre-optic cables ran through Greater Einland; it was just that no one used them. Maybe the fact that it was such a clear break with everything that I had known was the reason I integrated myself completely.

However, what finally sealed this sense of arrival was the house.

The perception of time has to overcome three thresholds:

The fusion threshold permits humans to understand two events as separate from one another, whereby the various sensory organs have different minimum requirements. While the eye is more forgiving and needs twenty to thirty milliseconds to separate two elements, the ear can distinguish between elements from just two milliseconds. The second is the order threshold. This makes the sequence of two stimuli comprehensible, which requires both to be separated by about forty milliseconds. The third threshold concerns the present: this is formed by a three-second space that blocks the view of the flow of time like an endorsed barrier.

I spent the whole weekend in bed. Awoken intermittently by the knocks of Frau Erna, who brought my meals to my room at the usual time, I hardly knew when the day ended and the next one began. I slept eight hours, was woken by the chiming of the church clocktower at noon, went to the bathroom, ate, and lay down for another eight hours, until my biorhythm had liquefied and I no longer knew whether it was day or night. It felt like the blinds had been drawn, until I realised that it was dark outside, or I gave a start because I thought I'd left a light on before realising that it was the sun.

It wasn't until Sunday evening that things turned around. I was lying on my squashed face, watching the sunset with indifference, when I remembered the house for no reason whatsoever. A few days before the events at the funeral home, while walking with Philipp to the salon, I had noticed an empty house. It was a beautiful old building with half-timbered gables, a carved balcony, and a garden out back with fir and walnut trees. It caught my eye because it had FOR SALE OR LEASE in almost obnoxiously large letters, red and glowing, out front.

To own a house, a so-called home — the idea rose up into my brain like a bewitching scent — would lead me out of my misery, I suddenly suspected. I wouldn't have to go back to Vienna, and the question of whether the university would have continued to employ me would have resolved itself. I wouldn't have to explain to anyone why I disappeared before my inaugural lecture, wouldn't have to count the annual output of publications, wouldn't have to make an appearance at the despised conferences. I wouldn't have to exchange one further word with my aunt. I would settle down, and why not here? *Why not in the countryside?* I thought, before I remembered that I barely had enough money to even pay my tab at the Pumpkin. Everything hurt from lying around for days on end, and I decided, in spite of my miserable financial situation, to take a walk to this very house. Although it was only November, it was snowing, and after having not left my room for three days, the light blinded me painfully as I took a right turn past the town wall towards Johannesstrasse. I found the same sign as before: FOR SALE OR LEASE. Beneath it was a number, which I noted down on the back of my hand so I could call it once back at the tavern, even though it was a Sunday and evening time. Oddly enough, someone picked up straightaway — a smarmy young real estate agent, who was able to offer me a viewing the following morning for the *detached property*, as he called it. A brief telephone conversation clarified that the house was dirt cheap — no wonder, I thought to myself, if the foundations sink by a foot a year and you didn't know whether the walls would still be standing next winter. But what was the point? I didn't even have this ridiculous amount in my account, and I would have to think carefully about whether I could apply for a loan in my position. The university would no doubt be firing me any day now. Early in the morning I met the agent, a slick and polished boy with the face of a law student who threw open the curtains with a pompous gesture and let the doors swing open on their hinges. The house was magnificent. It had seven rooms across two floors — a beautiful wooden staircase, herringbone parquet made of walnut (which originated from the trees in the garden, the agent assured me), bright Art Nouvelle windows, and a ground floor that looked like a former cattle shed. On that lower floor, the walls were exposed, like in a loft — the building had previously been accommodation for workers at the nearby timber factory. A small cutting machine had once stood in the so-called salon, which gave the room its factory-like appearance. Since the previous owners had only recently died, and, as the agent put it, the estate was handled a little differently in Greater Einland, the house was for sale including all the furniture: a small library filled with classics, a beautiful French kitchen, and a large double bed on the upper floor, from which one could see the firmament through a skylight.

Most of all, however, I was impressed by the desk. It formed the central star of the study, consisting of a wood panel resting on two hand-carved trestles like those used by craftsmen, with a dark pattern, as if the tree it originated from had had to survive harsh winters during its livelier days. A black chalkboard covered the whole of one wall so that one could use a sliding ladder to distribute formulas crossways all over it, and a chaise longue on the other side invited you to reflect upon what had been written.

The house looked like someone had climbed into my head and made a mould based on the patents to my desires. It was like the treehouse one had begged for as a child; like the big cardboard box one could crawl into and make a spaceship out of; like the tangle of interconnected compartments under the hollow hedge, which I'd pushed through with my friends and then sanctified as rooms. Here, I would be able to finish my postdoctoral thesis. It was a dream factory — a sacred place of my production.

I asked the young man to prepare all the necessary documents straightaway; I would prefer to move in that same week. I just had to get a loan, but I would manage it somehow, with my professorial title and all the promises that went with it. I *needed* this house. The speed with which the agent agreed was, however, still surprising, because out from a folder he pulled the purchase contract ready for signing, and, one after the after, a notarial notice, a credit check, and confirmation of acceptance, all of which were already made out in my name.

'You're welcome to move in immediately; I had a suspicion that you wouldn't be able to resist the property,' he said.

'But who paid the deposit?'

'The Countess, of course.'

We arranged to meet that evening for the key handover: I would in the meantime, I explained, find out more about the financial arrangements I had to make. Handshake, exchange of business cards, then I was hanging on the telephone in the Pumpkin, attempting to locate all the banking institutions in the vicinity.

In any case I would have to, this went without saying, go to the nearest larger town, as there wasn't even a cash machine in

Greater Einland. When I put the phone down, I registered, to my surprise, that the prospect of moving around a city evoked a not inconsiderable amount of disgust in me. For one thing, I still didn't have a car — but that was by no means the decisive factor. Rather, I was suddenly tormented by the thought of the noise, the pace, the passing of time, which lay here so wonderfully fallow, like a regenerating field after harvesttime.

I asked Frau Erna, who was just then carrying two plates from the kitchen into the parlour, where a bus to the next town left from.

'There isn't a bus,' she said absently, and flew away from me to the regulars' tables.

'What do you want there anyway?' someone shouted around the corner, but I had to walk around the bar in order to see that it was Master-Builder Keinermüller who had asked.

'I want to apply for a loan,' I replied, sitting down opposite him. His hand, already raised threateningly above his head as if to knock someone over, thundered down onto the tabletop, causing his soup to spill. 'You don't need a loan! We always lend to each other here. You can borrow anyone's money and you get given a borrower's note for it. The whole thing's settled with the Countship. It's far less hassle than an account.'

'It's ninety thousand euros,' I said.

'Oh, that's chicken feed.' The Master-Builder shovelled what was left of his soup into his mouth. 'These little transactions are always going on, didn't you know? You borrow something and are indebted to the debtor of your own debtor. Allow credit to be given and tell someone who still owes you to pay there, and so on and so forth. That means that ultimately you pay your own debtors. So capital never leaves the town, everything stays local.'

Because I was sure that I wouldn't be able to get to the bottom of these absurdities, I responded to his explanation: 'Who can I ask for the amount for the moment?'

'In principle anyone, even Erna here,' Schlaf chimed in. 'Or, for my part, me — I can issue you a borrower's note immediately.'

'And in what instalments should I repay you?'

'Oh, you don't, you issue other people borrower's notes, which in turn relate to me.'

My head was spinning. What kind of strange constellations was I — and everything without my direct cooperation — already involved in? Maybe someone was borrowing something in my name right now.

At that moment Erna came around the corner. 'Ruth, I think the Countess has already issued you a blank borrower's note. Feudal model. Just buy whatever you want, it should be paid for.'

'Where did you get that information? I never asked the Countess for that,' I called back.

'I know from hearsay. And officially, well, what can I say. Purchase agreements, rentals, loans. It all ends up on the Countess's desk anyway,' Erna explained. 'And because there's no cash points here, the withdrawal is sort of shared out.'

'But to whom do you owe money when you borrow something?'

'It's not that easy to say. Could be someone different in the morning than in the evening. The best thing to do is to just borrow as much as possible yourself.'

131

'In this case, of course, you only owe the Countess, as we also have a feudal lending model. Here' — Master-Builder Keinermüller scribbled something on the back of his receipt — 'I assume that the arrangement with the Countess is tied to a job? You work, receive a salary, and an interest-bearing tithe goes into the house. The employment contract is binding until you've paid back the money for the house, otherwise you'd be liable for the agreed advance amount.'

'Tithe?' I asked helplessly. 'But I haven't signed anything.'

'Seems like you have,' Schlaf said, ordering another scotch.

When it got dark, I packed up my clothes, which were lying in every corner of the room, and arrived in front of the house at the arranged time.

'Everything's been paid for,' the agent beamed, as he opened the door for me for the second time that day. To be on the safe side, I had fetched all of my belongings from the guesthouse and thanked Erna (unsure of for what, exactly), but as the keys were handed to me without delay, I was still astonished. Now I had to accept the job, I thought, and was suddenly happy about it. It seemed I *would* finish my postdoctoral thesis. After the agent had left, I lit the stove with wood already provided, barricaded myself in my new bed, and lost myself for hours in natural history books. Some longings we don't have until we encounter them; for the first time in my life, I'd arrived.

It was only with great reluctance, when my eyes were exhausted, that I took a look at the contract that I still had next to me on the mattress. Already pinned to it was the statement from the land register, in which I had apparently been entered at lightning speed as the new owner. In the lines above my name it stated the former owners, and when I was able to decipher the cursive script, I was stunned: *Petra and Joseph Schalla*. I had, without knowing it, bought my grandparents' house. I was suddenly awake again. How could I not have noticed? This was the attic room with the window my parents had told me about: they had lain here and determined the constellations. I ran to the balcony: the hill behind the house where they could ski! And now it made sense that the house, which had been pitched to me as 'the former home of woodworkers, inclusive of a workshop', had belonged to my grandfather, the owner of the timber factory. The memory map I had made three weeks ago tore itself from the imaginary and descended over the landscape down to my house, where its nodes and junctions found their position absolutely perfectly. When I was finally in bed, I imagined that one of them had just laid down here — and suddenly I was once more seized by the question of what the both of them were doing here every week. Was it something to do with the house? I made up my mind to do some research about the history of the town the following day. This issue, however, had become superfluous: when I left my house the next morning to discuss my future tasks with the Countess, I found the local chronicle hammered into my post-box. I had become a Greater Einlander.

The following day I read the story of Pergerhannes, the mythical founding figure of the town, which had up to that point been kept from me. Remarkably it took up most of the local chronicle, even though it was obviously a legend:

> Hans Perger, Pergerhans, in other sources also Perger Hannes — a rich craftsman who occupied the post of master leather–tanner — lived close to the Market Square, where he had a workshop, between 1595 and 1636. A journeyman's examination from 1611, and the apprenticeship of three local boys five years later, are verified. There is also evidence of the purchase of another building on the corner of today's Hebelstrasse. In a letter from the vicar Steffan Herman it is reported that Hans Perger maintained a private library that contained sacred writings, including a minuscule from the Bamberg monastery, as well as reports on various handicraft techniques of the time. Such a book collection can be understood as an indication of extraordinary wealth, and the barely twenty-five-year-old is likely to have had a not inconsiderable influence in the area. In any case, it is indisputable that, in 1629, Perger had already started to excavate the infamous shaft that would make him immortal.
>
> At that time, the main entrance and the water tower were bordered by the Korngasse area and today's Schlossstrasse that now leads directly to the castle. This first tunnel, which was created with gunpowder using the blasting technique customary at the time,

is still connected today with various superstitions: In the 1980s, for instance, the new elementary school building was relocated away from the intersection of Siedlungsstrasse/Bachgasse, because a planned football pitch would have been near the uppermost shaft entranceway, and the majority of parents had spoken out against this positioning.

Little of the story of Pergerhannes can boast real authenticity; the entire set of issues around him was, for the most part, passed on orally. The most detailed written source is only a century old and formulated in an extremely unusual tone. The fact that this report, which was set down in 1897, was not signed by a named author also proves that the material was an orally transmitted local epic long before it was committed to paper:

Perger Hanns is a wealthy businessman of around forty-five and well known in the town when one day word gets around that he has succumbed to a silver rush.

Even though Perger Hannes is already served by twenty serfs who scratch the skin off their bones for him from the anthrax tanning agent, he can't get enough. The stinking holes proliferate on the outskirts of the town and make the surrounding soil rot into infertility through lesions. Nevertheless, one sells the exotic products of this weathering work, which include: cow and goat leather, but above all the wolf hides, which, known far beyond the local borders, attract traders to Greater Einland.

Pergerhanns is respected, but despised. The symptomatic manifestations of the tanning profession, whose unclean trade always makes one into a leper, ensure that he is avoided. He remains unmarried for life.

It can be assumed that Hanns Perger solely used his own assets to expand the facility, which he ultimately sold again. The historical report claims a 'silver rush' as the reason behind this: in 1629, Perger invested all of his savings in mining, the same year in which the first Greater Einlander borehole bottom was commissioned. However, dealing with the sources becomes difficult at the point where the digging of the very tunnel is described. Here, the report seems almost mythical:

The conspiratorial stones lie deviously close together as Pergerhann's men use hand chisels and horse-drawn winches to dig into the rock, driven forward by fifteen sprightly climbers who rotate in shifts. He himself is caught in wet dreams of the mountain, the wet walls of which appear to him like the sweet enthralment of coitus. Once he has been on the surface for more than a day, he can hardly stand it and descends again, where sweet voices whisper promises about the treasures in the deep.

The exploration team quickly came across exploitable substances, and after a month the rumour spread that silver had finally been found. However, the quantities did not seem to have satisfied the master leather tanner in the least; under the hard hand of Pergerhannes, they dig deeper into the rock. Twenty-four hours, around the clock, the entire course of the sun that nobody sees anymore. They rest and pray and eat and sleep in never-ending darkness. Due to the increasing confusion and the perennial cold below ground, it soon becomes difficult to keep one's bearings. More and more jeopardies are hazarded for the tunnelling. A sixteen-year-old boy is the first to be devoured by the rock. When the thin youth with his bronze lamp is believed to have been crawling through a narrow shaft with a suspected cave behind it, an unexpected inrush of water occurred, washing in a large amount of debris and restricting the return path and the breathable air of the young miner. For three days, the miners heard his screams while finishing the borehole bottom, then it went quiet.

This first mining accident was the reason a few passages and side tunnels were created, in order to drain the water that kept seeping in during the work. Deaths are not uncommon in the mining industry, but the adolescent's painful death had a disturbing effect on the workers, who for the most part were trained tanners and had no underground experience. In view of this, it is all the more remarkable what depth was reached by December 1630.

Because the tunnel becomes ever more unending, it is soon no longer worthwhile for workers to climb up between one and the next shift, that is, overnight; no lifts to bring you back up from the earth's crust, no electric light from which the security of permanent illumination could have been granted. Lamps in which animal fats cast a greasy glow over the minerals flicker hesitantly over everything.

The workers descend into the abyss for weeks on end, work twelve hours, sleep eight, pray for two, and eat the remaining time. They no longer feel the dust that lies on their skin like a second mantle within the first. To keep them alive there are rusks, soup, jerky on Sundays, and litres of watered-down wine at all times that keep fear at bay.

Even though workers disappear or perish time and time again under these conditions, more and more fearless young men climb down into the depths. A sacrificial will is rife in the village: it is understood as a pious surrender to the land and its gifts to penetrate the mountain — to deliver oneself to the will of the damp earth.

Pergerhanns, unlike the other mine owners of his time, makes himself comfortable in this eternal twilight. He wants to be the first in every newly developed section and nestles his body with ardency against the stone, even though it has still not brought him any significant silver deposits in a year. Fifteen water scoopers have to keep the shaft dry, but Hans Perger is always the first to stand in the damp with soaked trouser legs and bloated leather shoes. He is notorious as the cruel captain of this odyssey: Pergerhannes has crews dig at opposite ends of the tunnels, then breaks off their work whenever he pleases and tells them, contrary to any statics, to rebuild a shaft in the middle of an intermediate corridor.

It is during this time that things begin to get out of hand: in the by now completely confusing network of paths, he, the leather tanner, is suddenly overcome by a distrust of his men. This is why he creates new rules. He divides the ramification system, a kilometre in size, into four quadrants, a north, south, east, and west quadrant, and assigns a foreman to each. Fifteen men are made available to the crew. The key requirement of Perger, however, is that the foremen only see a plan of the quadrant where their pit is located. Exchanges between them are severely punished. Due to the lack of coordination, another tunnel collapses due to moisture in October 1631 — only this time twelve people died, because they did not know about the nearby western exit from the sole.

Over the course of decades, the figure of Pergerhann became a kind of motley figure into which melted several historical people, but especially those who disappeared into the pit in the period from 1632 onwards. At one point Perger is also referred to as the owner of a dairy, and later even as mayor and town administrator, which can be considered out of the question for the historical figure. The events of the narrative that have been sketched up to this point are also referred to as the so-called 'Little Story'. Not only was it added later, but it also mainly originates from oral sources. In contrast, there is the 'Great Story', the passages of which can be repeated in unison by every child in the region:

In March 1632, people in the village were very suddenly saying that Hans Perger had disappeared, that is to say:

not disappeared in the true sense, because it is a generally recognised certainty that Pergerhanns met the devil in the deepest ravine of his pit. It is impossible to say from which source this knowledge first arises, but it is known that it happened on the third of the month: It is early morning when Pergerhanns learns that the southern crew has encountered a large underground cave; a kind of grotto, oppressively humid and spread out like a lake through a dripping stone cave system — devouring everything right up to the last flood basalt vein. He immediately stops all work — Pergerhanns gets into the branch and orders that a boat be made ready. He urges his men to leave the cave so that he can be alone, and climbs into the tunnel with nothing but his miner's lamp. He pushes the skiff along with a willow stick and disappears into the cusp of the lake.

That is the last the men see of Pergerhannes.

When he does not come back after a few hours, they gather at the western tunnel exit and wait for their master to return — many are in the sun for the first time in weeks and have to spread their palms over their eyes for hours before they can identify the nature of Greater Einland again and return home to their families. The hoar frost lays on the stalks that discreetly intertwine over the northern entrance hole, over which a child steps at this very moment, sliding silently into the tunnel. Falling fifty metres into the ground like a projectile, the child becomes one with the land. The child will not be missed because it belongs to the travelling people and cannot be assigned to any name. A gypsy woman complains that her son has disappeared; people laugh at her, and the day comes to an end without anything of note happening. And yet everything holds its breath.

That was the beginning. While the master went missing underground for six weeks that spring, another eight children disappear without a trace and nobody wants to get anywhere near where it happened. Whoever is embraced by the mountain is simply lost to it. Now nobody has the courage to dig: it's believed the mine is already lost, and they pick up their plough and pickaxe again to do the righteous work up on the surface. But no one dares set foot on the meadows and farmland plains anymore, because everyone dreads the hollow space that opens up below. People huddle together in the inns, wet with sweat and fearful. It only affects the spawn at least; not a child of a full citizen and certainly not a full citizen himself. Nobody sees any of the children, thirteen in all, that disappear, as if the mountain wanted to draw them in at the most intimate moment.

In some sources, it is stated that this period only lasted two months, but that people felt it stretch like a decade. Many a villager saw Pergerhannes climb into the hole as a young man and come out as an old man. In other documents it is even said that time stood still, and that the moon did not move a metre in those weeks before the inconceivable happened.

Finally, on May 31 1632, Whit Sunday, Pergerhannes, the Loden Hannes, the Mine Perger, rose into the light once more, and although he was underground for weeks and weeks, he climbed out of the pit that day in time for the church service, in perfect short lederhosen and as if he'd freshly got out of the bath. In a wool sack he carries a multitude of shiny, precious stones, which he begins to hand out in the church: diamonds, rubies, emeralds, sapphires, until every child who walks through the village behind the Whitsun Quack shouts with joy.

In the coming weeks and months, Greater Einland sees an increase in wealth, indeed even the awarding of a town charter. In particular, the aristocratic Korb-Weidenheim family, who were respected but impoverished until then, managed to rehabilitate their circumstances through owning the land on which the western entrance was located. The sum for this is grotesque:

The house fronts straighten up tautly, as if they had been treated with bellows — the wrinkles smoothed out through the stream of air from a sudden inflation. The cracks in the facades are filled without anyone ever seeing who did it — the potholes in the steep road are paved over, and people are dressed in beautiful robes.

It restores the stricken hunchbacks of the workers of Greater Einland: a wealthy Jew invests in the town for no apparent reason, and everyone now has well-paid jobs. Although nobody knows exactly how or where the revival of their so-called circumstances comes from (seeing as nobody ever sees a piece of silver coming out of the pit), they are gratefully received. Except for in the evenings, nobody really dares to leave their own house. The taverns are as if swept empty; the shining oil wicks in the lanterns never need to be lit, because nobody wants to go outside anymore.

In March 1635, after the church service, Pergerhannes descends the ladder at the north entrance for the last time, and stays underground forever.

In the first year after this last descent, twenty-two people disappear into the labyrinthine tunnels of the mine — adults, too, this time — the first being a knife grinder by the name of Jajo. He's witnessed in the twilight of dusk, not long after the disappearance of Pergerhannes, definitely going to the south entrance and climbing down the ladder. In the village a firm belief continues to spread in a whisper: that a time will come when Pergerhannes will return, and that this very return should bring time to a standstill.

Over the centuries it has been called into doubt over and over again as to whether Pergerhannes even existed, or whether he was rather a founding myth that allowed people to understand certain movements in nature that would otherwise have been unfathomable to them.

A second possibility that was discussed is the person of Pergerhannes as a kind of amalgam figure; a basin for all those memories that in reality were not undertaken by an individual, but rather by the collective. In this respect, it is also plausible that the whole of Greater Einland succumbed to the silver rush, or that the fateful quadrant system that cost so many lives was in fact decided collectively. Be that as it may, at the end of 1640, the Perger Pit came to an abrupt end:

In the early morning hours of 28 December, an earthquake shook the town, catapulting people out of their deep sleep; when the first of them lean out of the window, the Market Square is already a good three metres lower: above the main basin of the lake, the honeycomb-like and, from lack of coordination, completely arbitrary soles collapse. The water that has accumulated in the various drainage shafts frothily unites, the water gauges hiss upwards, and now the last entrance is also impassable.

10

The care home was still holding together on the lower floors, as if someone had split the building in half with an axe, but the blow had been struck with hesitation. It was an arduous walk up to the rooms, because the lifts had long been out of service, and the steps had unfolded like the bellows of an accordion. The tiles in the dining room, the floor of which having fallen away on both sides of the space under the pull of gravity, stuck up splintering from the concrete base, and they had to hang the seniors' wheelchairs on the doorframe with straps to prevent them from rolling away. If you looked in briefly, you might have thought you had come across a roped party on Mount Everest, but then you would notice the heads sunk to their chests and the infusions dangling over them.

The higher the buildings were in Greater Einland, the worse the repercussions of the subsidence — since the torque of the lever arm in the depths could cause the greatest devastation. In the patients' rooms that the nurse led me past, tufts of cables protruded from the walls like roots. Breathing tubes and catheter leads, which had to at one point have run through sheaths, were exposed: the hidden aspect of human decay was now coming to light at the same time as the architectural breakdown. It shook me. Juices and saliva and gases: all of this was only quasi-covered with cotton wool, as if for the sake of appearances. I was led along a corridor that was already secured with wooden platforms just below the ceiling, like the ones found in mines, and I admired a carer who was clambering over the expanse of rubble cordoned off with caution tape despite carrying a tea tray in his hand. Everything about the people's bearing maintained the appearance of utter normality. This indicated that the situation had changed so slowly that the adaptation processes had happened almost imperceptibly. The quick glimpses in the rooms, the smell of disinfectant for floor and bodies lying over everything, the electric light that had intensified to a glare for tube extraction: death was at its most tangible in sterile places. I was shown into a room, and the nurse left me.

So that's it, I thought to myself nervously. I'd had to spend a whole year here to find out about this place, and even that had been by accident in the end.

'The retirement home is about to fall apart,' Sister Elfriede had said, who was supplying some of the patients there with her soup kitchen. 'Maybe we ought to get together and give them a hand?'

'Absolutely,' said a woman I knew as Resi, and who delivered the mail twice a week. 'How do you do it, Ruth?'

'How do I do what?' I asked, looking up from my newspaper.

'You know, with your grandmother. Are you paying extra for her to be in a better room, or did the Countess put a good word in?' I was stunned, while the others began debating about their loved ones in the home, and I needed some minutes before I could muster the courage to enquire further.

'My grandmother's alive? Gerda Schwarz?'

'But of course,' Schlaf said, slurping a piece of spaghetti into his mouth. 'Of course she's alive.' A phone call confirmed what had at first sounded inconceivable to me.

In the room I'd been led to, there was a single bed, a sofa, along with a television mounted in the upper corner of the room, which was currently showing ski racing. Voices penetrated through the closed doors — lowered, as if not to disturb those who no longer participated fully in life during their process of drifting away. For a moment I sat in an armchair in the care-home room and didn't know exactly what I was waiting for. It was only when I walked past the bed to open the window to let out the stuffy air that I saw a thin figure was lying on it, clad and covered in the same white of its skin. I blinked a few times before I could say with any surety where the body ended and the mattress began. It was a woman; on her chest lay a white bunny, a horrible thing that was almost greasy from manhandling. So this was my grandmother. I stared at her for several minutes without knowing what to do with myself, then I moved closer.

There was a strange ambiguity in the way she held her body. It was unclear whether she was asleep or unconscious, and it was just as unclear whether she had noticed me or not — I sat down as gently as was possible. Those familiar phrases came to mind: *skin like tissue paper* or *utterly fragile*, and yet the body lying before me seemed so much more fragile than I had imagined. The entire frame of bones hung together with the last bit of its strength. From the look of the tendons, everything had wanted to let go a long time ago. *Ninety-six*, I thought, and in the same moment she opened her eyes.

'Did I wake you?' I asked, embarrassed, and immediately regretted being so familiar with her — we were basically complete strangers. But there also wasn't any time to take it back: the woman sat up and drew her legs up to her chest. She without a doubt looked like my father: the same deep-set eyes, the same small forehead — but that was, of course, a banal insight. As I reached for her hand, I began to tremble and drew it back.

'Hello,' I said. 'I'm Ruth, your granddaughter. I live here in Greater Einland now. Did Mum and Dad tell you about me? Erich, your son, I mean. I'm a physicist and I'm researching Eternalism, did you know that? I live down there in a house that I bought.' I pointed preposterously at the white wall, while this torrent of randomness broke out of me.

'It's hot,' I said as if to myself, and finally threw open the window. Now that I could finally breathe again, I remembered all the questions I wanted to ask her. But I got stuck before I had even started.

'I have to tell you something. Erich and Elisabeth — my parents' — I turned back to her again, but looked at the floor — 'they died. About a year ago. I'm so sorry. They were buried in Vienna, and I wasn't even there.'

My grandmother was still quiet, but for a moment it was as if this confession had at least rolled a weight from my chest. Then suddenly a response came from the bed.

'I know, the nurse told me, I remember. Of course I remember,' the woman said, and I recognised from her voice that she was my grandmother. Strange, I had never heard it before.

'But I don't know — what did they die of? Can you help me, Sarah? I want to sit over there.' I watched in amazement as she moved to the edge of the bed on her own. I had intended to gently hold her under her arm to support her on the way to the seating area, but had underestimated her feathery lightness and practically took her off her feet, so that for a moment I had the feeling I was carrying her to the other side of the room. We sat down, and I poured water into the glasses provided. 'My name's Ruth, not Sarah,' I said after a long delay. It was incredible how clearly she could formulate her words when she answered.

'We haven't spoken in a long time. I've been travelling and just settling back in again. No one wanted me here at first, and now you come here after all these years. You're trying to poison me, aren't you?'

'No one wants to poison you. I'm visiting you,' I said.

She had put her hands over her head in a kind of pleading gesture, with which she now begged for forgiveness between her knees.

'Your parents poisoned me for years, everyone poisoned me.'

I had heard that this kind of paranoia was very typical for people with dementia, and that one should try and dispel it with the greatest care.

'How are you getting on here? I'm your granddaughter, and I wanted to introduce myself.'

'Yes, yes, now I see it. You're Ruth, my Erich told me about you. You are so beautiful' — now she had tears in her eyes — 'such a beautiful girl. Look at you.'

'So, what do you do here all day?' I asked her, slowly, as if I'd just learned to talk.

'Who are you again?'

'There are some lovely things on offer outside, leisure activities, do you take advantage of them?' I said hollowly, and immediately dropped the hand I had raised for emphasis.

'What was my husband's name? Leopold, wasn't it?'

'Yes,' I said, 'and I was about to ask you a few things about him. Do you maybe remember what happened to him after the war? Did he go to war?'

'The war?' she asked, once more shocked. 'Is there a war on?'

'No, not for a long time. I mean the Second World War.'

'Oh that,' she said, relieved that it was nothing more. 'We had to be frugal —'

'Yes, yes,' I interrupted. 'And while you were being frugal, what happened to Granddad? Look.' I pulled out a piece of paper from my bag. 'Granddad didn't appear in the register after 1945. But you do, here. And here. Did he not return from the war?'

'He's dead, isn't he?' I nodded. 'That's a shame.' She gripped the battery-operated bunny still lying on her chest, whereupon it activated and rattled out the song 'I Just Called To Say I Love You'. Irritated, I tried to turn off the animal, but she held on to it tightly.

'Who are you?' she asked again.

'It's nice that the nurses come and pick up you for dinner every day. You must know a lot of the other residents, right?'

'He never came back,' my grandmother said, so quietly that I could barely understand her over the blaring bunny. 'When the hollow space under the parquet was cleared out.' Suddenly the song was over, and there was silence.

'What hollow space?' I asked, but was relieved when she didn't answer. 'Listen, I wanted to ask you something,' I said, changing the subject. 'Did my parents visit you very often?'

'Who?' she asked. 'Who are you?'

'Erich and Elisabeth. Your son and his wife. I'm Ruth.'

'Yes, they came,' she said with surprising clarity. 'We talked about you.'

'And what else did you talk about?' I asked. 'Maybe something about what happened during the war? Or about your life during that time?'

'They asked me a lot of questions. Always a lot of questions. And then we ate lunch together.'

'What did you all talk about?' I tried again.

'They always waited for the food,' she murmured, lost in thought, 'so they could poison me.'

This was the moment I gave up. I pressed the emergency button that summoned the staff, and the nurse that had led me there entered the room almost immediately. 'Finished already?' she asked, inappropriately cheerful as we stepped back into the hallway. The whole rural-town atmosphere had tightened around me, and I was breathing hard.

'She has severe dementia,' I said, even though the nurse would have known that. 'Could I perhaps help her financially?'

'How do you mean, financially?'

'Doesn't matter,' I said, ashamed that I had considered never entering this place again and easing my guilty conscience by other means. It was out of the question. I had to see her again — she was the key to my parents' visits.

'Your grandmother's confusion, to our amazement, has improved over the past year. She was a wreck before that, hardly spoke coherently at all. It's got a lot better, which is a miracle because normally things only go downhill at this stage.'

'I had the feeling that she's not all there. Is that the way out?'

'You should just stop by more often, maybe she's just not used to you yet? We notice that the patients gain astonishing amounts of mental strength if a relative visits them every week. Your grandmother is in good shape for her age and her medical history. Did you know that she's been with us since she was forty?'

'No, I didn't know that. Can I get through the doors without a pass?'

'Yes, if I'm not mistaken, she was brought in by your parents' father. That is, by your maternal grandfather. And he also visited her regularly until his death.'

'What were her symptoms when she was admitted?'

'Oh, your parents asked that, too. Hardly anyone understood the clinical picture. If you like, I could take a look at the files? Your parents had the symptoms recorded in detail.'

'No, that's alright,' I said quickly, relieved that we were finally at the exit.

I took the way back into the valley through the forest, where the birds had already struck up their courtship songs. In the past two months I hadn't interrupted my walks for even a day, and had watched in fascination the way the landscape slid into winter. Back in town, I did my grocery shopping for the weekend, and felt the way the turmoil created by the visit to the care home slowly subsided as I walked up Johannesstrasse. Even though my house was less than a hundred metres from there, I took the detour via Quergasse so as not to have to walk by a certain building, which I avoided passing whenever I could: the Glottersaat house.

I can't remember when exactly it was that I first heard the story of Herberg Glottersaat, but I do know how shocked I was that no one had told me before I'd bought my house, as his was located only a stone's throw from mine. It wasn't until some months after I'd moved in that someone told me about his so-called case.

Nobody could understand my horror — the matter was told to me without any additional explanation and, oddly enough, without any concealment, one evening at the Pumpkin: it concerned a man with the unusual name Herberg Glottersaat, who lived at 31 Römerstrasse and who would sit, just like we did, at one of the tavern tables to take his evening meal. I had noticed him many times in the morning when I left my house for work due to his sheer size. He was well over two metres tall, probably in his early sixties, but still had dark hair, and every single day he wore, along with a plaid shirt, a classic flat cap that one could attribute to a farmer, a truck driver, or a common drinker. The story of which he was the protagonist, however, was abnormal, even downright despicable. Which is why everyone in the town knew it.

'Do you see that man over there?' Sister Elfriede had asked, nodding her head in his direction. 'Everyone knows him here.'

'Everyone knows everyone in Greater Einland,' Ferdinand interrupted.

'Yes, alright. But they know him even more. Something happened in 1984. They were completely normal folk at the time, the Glottersaats. In construction, nice family, wife stayed at home. Everything normal.' At this point she fell conspiratorially quiet, and the others went silent as if responding to a cue. 'I'll tell it like this. One day, it was in September, his children disappeared. Four of them — three boys, one girl — all between seven and twelve. Apparently on the way to school, maybe they were just playing truant, it's not that uncommon at that age. Until people noticed that his wife couldn't be found either.' All heads turned once more towards his table, but Glottersaat calmly ate his soup. 'On the fourth day after they had been reported missing, the police finally searched his house. And you wouldn't believe it. All five bodies were in the basement, he'd killed them with strychnine. Still to this day, no one knows why.'

'Then why's he free?' I asked, not yet entirely convinced about the credibility of this story.

'Miscarriage of justice. A technicality? No one knows for sure.'

'What does that mean, no one knows for sure?' I wondered how someone could be so interested in the details of a murder, but not in the apprehension of the murderer.

'He works for the administrative office now, never did anything peculiar again,' said Sister Elfriede.

The fact that he planted flowers in front of the elementary school was apparently enough for the Greater Einlanders to believe in his complete rehabilitation. It was talked about openly, as if it were just an anecdote about an eccentric — not something you might want to keep secret from anyone, but also not something you wouldn't want to lower your voice for in order to make the most of a good story. I often pondered that Glottersaat himself, sitting there, had to sense that someone was being initiated in his abysses and tragedies, indeed, that he might even have been primed and was silently participating in this dramatic depiction of his life.

11

My daily route to work began with the sight of the lush green forest behind my house — an image that invigorated me time and time again. The difficulties began, however, as soon as I entered the town centre. The subsidence had progressed much more quickly than we had all expected in the last few months. The end of the winter and the melting of the snow a few months ago had, in a short amount of time, made the town sink more than a metre, and the roads were in such a desolate state that when crossing them you felt like you were wading through a quagmire. All of the cobblestones that made up the historical surfacing of the town had been forced up and dislodged by the subsidence, and now lay loose on the squares and streets. There had been attempts in the meantime to cement them back in, but they broke free as soon as the hole sagged by even a millimetre due to a damp night. All year round, there was an acute risk of slipping; we had all become masters at getting around. Even the elderly, normally barely able to keep their balance on solid ground, skilfully stretched out their walking sticks, as if they were walking on high ropes. The church tower had developed a new menacing dimension: some claimed that it was at a 45-degree angle, and even if the official measurements confirmed the exaggeration of this statement, its tendency to tip could not be completely dismissed.

When, like every morning, I went to the bakery next to the primary school to pick up my obligatory coffee, I had to climb over a wall that shielded a cracked hydrant. Then I turned into West Town. I looked around carefully before entering the pharmacy, making sure that there were no other customers inside. Pharmacist Stuhl was expecting me, and he brought out a bag of my medication from under the counter, the cost of which I paid for with an enormous sum of cash. If I hadn't been earning double from the Countess what I used to make in my old job, my funds would have dried up within a matter of days.

'It wasn't easy getting this amount of codeine. I had to stretch it a bit with one for children,' he said quietly.

'Codeine is codeine,' I replied, taking care not to loosen the cobblestones in front of the door by kicking them too hard. Then I continued in the direction of the castle.

Apart from the church, the main square was the core of the collapse: its centre hung a full three metres lower than it had a year ago. The stones weren't just loose on it, but had slid right into a heap in the middle — it funnelled downwards to the image of the former archangel. Down there, that is, at the low point of the parabola, the first breach into the mine had occurred last month. As thin as the needle of an eye at first, then soon as thick as a fist and then a leg. I saw this black void, which I knew from my calculations to be over the deepest depression of the hole, every day on my way to work, and imagined how a stone, thrown into this hole, would fall a hundred and fifty metres into the mountain.

You could only move around the funnel-shaped main square on its stony pizza crust. The others and I, who had to pass it nevertheless, edged along the narrow ridge next to the house fronts, politely, as if passing on a driveway, giving priority to one another — waving to acquaintances when they clambered up the street lamps on the opposite side of the square. We were standing on the same structure, and were still unreachable to one another. With my back against the wall, I shuffled past the east side of the square, more slowly than usual, because at the same time a group of primary school children, joined to their teachers by ropes in front and behind, were on their way to school. In spite of the desolate condition of the town, the Greater Einlanders had had the good cheer to plant flower bulbs in the planters, the bursting shoots of which were now rubbing against my neck. It felt like we were occupied for hours with crossing this square, but it only took a few minutes.

Perhaps the strangest thing of all was how much the rhythm of the collapses carried over to the sense of time of all the Greater Einlanders: in the weeks in which the collapses happened rapidly, time seemed to race, and one barely had the chance to notice the many changes in the townscape, so that it seemed as though the weathering of years had taken place in a few moments. But if everything remained constant, the flow of things took on a certain viscosity, and the months rolled over me in insignificant indolence. I would hardly notice how a whole autumn had passed. Just as nature usually influenced the perception of time through the rhythm of its four seasons, things stood still and flowed here very much with the subsidence. Leaving the main square was a blessing. The rest of the town was also devastated to a certain extent, but one didn't have to deal with such extreme inclines. Quite the opposite: I was pleasantly surprised how intact everything seemed today in North Town, even if this impression was nothing more than an optical illusion. Only a few weeks ago, we noticed that the landmarks, all of which were clustered together, were tilting more and more, so we decided to simply incline the pavement at exactly the same angle. It was only by ten degrees, which we had mastered with hydraulic mortising and supported with injections of concrete, yet the impeccably straight impression preserved the mind through this farce.

To leave the town centre, I had to overcome one further hurdle: a single step, which had grown from twenty centimetres to half a metre. Only the castle, since it had been built on bare rock, stood in the same position it had for the last four hundred years.

'Good morning, Frau Doktor,' said Karl the butler as I entered the castle. 'Tissues,' he warned, pulling a packet out my pocket, which he replaced with a new one, before he — always the most unpleasant part of this procedure — poked his stiff fingers through my bun, to check that there wasn't a listening device or something similar inside it. His bony, cold fingers gripped my temples, until the paranoia of the Countess, who constantly feared that her employees were spying on her, had been satisfied.

'Good, you may go in, you have a lot of catching up to do,' said Karl, regardless of the fact that I wasn't even a minute late. I felt uncomfortable, as I always did when I was reprimanded by him. Even though I did my work to the best of my knowledge and belief, actually even performed better than what was expected of me, I felt permanently guilty. After all, I not only owed the Countess for my income, but also for my house. It was an infinite minus hanging over my head, not immediately urgent, yet subconsciously always present. In this respect, I soon discovered, I was not alone in the town — everyone owed the Countess in one way or another. I walked up the two flights of stairs to my office and pretended to immediately immerse myself in my calculations.

For almost a year now, the mimicry that I'd nurtured here had become second nature to me. Five hours a day I busied myself in my towering paperwork, without moving a single step forwards with anything, while at the same time the Countess brought new, either unsolvable or senseless tasks to me. This meant: for a salary, which I received from the Countess monthly and in cash, I cultivated a fallow field of paper.

Above my desk hung a blackboard listing the three catchphrases by which my work had to orientate itself: *refining, broadening, filling*. Refining — I had learned that this meant leaving the data as it was, but transferring it to a different, more tolerable aggregated state. I spent endless hours converting units into one another, and subtracting the margins of fluctuation from the results. The figures obtained in this way, which were visually soothing, but were by no means less apocalyptic in their prognoses regarding the subsidence, were presented at the weekly salons, where they acted like balm on a gaping wound. The second measure we called broadening. Certain factors were subjected to a so-called revaluation, which could be ecological, physical, but also moral, in some cases even spiritual. The aim was to put unchangeable data into a positive light through invented advantages: the dampness of the ground, which began to dissolve, squelching under the soles of our shoes, as a sign of fertility — or establish recent collapses as a good omen, since the entire town was approaching a common level at least. The term broadening related to the broadening of words: the subtle breaking of contexts of meaning. On a basic level, it was a matter of straightforward propaganda tactics. So for the moment all I did during the day was move numbers from one paper margin to another, and use them to create pleasant PowerPoint presentations once a week — and it suited me just fine.

This was because these first two points, which ate up a large part of my energy, constantly kept me from tackling the task for which I had been hired: the development of a supportive substance that would accomplish what the Countess did not trust any and all professional service provided to do. I was not totally unhappy that this agenda was to a certain extent delayed by other activities. For one thing, in spite of my studying of the material, I still had serious doubts that such a miracle formula could be squeezed out of a theoretical physicist like me. What was much more important, however, was that whenever I had undertaken to do it in the last year, I had come up against peculiar irregularities. They were so obvious that I had wondered why no one had ever noticed them; not a single number matched reality. The first thing I noticed was that the volume of the hole was much greater than the figures stated in the official documents that had been made available to me. In my naivety I had simply corrected it, showed up in the office a week later, and, looking through the papers, had found the wrong figures again, without anyone having even mentioned the matter. I soon gave up informing anyone else about my findings, and more than that, from that point on, I showed a certain degree of caution while researching during the day.

Even today I noticed one such discrepancy: a certificate from the year 1950 listed a side entrance to the mine that I did not recognise from our directories. I looked around hastily, then stuck the document in the machine to make a copy for my private research. I had decided, out of principle, not to work on a filler until I understood how so many errors could have got into the documents. After all, even if none of it signified anything, it would senselessly slow down my work. But maybe something revealing would be discovered this evening. I slipped the copy into my handbag and took a deep breath.

At midday, only an hour after I'd started my work, I checked the clock. From the very first minute I had felt uncomfortable in my office: it was arranged like the interior of a Rococo egg and wallpapered with bizarre depictions of young boys and graceful deer on the heath. I had to regularly take a breather out in the corridor: the air in my office was as hot as an oven, especially in winter. All about the place, overzealous personnel lit fires in the fireplaces, the heat from which was retained by the thick carpets — and on top of that the four-metre-high windows could not be opened, but were rather flush with the wall. The boredom was unbearable; and the closer the hand moved toward the two, the closer came the time of day that I feared the most. At that moment,

I could already hear the sharp tapping of steps approaching: at this time, and with monstrous assertiveness, the Countess entered my office, where I was still doing my so-called work.

'Oh, there you are,' she said sternly, and had already entered the room with the full effect of her presence, laying her wide-brimmed hat on my documents. Most of the time she came from meetings with distinguished friends.

'I wanted to speak to you regarding an urgent matter we have agreed to talk about,' she said unnecessarily, as she sat on the edge of my desk. Of course, we hadn't discussed anything of the sort. 'Here, I have the plans from the old steelworks. I don't know if you need them. If not, I mean, if you don't, then I'll just take them back. In any case we have to compare notes soon,' she said nervously. 'We urgently need to talk. You know that Sister Elfriede's house is, some might say, subsiding. It's causing quite the stir. It's well known that Sister Elfriede is an important part of the community. Could you do a little research for me by next week?' I moved closer to her in order to look at the plans, and felt her body stiffen.

'They're not just saying it's subsiding, they're saying it's already started to break down the middle,' I said carefully.

'However that might look in reality — the key thing is that we don't want to upset such a long-established citizen and then have to mediate by intervening. We should find a way for the problem not to be noticed.'

'What do you mean? How are we supposed to hide that a house is breaking in half? I believe the electricity wiring is hanging free.'

'I see, well, do I need to complete all of your tasks then?' the Countess shouted, throwing a pile of papers onto the floor, but calmed down again immediately afterwards. 'Oh, there's no rush. I'm only talking about the ground work, provided you can be expected to do it.'

On a daily basis the Countess came to me with these kinds of ideas, which bore no relation to basic physical laws or financial realities.

'You're spreading yourself too thin,' the Countess said, as she saw that I'd turned back to the papers lying before me. 'But let's talk about something else. Yesterday I asked you to do the calculations for the proposal, you know what I'm talking about. Take care of it as soon as possible.'

The Countess remained sitting in front of me.

'As in … right now?' I finally asked.

'If you have nothing else to do, please.'

I dutifully picked up my pen and, sweating, familiarised myself with the folios that the Countess had put on my desk for me yesterday. It was the most foolish nonsense that I'd ever read: an application for the construction of a kind of underground suspension railway that was intended to illuminate mining in the nineteenth century. It ought to be completed in time for the great art action, and be a draw for tourists despite its outrageously expensive tickets. I saw with an initial glance that not only was the cost–benefit calculation completely unsustainable, but also that the guests, moments after entering the mountain, would suffer an inevitable death from falling rocks. The Countess, however, sat stock-still and observed my obsolete arithmetic — the longer the situation lasted, the more I had the feeling of wrongdoing on my part. I was overcome with shuddering, time didn't seem to pass, precisely because this situation was repeated almost daily. Dripping with sweat, I finally submitted the application with the calculations.

'Thank you,' the Countess said, pulling a piece of paper bearing her signature out of her pocket.

'Your holiday request. I have approved it, of course, as I always do for my best employees,' she said, and I breathed a sigh of relief.

She was already making her way back to her office when she stopped again.

'I wanted to ask you something else.' She looked sheepishly at the floor. 'Would you like to come to the theatre with me this evening? My husband doesn't have time. It's *Macbeth*.'

'I already have plans this evening, unfortunately, otherwise I would have liked to have gone,' I replied.

'Fine, if *Macbeth* doesn't interest you, there's nothing that can be done,' the Countess said, as if I had rejected her personally. 'Not in the mood for Shakespeare, very well,' she added, ignoring my assertions to the contrary. She sat down again next to me, ruffling her hair, then, after lightly clearing her throat and mumbling a few words, returned to what she had been saying.

'Well then, where are you off to this evening, if you don't have any time? You don't have to tell me,' she added hastily but aggressively.

'I'm meeting someone for dinner,' I replied deliberately vaguely.

'Oh. Yes. I understand then it's not going to work. If you're not interested in *Macbeth*,' she repeated again. 'I'll see you tomorrow then.' And her outfit slid across the floor out of the room.

At exactly three o'clock, I was released with official precision from my daily duties, with the intention of giving me time for writing my thesis. I had an almost daily hangover from the conversations with the Countess and needed the way back home to regain a clear mind. Furthermore, my grandmother floated like a ghost in my head. The hollow space under the parquet was cleared out, I thought, and unlocked the door. However, as always happened when I entered my house, an immense calm fell over me.

In the garden, the herbs I'd planted had already broken through. I picked a little basil for my lunch, sat in my armchair, and thought about what had to be done next in the garden. The feeling of having taken over the management of something that had been given to me from the previous generation grounded me — I had paved the driveway and repaired the facade myself, invested what I had left over in a new central heating system and a garage, even though I still didn't have my car. But there was an uncanny feeling of happiness over all of it: in the end, my parents had been able to pass something on to me, even if it had been under unfavourable circumstances. I was not uprooted, but embedded in a continuum, even if it was only a material one.

I heated up my food and began working on my scientific studies; time was already pressing. Week after week the workload for the Countess had increased, and the time I had for my thesis had decreased. Half a day, as I had understood for a long time already, was too short to really immerse myself in the theorems. Just as I was starting to get going, I had to leave the house again, and walked down Oberschenkelbacherstrasse.

I found Ferdinand standing in front of the wine tavern, where he was having trouble typing something into his phone with his huge sausage fingers. He panted from the exertion, and didn't notice me until I was already standing in front of him.

'Ruth,' he said, 'there you are. I was just trying to message you. Say, how come we're not meeting at The Pumpkin? It's difficult getting around at the moment, I've been stage 3 since last week.' Only now did I see that a tube was sticking out of his nose — and that this was connected to an oxygen bottle in a little trolley via a transparent hose.

'I don't know,' I said and looked around, embarrassed. 'I thought it might be nice, and, you know, the good air.'

I gently urged him to go in, and we sat down in the corner of the garden. A wooden sign bobbed on the branch of an oak tree that read 'Storm and Chestnut'.

'How's the swimming going? Good enough for the Olympics yet? You and Anita, you're in the same group, right?' asked Ferdinand, who had to break off after every three words to noisily draw air into his lungs. I became a little breathless myself from listening to him.

'Good, but we're short one person for the relay team. There's only three of us in the club, so one of us always has to swim twice,' I replied and hastily waved over the waitress. It was already darker than I'd expected it to be. Ferdinand ordered a litre of wine for himself, along with an oozing schnitzel. I winced when I saw a bite of potato salad fall out of his mouth and onto his football scarf. I wondered whether it was bothering me that I was ashamed, or whether I was already ashamed about being ashamed in his presence.

'We meet far too seldomly, Ruth. I've wanted to show you my new apartment for ages. I live down on Genossenschaftsstrasse now. I have my own garage and a new kitchen with an ice cube machine.' He smeared lingonberry sauce on a piece of lettuce.

'It must have been hard leaving behind your house; you grew up there and everything. Has it completely broken apart?'

'Completely,' he said, and shook the final drops from the litre carafe. 'Wasn't hard. My dog fell into the crack in the cellar and died down there in the end. Didn't notice for a whole three days, only when it started to stink. So I decided to move out, before the same thing happens to me.' He laughed uproariously, but it took three or four intakes of breath before his oxygen supply normalised. 'I mean it, you should come over to mine some time.'

'I've got a lot of stuff on at work. It's going to be intense for the time being,' I said quickly. I was agitated, and I looked at my watch. 'What else is going on with you?'

'Nothing, I'm doing fine, but I need a new car. For the football games.'

Was he really that insensitive to his own physical state? Or did his rural upbringing forbid him to show his suffering too much? He seemed, in any case, in good spirits.

'Ferdinand, I wanted to ask you something else.' I tried to begin as innocently as possible. 'You once said something about an entrance to the hole that someone could go down into.' He answered in the affirmative with an inarticulate noise over his schnitzel.

'Could we quickly go to it later? Is it even still open?'

'What, today? It's almost dark, and I can hardly climb steps.'

'It's important. Let's go for a walk. I need fresh air,' I said nonsensically, as we had been sitting outdoors the entire time anyway.

'I don't know,' Ferdinand said slowly. 'Couldn't we wait till after my treatment? Besides, it's forbidden.'

'Just for a second,' I insisted, until he finally gave in, and I paid for everything that we'd consumed as if by way of apology. We made our way to Edelweissgasse.

'It's at the western entrance,' he said, already completely out of breath from the short walk uphill.

I fervently hoped to find an open entrance through Ferdinand — in truth, it was the only reason I had met him today. In the place where we were heading, there were particular discrepancies — the geological reports showed strange hill profiles, as if someone had attempted to fill in the soil there by force. Nothing had been found in the official documents.

'Ruth, it's not worth it. You can't see anything.'

I had to push Ferdinand forward every metre, and he was visibly in pain — yet he was the only person I trusted. After a terribly slow walk, we arrived at a steep section north of the Scheinbacherstrasse. Ferdinand, panting, clung on to a tree trunk, while I climbed into the thicket,

'Shit, the entrance has been nailed shut!' I shouted to him.

'Told you, didn't I?'

I considered for a moment whether I could do anything about it, but the slats, which had been fixed into place with nails as thick as fingers, wouldn't budge even a centimetre.

Even within the general theory of relativity, there are points where time comes to a standstill: black holes. If a body has so large a mass that it not only holds itself together, but also binds more and more particles to itself in a noticeably stronger gravitation, a chain reaction is triggered. A greater mass means a greater attraction, which results in a denser centre, which in turn draws more mass into itself. If a particularly strong pulling force has developed, neither bodies nor light nor information can leave the hole again.

The outer sphere of these singularities is called their event horizon: it is the boundary between the black hole and the universe that surrounds it, the crust where being and the nothingness that eats away at it meet. The name event horizon is, of course, deceptive because, by definition, no more events can be located there. All movement is suggestion; the gravitation emanating from the hole distorts space and the passage of time, everything is broken by the force of the infinitely compressed mass.

12

The hollow space underneath the parquet was cleared out. For many days, this sentence rotated in my mind. It distributed its composite parts before my inner eye, all of which I had to push away from myself, one by one, because they were far too opaque to be able to glean anything from. *The hollow space underneath the parquet*, I thought to myself in inattentive moments. Did this formulation perhaps indicate something repressed in her mind? That was a depressing thought: that she finally had an awareness of her decline.

It went on like this for days, and as I was thinking about it for the hundredth time, a further idea popped up behind this sentence. One that was so improbable that I began to get annoyed about its persistence. I diverted myself with my work or agitatedly left the house to disappear into the forest. It was only after three gin and tonics during a visit to a bar with Anita that I finally succumbed. I lay on the sofa, the room spinning, while an impulse made its way through my disarmed mind. I crouched down on the floor and probed the cracks in the herringbone parquet, in which centuries' worth of dust had settled. I couldn't penetrate it with my hands; I fetched a coathanger and ran the wire through the crevices, to satisfy this suspicion once and for all. It got caught

173

near the window. I pulled the hook in surprise, and the wooden floorboard popped up. It took some time before I understood what had just happened. A wooden staircase led into a recess in the floor, which I could only barely make out due to the shadow cast by my ceiling light. I climbed reluctantly into the hole, which smelled of heavy earth, and I stood on the clay floor of an old cellar compartment, which had a bare lightbulb on its far wall.

At some point, the two mysteries need to be discussed.

In the mornings and evenings, I would sit for two hours cultivating my private investigations like a clandestine civil servant, which the Countess's workload couldn't keep me from. Only my thesis suffered even more than it already was. The thing was: from the very beginning I'd had the feeling that something wasn't right about the history of the hole, and that the filling, in addition to the obvious structural need, also had the purpose of transforming this vagueness into a solid mantle, an ossification that could never again be broken. The Countess's wish for a binding agent to be developed had increasingly faded into the background for me. Instead, the hole and its causalities, its condition and its preservation, but above all the processes that had led to its formation, had in the last year become my hobby.

If I came across information, it was mostly a byproduct of the work that I carried out for the Countess. I photocopied the more interesting papers at the castle and took them home. If you put them together and, where applicable, added missing pieces, it resulted in a picture. As if I had accidentally tipped out boxes of matches, and the matchsticks had merged into a clearly discernible motif. Or I should say, two motifs arose: a general one and a special one.

The first mystery was the tunnel system and those incidents that lay within them beneath the surface. It took months for me to realise that something was missing in these stories, because the gaps had been dutifully plugged up. It foremost required a trained eye on the local environment, a practically native eye, to see that the threads that converged over the hole were different from those of the original fabric. Only the subtle shade of the stories disclosed them.

The object of the mystery was this story of the missing forced labourers that I had first learned of a year ago. Generally speaking, this wasn't anything remarkable in Austria — i.e., the fact that the crimes under National Socialism had been carefully covered up and then came out in the end after all.

It turned out that not only had around seven hundred and fifty bodies been lost in the collective memory, but that even the grave itself had started to move in people's various stories. Its location was constantly changing in the documents from various decades: at one time, it was supposed to be on a hill behind the protected forest; another time, it was described as being on the main road, or directly on the land of the former concentration camp, where the memorial had been erected in 1988. That alone was remarkable: that a mass grave had been forgotten. Far stranger, however, was the disappearance of the seven hundred and fifty people: a mountain of corpses that the earth had swallowed without a trace.

A final partial mystery — perhaps it was simply incomprehensible to me because of a lack of imagination — was the question of how ten guards had managed to kill eight hundred people. I had long suspected that the guards must have had help, yet even this was a formulaic, picturesque, deplorably banal version of things: the Wehrmacht had done it, the Wehrmacht, the Wehrmacht, the Wehrmacht had sequestered everything. That is to say, it really wasn't that easy, because in three or four places in the history that someone had tried to smooth out again after its unfolding like an unruly table cloth at Sunday lunch, the obstinate earth's crust was surprisingly torn. A real estate agent had bought some land near the South Town in the eighties, and when he started the excavator, there appeared, to the honest surprise of everyone in the community, bones, tumbling from the earth by the hundreds. The ground was pounded down, an unmarked cross was stuck in it for the sake of decency, and the matter was once more collectively forgotten.

Then I found something else: I had to write a report on test drillings and their geological results from the year 1989, when I found a reference in a note in the margin of some old plans. Apparently, during these tests first one body, then a second and a third had been found on someone's land, far from the first two graves. When they looked in the outflow, a vertical bore pipe behind a villa, they found a further ten people. These weren't isolated cases; I dug deeper into the files, and soon found out that there had even been a hearing in the fifties at which a family stood trial, because someone had come across three bodies in their yard. I was surprised when I read the names of those involved. In the absence of evidence, the matter had ended in an acquittal, and people went back to creating a so-called good impression. Every time there is a spillage, a runner is thrown over the tablecloth before the guests arrive — a white-washed piece of fabric, with small animals or skiers or other patterns printed on it that distract from the stain. It soon became clear where the expensive, water-resistant waxcloth was coming from: the Countess had bought all of the relevant land in these unpleasant cases, and consequently things had been quiet ever since.

When two issues are interlinked and their moving parts fit together perfectly, both of them start to move. It seems like a lucky coincidence, because you think you can measure one by the turning gear of the other. For me, it was the personal and the societal. Yet this motion is deceptive: in order to grasp the mystery, I would, in fact, have to separate these gears from each other to a greater degree. Had I not been so absorbed by their synchronisation, I might have understood that collective forgetting is different from individual forgetting.

Because then there was the second mystery I was constantly working on. It was the mystery of my parents and all of the things connected to it. It was much more precise than the first and had a clearer goal. It was as follows: why had my parents visited Greater Einland every week and why had they never told me? What had led to such a radical break between them and the community — and what had led to their putting it into perspective?

I gathered material on this mystery at every opportunity — details about my family history, which in turn raised further questions. One in particular drove its way to the top: Leopold

Schwarz. My search for him in the land registers and indexes had been in vain. I found neither his notice of indenture (because I suspected he might have been drafted) nor any indications of what had happened to him after the war. Leopold Schwarz was the gap in my family: I had found three grandparents, but one's existence remained dependent on me.

He was the first explanation I found for what my parents might have been looking for here. The problem was that I hadn't found the slightest proof: I clung to this parallel between me and them, and yet knew nothing of their motives. I just always remembered that on the first day in the town archives, Anita had said that my mother had come by almost every week to excavate documents, just as I was doing now, and with a discretion that I now assumed was calculated.

I lay in wait for the unspeakable thing I was after: had my parents also noticed that people had disappeared? Had their research gone deep into the hole, or had they begun with my grandparents — with the sudden disappearance of Leopold Schwarz? Or maybe it had absolutely nothing to do with it at all, I thought on some days, when I lay alone on the couch in the living room they had both played in as children, and then I was ambushed by the strange feeling that I didn't know anything about them at all.

For the work I was performing for the Countess, I had burrowed my way into lithology at an alarming rate, and after three or four months I began to read the physical properties of the sediment like the morning newspaper. Because we were working with borehole geophysical data analysis — that is, drawing out our information through narrow eyelets that we had to first chisel out — we only had data from imprecise measurements at our disposal. We couldn't enter the hole — it was a hostile, permanently collapsing terrain that we were researching. This method was called remote sensing. I had mandated the Schlumberger method: an alternating current for exploring the subterranean nature of the soil, and then itemising the cavity using sonographic methods. This was in the spring of 2011. After realising right at the start that the data on the size of the caves did not match our plans, a further inconsistency was soon revealed. I had the radargram in front of me, which should have produced a uniform, linear diagram in tune with my expectations, but instead I saw wild, jagged clusters of fragments. Where some parts of the underground had been tidied up, and fine stone chambers had been cut out for the miners, in other places someone had, without it ever having been recorded, indiscriminately detonated explosives. And in some places, there was no stone at all, and that's what most caught my eye: there were non-mineral materials in the tunnels, perhaps tonnes of wood. I sat perplexed in front of the sonographs' densely sprawling tangles of lines. There was no way of pursuing it any further, because all I could draw my conclusions from were mere return signals from sound waves.

Once again, something prevented me from drawing anyone's attention to these finds: the way the papers appeared to have been falsified made me suspect that it couldn't have been an accident. Or was I just paranoid? Was I bored? When I dared to include the deviating results in a weekly report to the Countess, and even wanted to add something further, I saw that Philipp had marked them for deletion.

The mystery itself lay in layers that kept needing to be drilled: there were hundreds of tiny inconsistencies. For instance, that the hydrological reports clearly showed water ingress that was never included in the data. Or that a child had allegedly fallen into an abyss four years ago, in a place where in reality there was no such opening at all. That a concession had been in place for the mining of iron ore for fifty years, even though there was no iron in the mountain. I collected these documents on my desk and later in my living room. There were small shifts, yet the deeper one drilled, the more fluid whatever I was holding onto became. I suspected that it must be a deception coordinated with the authorities. When I later decided to go to the town archives to note down the details of the mining and all the explosions, the system told me that I was unable to: the volume in question had been loaned out to Elisabeth Schwarz two years ago.

I put the facts to myself every evening and annotated them with footnotes, so that I knew exactly where they came from. I drew question marks wherever there was an ambiguity, and collected ideas on how to fix it.

Seven hundred and fifty disappeared people, and a community in which a monarchy had been reinstated practically overnight.

Explosions underground, see footnote 1. Here: a geological report that shows that activities took place in the mountain post-1945. Question mark: my parents took out the volume. I shook my head, no, at least seven hundred and fifty disappeared people, fact, and one of them was Leopold Schwarz. The miners who left the mountain after 1945; my parents left on 21 September, the documents on the backseat, then a collision: an exit, a demolition ten years ago, recorded nowhere, see no footnote. And one thing had bled into the other: the sinking land and its inhabitants, some of whom had irrevocably liquified others into the mountain because they thought that, unlike them, they didn't belong to it. This humus prepares the ground for rapid growth. It is easier to put down roots where much of what is in the soil is rotten.

From the beginning, I knew that my chances of solving both mysteries were extremely slim. All the materials that reached me were disordered, anecdotal, and obfuscated by the mudslides of memory. To be buried and carried off also means that the layers get mixed up. When I wanted to look at the hole, I found my parents. When I wondered what they had been doing here, I found nothing but the hole and what I thought I had lost in it. No matter where I went, I was constantly being told about my parents, with anecdotes and pieces of information. I could be eating my supper and someone would slip me a photo (in it: my father, maybe fourteen, tanned and astride a chopped log) or tell me a story about my mother's parents' house, in whose kitchen poppy-seed cakes had been baked in an assembly-line-like fashion. It was the disconcerting touch of a past I had nothing to do with, when someone approached me while I was having breakfast in the café in town and said: *Your parents were always here too!* What I could believe of it remained to be seen: I only had information from indirect conclusions at my disposal. It was biographical remote sensing.

Whenever I switched to the mystery of the hole, because I thought I would be able to deal with the factual there, I noticed that the main source of my knowledge was likewise only hearsay: no different from the case of my parents, everything was conveyed via old stories, bon mots, and the dispatches of my own grandparents. What had actually happened and what had been embellished or even only surmised was difficult to determine. In the nineteenth century, it was said, seventeen men supposedly on the search for gold disappeared. In the eighteenth, they were looking for copper — at the beginning of the twentieth century, a desire for uranium drove people into the hole. You would be told these things in the inn over a beer or someone would find it in an anthology of fairy tales, but the same thing would be later invoked in an historical work. At first glance, none of these stories had a causal relationship to the other — indeed, I didn't even know whether their role went beyond the purely metaphorical, that is, beyond what was already laid out in the myth of Pergerhannes, for instance.

The problem resided in the fact that the camp-prisoner story was handled in a very similar way. Everyone was used to telling the history of the mountain a little differently, and because everything came from word-of-mouth accounts, inaccurate formulations kept cropping up that made clear knowledge impossible. One would turn, full of relish, to the horror stories, and with love to the mountain transfigured by mystery, which in turn seemed to form a tight-knit community between its inhabitants.

I couldn't see anything underground.

I had to give my eyes a few minutes to get used to the darkness, before I could turn off the light in the darkened chamber. I was standing in a kind of recess in the foundations — a gap that had been placed in the middle of the wooden gables. The chamber had an uneven, tamped-clay floor, and the bricks were exposed — I felt the coolness of the earth emitting from them. By my estimates, the whole compartment couldn't have been more than three metres square, and it was completely empty except for a table, on which lay a book. The surfaces were covered in a finger-thick layer of dust — it was a place with an oppressive atmosphere. Its emptiness in particular was oppressive, and precisely because it was so empty, I looked for details that I hoped to see: I found two sturdy hinges protruding from the left wall, and a hanging cord at the entrance that made it possible to slide the doors open from the inside. I had spent only a few minutes in this strange cellar when the claustrophobia hit me. Before I went upstairs, I wiped the book on the table with the back of my hand and saw its title: *The Iliad*. Breathing heavily, I went back into the living room and dialled the number for the care home. The night nurse picked up.

'This is Ruth Schwarz; would I be able to come by now?' I asked. 'It's urgent, I need to speak to my grandmother.' Silence on the other end: *Of course*, I thought, *it's half past one in the morning, what an absurd question.*

'I'm sorry,' the nurse said. 'I thought you'd been notified. Your grandmother passed away three days after your visit.'

13

The first incident I personally witnessed was the one at the swimming pool. In early summer, just as the swim-ringed children were jumping from the diving towers on the first day of the season, the water level rapidly dropped at around 1pm, and around ninety seconds after the first person had noticed the suction, the water had completely drained. No one even had time to shout for help or to fetch a lifeguard who could have thrown the buoys into the pool. Between the children sitting on the blue bottom you could see a crack as thick as a leg in the concrete. As time passed, an awkward silence took hold; no one dared to call the fire brigade, because, after all, no one had been hurt. The mothers lay on their stomachs and dragged their children out of the pool by hanging towels. The very same day, after the lifeguards had provisionally repaired the pool, they filled it with water again — but the invisible cracks continued to pervade the whole structure like fine capillaries, and so they had to pump thousands of litres into the slowly leaking basin every day for the whole of July, just to deal with the situation.

It was true that what was going on was part of a natural event, but it fostered a charged atmosphere, generated by the infinitely slow cracking of the stone foundations on which we continued our everyday life without a care. A month later, still in the hazy heat of the summer, one could gather from softly worded newspaper articles and whispered conversations that reports of burglaries had skyrocketed. Initially, these were individual cases that were unrelated to one another: burglars are said to have climbed behind the bourgeois house facades that had given way to the earth's erosion and subsided. Then it gradually became clear that the unsightly sides of the houses, the long-standing cracks in their facades, had been obscured by swings and tarpaulins that had hastily been thrown over them, and that cunning criminals had realised all this before the rest of the population did. The private erupted into the public, even if one sought to cover it up.

The streets slowly, and without anyone being able to determine the precise transition, took on the character of the provisional, a never-ending sequence of transient states. After the school became in acute danger of collapsing because of its roof, the children were temporarily hosted in containers. Everyone got used to them so quickly that within a few weeks the blue metal boxes, which could be stacked and adjusted, were considered buildings in the real sense. The whole townscape slipped a small, but disturbing bit further towards ugliness. The same thing began to happen to the private houses, too: where there had previously been flat concrete garage roofs, there were suddenly ones made from corrugated iron, which tolerated the tectonic activity better. Fine wrought-iron fences were replaced, little by little, with wire mesh equivalents. Surprisingly, what shocked me the most was the fate of the beautiful, willowy statue of Lady Justice in front of the district court (blindfolded and holding scales in her hand), which not only broke down the middle, but also both halves — that is, the left and right — had drifted apart from one another. Instead of dismantling the bust however, the gap in the middle was constantly being filled in, so that Justice's physical size visibly increased. Ultimately the community considered, since the figure looked more like a caricature, remodelling her into the founding father of the town, Karl Stiefel, for whom this potbelly would have at least been authentic. But this was dismissed as too ridiculous. In other words, a second coating of glaze was overlaid on the baroque cityscape: a layer of fillings, substitutions, and imposed eyesores.

In the autumn of 2009, a certain anxiety began to mingle into my thoughts, too. I checked the doorframes, and began using a spirit level — at first only occasionally, then several times a day — to check the shelves. I studied the plans I had in my office, which were updated with every fissure, until I was sure that the groove of the subsidence didn't go through my house. It had become a running joke in the office — when I got to my desk in the morning, Anita or Philipp would often throw me a geological profile on which the distances between the damp places to my house were drawn up in marker pen. I didn't find it funny — the idea that it would get hold of my property tormented me day and night.

The house: sometimes I felt its foundations within me, as if I had deep, root-like wreaths of nerves in its floor slab. I lay in my bed and felt the beams creak, as if it were my own joints making this sound. I felt a liveliness in the walls that I had never perceived in something inanimate before — the way the wood stretched in the sun and the shingles twitched under the sleet that fell regularly. When it rained I felt the top of my head become wet. On other days I laughed at myself for this pathos, and yet it was undoubtedly the reason that those processes, which would later come to a head, kept running unnoticed in the back of my mind. On the surface, I was completely satisfied with my conviction that I would not work on a filler until my fears about the hole had been proven groundless. Yet when I was first affected by the thought that my own house could sink, automatisms were set in motion within me. It was 15 September when these hidden thoughts found their way to the surface.

I'd lain awake half the night before I got up. Cold air whistled into the study and pushed aside the heavy curtains, against which the glowing end of my cigarette almost brushed as I stretched in the darkness. I'd been smoking again for the past two months. At first ashamed and under the self-appeasement of *only doing so when drinking with others*, then while working if the task was especially demanding, and finally on waking, or even, in fact, while trying to stay awake. I stared into the darkness when I heard a simmering from the kitchen, and remembered that on my way to the study I'd put the espresso maker on the hob while on autopilot as usual. The heaviness of the bed was still in my bones, even though I hadn't slept at all. It was pitch dark as I fetched a cup of coffee from the kitchen, went back to the window, and, with the boiling hot coffee in my mouth, grasped the decision to work.

I sat at my desk and my head ached — but I held the pen firmly. Perhaps it was due to the late hour: I had a magical peace of mind at my command, of a kind one often feels in dreams. On the right-hand side of the table were the specialist journals on replenishment I'd ordered countless copies of and had never opened — in the centre were the graphical representations of the slumps, which I usually only stared at for a distraction. At that moment I had an idea. Without any effort and without my involvement, the answer revealed itself: *the binding agent had to be of the same composition as the hole.*

Within moments, I had started covering sheets of paper with formulas. One would need, I determined, small canals through which the water could drain. My ludicrous idea, which, I assumed, also contradicted all technical rules, was to mix a fungus in the still damp amalgam — a mycelium that grows quickly and in the dark. The filling agent would have to be prepared in such a way that it would require many days to harden. During this timeframe, the massively multiplying mushrooms would embed small tubes of the desired quality into the filled space — and simply die off after the amalgam had hardened. By the time the sun had started to rise, I had gone in the kitchen countless times for more coffee, and within a few hours I had got down a formula. It didn't take long for me to identify two main problems: first, I would have to produce a petrol-based mixture that would render the land barren a few hours after the injection; dead, flora-murdering castrato soil. The water and thus the nutrients would not be completely transported through the extremely thin tubes, at least that's what my biological lay knowledge told me. It was a moral problem, I thought, and wiped viscous fluid out from the corner of my eye. Second, and most important, due to my lack of experience it was not clear whether the binding mixture would hold at all. This was, however, a technical question that could be solved through trial and error.

An innocent, enthusiastic impulse was now keeping me awake: the urge to research — the question of whether what I had written down on the paper would also prove itself in reality. I sat impatiently in the winged chair in front of the wall of books to calculate the unfamiliar quantities. It was six in the morning, which meant that the shops wouldn't open for two hours, and I would only have a short window of time to get everything before I had to go to work. I began to write down a list of substances out of which I could fabricate an at least roughly similar mixture. The things I needed for the trial run were common products from any hardware store. I made more coffee, keeping the grounds and those from the last brew in a bowl, and left it to cool, before I got dressed and ran to the hardware store. It wasn't too difficult to find the things I required.

Back at my house I used the kitchen scales to combine the chemicals in a cleaning bucket. A lot more coffee grounds would be needed to give the fungus enough contact surface. I had seen a documentary about an Australian inventor who had developed a building material from coffee grounds, it now occurred to me, but I didn't know what to make of this idea. The rest, that is, the hardening element, had to consist of slag, but, of course, it was not possible to mix slag — which had to be concocted in a blast furnace — oneself. So I switched to bitumen and coarse-grained sand, pressed the nets of fungus in small coffee balls and mixed the rest of the grounds with the pseudo-asphalt that I'd made. I immediately carried two buckets as heavy as lead into my garden. A tiny canal had developed around the back of my house — this unauthorised fabricated filling wouldn't suffice for anything more. The hardest part was getting the artificial material deep enough into the little hole: I pushed the viscous tar into the ground with a broomstick until the last part I could reach was filled with it. As I left the house, still worked up by what had just happened, I vowed never to tell anyone about my discovery.

I had already been waiting for two hours in the still-empty Pumpkin, and had spread out my papers on the regulars table, when Hat-Maker Schlaf finally entered the bar, pulling his cashmere scarf over his mouth against the drizzly weather. He greeted me fleetingly, settled down in his usual place, and drew out the commercial gazette from his pocket — the same way he did every day — to fill his repertoire with anecdotes and complaints about the goings-on of the rest of the world in the half hour before the others arrived. Over dessert, he would once more assert that it would be best for the company to stay in Greater Einland.

I made sure that Erna wasn't in the room before I sat with him.

'Herr Schlaf, how's business?' I asked.

'May I help you, Frau Schwarz?'

He was taken aback, indeed unnerved, by my appearance at the wrong table, at an hour when no one had ever disturbed him before. In order not to let my nervousness get the better of me, I wanted to get to the point as directly as possible, before someone had the opportunity to interrupt us.

'Actually you can. You see, I haven't lived here very long, and I've been hearing a lot of things for the first time that are common knowledge to others.'

'Yes, of course,' he said absently, sticking his finger in the newspaper like a bookmark.

'And recently I read something at the castle … it was in the legal department, I work with all kinds of documents.'

Within a second all movement had been wiped from Schlaf's face. 'I'm listening?'

'You see, I read about what happened in '62 and would rather ask you directly than anyone else.'

'I don't know what you mean,' he said.

'Maybe I read something wrong. Yes, it was probably some wrong information. Because it said that you were in police custody for a week back then.'

'On false accusations,' Schlaf said, so quietly that I could barely hear him. 'And I was released and rehabilitated post haste. Kindly stop talking.' He leaned away as if the whole matter had been closed, but immediately added: 'Those bunglers. How do I know who buried them there? And now I'd like to finish reading my newspaper, if that's alright with you.'

'Were your parents still alive at the time? Why didn't someone interview them? You were only seventeen. At least, that's what it said in the newspaper.' Why were my hands shaking?

'They — my parents weren't involved at all. What do you want? This episode cost me enough. I don't want to talk about it.'

'I'm asking you for geological reasons,' I said, and knew myself how unbelievable it sounded. 'That four bodies were found in your garden is not irrelevant if we soon start digging up everything.'

'If you don't retract your accusation this instant, I will report it to the Countess,' hissed Schlaf, who had recovered himself. 'Someone placed subjects on my parents' property — that's done and dusted. There was a brief commotion at the time, fine, but you know how the media can be. It has passed.' Now that he had mentioned the Countess, I suddenly felt in a tight spot.

'I'm sorry, I didn't mean to offend you.'

'I'll tell you something: it could have just as easily been someone else's garden. Don't dig up all this stuff about my parents through your bumbling curiosity. These were old, frail people who were hard-hit by the trial. My father walked into the courtroom with the use of a stick after his son had been in custody for a week.' I didn't say anything, but by now Schlaf was in full swing. 'Things like this are distorted, they're bad for business. Back then they only fixated on us, never on Sister Elfriede or the others. Because we,' he pointed his rolled-up newspaper at me, 'had money.' With these words he thwacked the journal on the stable, and Frau Erna came into the bar, startled. He lowered his voice again. 'Only the devil knows why there were a few corpses lying there. It was the war. How many people do you think fell, here, from the town? If the Count hadn't saved us — it was a smear campaign. And you're dragging it back up, your generation especially. Because you never had to build anything. And now, get out of my sight.'

Without saying another word, I walked out of the inn, sat down, momentarily outside of my body, on the kerb and took a deep breath. *Sister Elfriede and the others, Sister Elfriede and the others*, I thought, and then hurried on again. I would take the way to the Kastelburg to calm down. It was a steep path that took around thirty minutes through thick coniferous trees, followed by a ridge over three or four hills, and ended in the spot-lit castle ruins, high above the forest, which were like a lighthouse towering up from the sea of treetops. While the others were partaking of their dinner at the Pumpkin, I tried to calm my heart on my way into the forest. I moved over these surfaces as confidently as I could find the way from my throat over my chest to my stomach with my eyes closed. As I climbed the ridge that gently led to the plateau above the town, my uneasiness subsided. Nature brought me into equilibrium, and I allowed it to seize me: agriculturally cultivated scraps of land, which the road had woven like a shuttle into a single piece of fabric. No sooner had I arrived at the Kastelburg than I sat on one of the walls left ruined by the Huns, and stayed for hours, never bored: I watched the wind sweeping the earth and smelled the moss behind me, until I wanted to infiltrate the soil myself.

I turned towards the familiar slope, but something seemed different to me this time: as if a plate of glass was lying over the panorama, as if I were sitting in front of a shop window with a model railway inside it, and all the people were only little men cast in plastic. On top of this, I was sitting uncomfortably, as I now realised, and had to move back and forth as if to be freed of something heavy on my back. When I stood up in frustration to get to the bottom of it, I saw that the back of my seat — this small wall on which I always wiled away my time — had sunk a good thirty centimetres. It had to have happened suddenly, because I had been sitting here just a week earlier. Evidently everything was following this sinkage in a viscous domino effect — some stone or other had shifted barely noticeably. But it shocked me no less than if someone had removed a bone from a face I knew.

All of a sudden when looking down into the valley, which lay before me like a picture puzzle, the scale of the subsidence was revealed. The surfaces were hacked into pieces — small, useless fields forced into shape. A crack went around the centre of town, as disfiguring as a deep scar. This panorama disgusted me — and at the same time, the more I backed away from it, the more it moved in, like an indiscreet person who doesn't want to let you go.

For the first time the landscape aggrieved me. More than that: I was overcome with loathing, so I decided to start making my way back. The moisture that had previously been evaporated by the sun I could now feel in my ankles. Then a gap in my memory, without my knowing how it had happened. I had been walking for about ten minutes, first turning left and then right, when I realised I was lost. The way had only been one road and yet I was standing on a bridge that I hadn't crossed on my way here. So I went back a hundred, then two hundred metres, but soon realised that I hadn't gone back but had actually taken a third, even more wrong, direction. It was getting dark, only the treetops stood out, pointed against the sky.

When I began to hit obstacles with my feet in the dark and could only progress very slowly, I experienced a moment of panic. Every direction looked the same as the other; there were no distinguishing features in the seamless black that surrounded me. I regretted not having brought a torch with me, cursed my lack of mobile phone, and continued to shimmy from tree to tree. I lost all sense of time. I felt that I hadn't been on my quest for even an hour, yet my feet hurt as badly as they did after twenty or thirty kilometres. I came to a decline, was relieved to be back in the valley, as I assumed, then a wall jumped up in front of me and I once more didn't know where I should go.

I gradually realised that I would no longer be able to find my way back home today, and attempted to turn this into something positive: it was still warm, I wouldn't freeze. *There's no real danger*, I said to myself two or three times, out loud, and lay down on the ground. I stacked some branches so that my body wouldn't roll down the slope, and lay my head on a rock, like I was pretending to be someone sleeping. Now that I was lying in absolute optical deprivation, what I had previously taken to be a wonderfully quiet forest was suddenly full of sounds. A hoarse owl screeched, and all around I heard rustling and hissing, so that time and time again, I sat up with a start. I now understood the wretchedness of my situation. When the miserable wind pressed the damp leaves in my face, I gave up. The sun was coming up, and I hoped I would be able to see soon enough and get home. For the last hour I sat and waited for my eyes to get used to the slowly returning light, then I finally comprehended where I was: I had spent the night in a ditch in the forest, less than five hundred metres from the path I'd walked in on, and had mistaken a forester's lodge for a rock wall.

I got home at dawn and brushed the leaves out of my hair.

14

I leaned my cheek against the soft, warm muzzle of the animal, from whose nostrils flowed a slow, calming breath that kept my own in check. Its chin was covered with bristles and yet was so soft that I could stroke its lower jaw. No resistance from the horse's docile flesh that let me go wherever I pleased: a feeling that I had always liked.

'How long?' asked a servant who was clearly underage, and who had just tied the saddle in place, but I couldn't immediately think what he meant by the question.

'I haven't actually ridden in a long time,' I said. Regardless of my non-answer, the lad lashed the stirrups deep into the brown mare's ribs. At this moment the Countess came around the corner, leading a mighty white horse, whose mane was woven into a baroque braid.

'Let's hurry,' she said, and I led the horse, the way I'd learned during my teenage years, following her out of the stables. 'I can't take too long because I have to meet someone at 3pm who will be making all the costumes for the festival. A master of disguise and deception. I've worked with him for years.'

'Are we really going hunting?' I asked, but the groom was already helping me mount.

I longed to be somewhere else, but there had been no escape that day. The Countess had besieged me for months about doing something with her outside of work, but I had always managed to wriggle out of it. The insistence she showed was inexplicable on the surface, and yet had a system: she criticised me incessantly and didn't even seem to like me very much, but at times she displayed a strange, almost excessive attachment to me. As if in some moments it occurred to her that she urgently needed a female companion. Then suddenly there would be a pack of lime-blossom tea on my desk, the kind she was constantly drinking herself; or she'd remember that I'd once complained of back pain, and draw exercises on a piece of paper that she said she herself did every morning in front of the open window.

The prospect of seeing her alone for a long period of time had something unsettling about it. I barely managed to hold a private conversation with her while walking a hundred metres along a corridor, and the few moments when evading her wasn't possible were pure torture. Nevertheless, the Countess had repeatedly made attempts to invite me to certain occasions — and I did not understand whether she simply did not notice the unpleasantness of it or whether there was a deeper motive tied to it, of which I had no idea. In my moments of paranoia, I feared that she was trying to find something out about me, as she was always doing with others. In those moments, I would respond to her advances as taciturnly as possible and withdrew as quickly as I could. Unfortunately, when a meeting had fallen through the previous afternoon, the inescapable occasion arose when she announced that the two of us, since neither of us had anything to do now, would spend the afternoon together. We would have to go hunting, she had concluded, and I didn't argue.

'You're firm in the saddle, I hear,' she said, which left me speechless.

When the horse, which apparently didn't need my assistance, trotted into the forest after the Countess, I once more wondered how she had found out that I'd had riding lessons for a few years as a child. Getting hold of this information was completely impossible, and yet, as always, she had managed to do so with ease. Behind the already spring-green paddocks, a forest path led between the trees. The Countess, too, wore her hair in a braid so tight that her scalp rose up from the base of it, and the riding jacket, worn high, came up to the nape of her hairline.

'This is where the trail begins,' she said, without turning around.

To my surprise a pack of dogs shot forward through the legs of the horses. I realised that I'd assumed that the term 'hunt' was being used metaphorically — but a small knife was actually hanging from the Countess's saddle.

'These lands have been used by the Knapp-Korb-Weidenheims for hunting for over four hundred years,' she said, unprompted, as if she were trying to practise a long-prepared speech for later.

I had trouble understanding her from behind, but she seemed to grasp this and whistled, causing my horse to quicken its pace to catch up with hers. 'We are tied to this landscape like the flora itself. People literally say: woven like a wicker basket in one's home.' Our horses fell in step, as if they had now smelled the trail themselves. It was incredible how well my body remembered the feeling of riding.

'Frau Schwarz, I want to be honest. I see much of myself in you, and that's why I wanted to speak at length with you and, so to speak, help you understand why this region and its people mean so much to me.' She turned in my direction and tried her best to look me in the eye, then turned away nervously.

'For us Knapp-Korb-Weidenheims, it is important to convey to others the merging with nature, that is, the environment that we feel we belong to. This is why we keep all of these beautiful forests privately owned, so they can't be cleared.' In all of her gestures there lay an awkward attempt to get close to me that left me half embarrassed, half suspicious.

'It's a form of protection?' I asked in a deliberately flattering manner, yet the Countess gave me a reproving look, as if I had asked something so banal it offended her.

'Of course. A patronage, but it is too complicated to explain now. You wouldn't understand it.' After this strange reprimand we were silent for a short while, before she turned to me again, struggling with what interpersonal relationships had put in her way.

'Well, what I'm trying to offer you is first-name terms. You may call me Ulrike,' she said, and suddenly her body was so close to me that I flinched. It was only then that I noticed that she had been riding side-saddle this entire time. This also explained how she had now, in a rash, intimate gesture, leaned over from her horse and grabbed my hand — so that I almost lost my balance and was in danger of falling off. She clasped my right hand and stared steadfastly into my eyes. It was almost comedic, how we dangled like a living bridge between both horses. But she was being deadly serious. We were carried for a few seconds before she rose once more to the vertical.

'We have to go after the pack; the fox should be close by,' the Countess said, once more business-like. I strained my eyes, but there was nothing in the slightest to see. The horses made their way into the undergrowth as if by themselves, following the alleged fox. Although the whole interaction had been so uncomfortable, something had shifted between us. The distance had decreased significantly, and I decided to take advantage of this semblance of closeness.

'I've always wondered who lived in the castle before you, Ulrike. Before your family, I mean.' The 'Ulrike' constricted my throat.

'My father, of course. He was a great lover of the arts. He died too soon in 1966. I was not even twenty and I suddenly had to manage everything all by myself. It wasn't the done thing for a woman.'

'That means that the whole area has always belonged to you? Your family, I mean?'

'To answer that question, there first needs to be a discussion of what "belongs" actually means and who counts as family. To whom is such a question addressed, to the present or to the past? Depending on what the ownership entails, it must be differentiated. One cannot always formulate questions in a basic way and pose them in the form they come to mind.'

I forgot what I actually wanted to find out, and was at risk of not keeping up. The horses were entering increasingly rougher terrain.

'You know, I've been doing some genealogical research,' I said, yet it sounded like an apology. 'And I was wondering who the mine had actually belonged to. It has had a turbulent history, just as much as some of the buildings in the town. I'm asking out of familial interest,' I assured again.

The undergrowth didn't want to end — at times I needed both hands to push away the vines and branches hanging in my field of vision. Finally we came to a small heath, a clearing that I had seen before from the Kastelburg.

'Do you enjoy the hunt? We could participate in one; my friend Baron Rülenwald puts on sublime spectacles,' she said. 'Of course, there have constantly been expansions, the Knapp-Korb-Weidenheims have worked hard for their wealth. Under my grandfather, and then also my parents, we purchased some of the land in order to better control the development of the area. But none of this is important, because if one discusses it, one can end up getting carried away and rambling on. I can tell you many things about your parents. You don't have to look far, I knew them well. Mankind can bear the truth, as Erich Fried said.'

'I'm wondering precisely the following,' I began. 'You owned the house I live in, my parents' house. Which I then bought from you.' I cleared my throat. 'But I've learned that both houses, that one and the one next to it, which my paternal grandparents lived in, used to be owned by the same person.' My voice was trembling; the horse was plunging headlong into the forest again.

'Could you formulate the question more precisely? I don't understand what you're trying to get at,' the Countess said after a long pause, and once more waited for me to elaborate on something I had been completely clear about.

'Did my grandparents sell the house?' I asked.

'We bought it at some point, that is correct, along with a few other properties. I must have still been a child. But as good as the whole town belongs to us. I don't think that this particular case is of interest to you. If so, you ought to look at the town law, otherwise you won't be able to understand the explanation.'

'I think it would be of interest to me,' I said quietly. 'But it's not urgent, it just occurred to me. Maybe at some point after the festival.'

'What a pity, the fox seems to have got away,' the Countess said suddenly and yanked the horse to the left by its bridle, whereupon my own turned off, too. 'But that's worked out well, we have to get back to work in any case.' And with that, the line onto which I had hoped to hold was cut. The horses fell into a gallop, and we soon reached the stables.

'Frau Schwarz, come to my office later. I have to rush now to my meeting,' said the Countess, abruptly switching back to formal terms of address.

Confused and disorientated, I stood off to the side while the groom put the animal in its box. I followed after the Countess, walking cradle step in my strangely stiff riding trousers towards the castle and up the stairs, where Anita was waiting at the door.

'The gentleman is already waiting, I've brought him coffee.' The Countess disappeared into her office — and while she was closing her door, I looked into the room for a moment as I passed. There, grinning at me over his cup, as if he had expected to see me at this very moment, was the mask dealer.

As the brass band marched and played 'Must I Leave Without You' pitifully badly, I considered for the first time whether I could take my leave then but dismissed the idea immediately. I hated the beery musical brunches: suckling pig on a spit, and beer mugs that had been refilled several times before it was even ten. That morning we had observed the christening of the new fire engine by the priest and a number of dignitaries, and when a selection of après-ski hits were put on, I longed for nothing more than to escape.

On the other hand, however, I had become part of the fabric of this society, and, while the Comradeship Alliance rose for an encore of 'Prince Eugen, the Noble Knight', I was stuck in the middle of a group of familiar faces, which made it impossible for me to escape. One could only wonder at the clientele of these beer mornings or the other beer-tent events: academics, who did not otherwise deign to socialise outside of their so-called circles, and who subscribed to three German newspapers for the sake of the features section, suddenly had a light infantry rifle slung over their shoulders to shoot plastic roses for their wives for two euros.

Among the firefighters and farmers' sons, patriots and screaming drunks, the more pretentious attendees clung to one another tightly, distraught at the idea of being alone; so in the end everyone had to stay for an arduous stretch of time, even though everyone essentially wanted to go home. Anita and Philipp were there, too, and every time I announced I wanted to be on my way, they kept me there with stories and schnapps.

It was already noon when we sat together watching grown people laugh while shooting Jägermeister bottles from the tops of their heads. Anita was drunk and was hanging off my shoulder, a little too tightly for my taste, while I made notes about everything I observed. I had no idea what was being celebrated, but probably no one did: a wine queen was chosen, but it was a bright June day, and the next vintage was still months away. The Countess did not appear at such events, which is why I had to, in order to be able to respond to her questions the following Monday: who had spoken and what had been said, how many dignitaries had been present and what they had eaten. Nearby, the whole gang from the Pumpkin was set up open-air to do the same thing they would have otherwise done in the same bar anyway. Even Glottersaat, with his flat cap pushed back and the same plaid lumberjack shirt as always, was sitting silently on the periphery of the table. Sister Elfriede, who was incessantly seeking to be included by everyone, winked at me.

'Three barrels of young wine have been given to the revellers free of charge in the name of the Count and Countess!' was announced from the stage. The crowd cheered, and the majority of people immediately jumped to their feet to fetch themselves a glass of the noble donation.

'Ruth, you grew up completely in the city, is all this very strange to you?' Philipp asked, and I shook my head, without looking up from my notes.

'No more than anything else. For example, last month,' I said to him, 'Anita and I had to go to the anniversary party for the Men's Choir. They've never performed, but they've been rehearsing since 1983! Isn't *that* unusual?'

'Last month?' asked Anita, laughing. 'That was the day before yesterday. You've been so all over the place lately.' I had to tense my facial muscles for a moment in order to verify that she was right. Greater Einland was like a loop; everything passed you by, confusingly similar, like a carousel, and what difference did it make? Then I quickly looked back at my list, concerned I might have forgotten to note down someone.

'But you're right, everything is strange here,' Anita said. 'That's why I can hardly wait to see more of the world.'

'Everyone has to live in America at least once in their life,' said Philipp arbitrarily, knocking back a schnapps.

'No, I want to go to Italy, *gioia di vivere*,' Anita interrupted. 'And the food, pizza in Venice.'

'Driving over the Golden Gate Bridge in cowboy boots, buy a small farm in Texas and shoot geese. *Bang bang* —' he fired fantasy shots from his fingers.

'Can you swim with dolphins there, too?' Anita asked. Fortunately I only heard this discussion in passing. The two spoke endlessly about travelling even though they'd never left the neighbourhood they lived in unless it was for work.

'Listen, I have a question,' I said, lost in thought. 'Have either of you ever actually seen the Count? Does he actually exist?' When I didn't get an answer to my question after a few seconds, I looked up and saw that Anita and Philipp, who had just been messing around, were looking at me in panic. 'Don't ask things like that, Ruth,' Philipp said, looking around, as if we were about to be arrested any second.

'What? Why not?' I asked, genuinely confused.

'You're still new here.' Philipp managed a nervous laugh, while Anita, who was much more uninhibited, leaned over the table towards me.

'You get a lot from hearsay,' Anita said, 'but I don't know anything for sure. My mother once told me that the Count is long dead. Someone told her in the pharmacy, and the pharmacist supposedly got it from' — she whispered almost inaudibly — 'the butler at the castle. The Count had multiple sclerosis, and the Countess had him shipped off to a sanatorium in Switzerland.'

'God, you two, you're going to get us in trouble,' Philipp interjected. 'There are a lot of people here.'

'Is it forbidden to talk about it?' I asked.

'Alright, *fine*,' he said. 'I once heard from Erna that the Count, who, by the way, was an Italian —'

'Never!' Anita shouted.

'Quiet! The Count fell in love with one of the staff and ran off with her to the Maldives ten years ago. Gave up his aristocratic title and everything. Gave all the land to the Countess because of it, but she's never got over it. Don't talk to anyone about this, otherwise you'll be actionable —'

'Actionable?' I asked.

'Of course, I've never seen him. So, it's all hearsay, Ruth. Maybe there never was a Count,' said Anita, whose mouth Philipp was now covering with his hand.

'I'm going to get something to eat,' I said, annoyed that my question had remained unanswered, and stood up to get myself a slice of suckling pig. *For breakfast*, I thought, vexed. Generally speaking, I didn't give a damn about the Count, and even if that hadn't been the case, it was clear it would have been difficult to find out anything definitive about him.

While I was waiting for my food, which I paid for with a coupon, I watched the mayor, who was sitting in the middle of the action and was greeted as automatically as he was impersonally by those passing him by.

'Good morning, Mayor,' the people said, and he nodded at everyone with the same gesture, his shoulders sagging, rounded as ever; his greasy antler buttons that threatened to burst open on his portly belly, but, taking into account the mediocrity of his whole existence, they failed to even do that.

He was just sitting there alone, and I was overcome by a sudden urge. With the idea that this would be an opportune moment, I sat down opposite him. Had he even realised who I was? We'd never spoken before.

'A wonderful party,' he said straightaway, and I smelled the booze on his breath. He was a strange sight that became completely perplexing close up: his hands waved effusively to everyone, but his face exuded a desperation that I'd never seen before. He had deep, dark circles under his eyes, which were combined with this lukewarm, fake smile, for which he apparently had to use all of his remaining muscles.

'Yes, a wonderful party,' I echoed. 'But it must be tiring if you know everyone, like you do.' In fact, he seemed so exhausted that he was about to fall asleep.

'It comes with the job. The two of us haven't really had the chance to talk, but I knew your parents well,' he said. 'We met every week, almost every time they came. For dinner. They talked about you and about how hardworking you are.'

My parents had eaten with him — with an opportunistic,

boring person, who hung over his roux soup like a damp flannel. Time and again with stories like these I got the feeling I was being told about strangers instead of the people who had raised me.

'Yes, we were good friends. *Peter*, they always said, *we're so glad that you're here so we can discuss these things with you that no one else wants to discuss with us. Thank you, Peter, for standing by us.* There were certain sceptics.' My ears perked up.

'Sorry, but what were your conversations about?' A bare tree trunk was carried in over the heads of some men in lederhosen into the large square. *A May Pole*, I thought, confused, but May was long gone.

'About certain developments that certain other people didn't want to see. I'm not talking about progress as such, which *is* advisable for people, but we are bound by a continuum of history, at least as a community.'

I had no idea what he was getting at.

'What developments were my parents interested in?' I asked again, and he replied after a hearty gulp, this time from a Roman-style wine glass:

'On the one hand it was, of course, about a very dark period in Austria,' he said, again being vague, raising his right hand to wave.

'Which period?'

'The darkest,' he answered. 'They had questions about, shall we say, ambiguities, regarding a certain course of action that happened from the top. And, as a certain kind of politician, my interest was purely in maintaining a tradition that is, on the one hand, human, and on the other hand, subject to reason.'

It occurred to me that after a year and a half in this town, I didn't know what party he actually belonged to. It could have been any of them.

The vagueness of his statement made me increasingly aggressive.

'Were my parents researching something about the National Socialists?' I asked in a provocative tone — though there wasn't actually anything provocative about my question. The mayor took off his hat, as if he were hot. An oily tuft of hair appeared from under it.

'One has certain … *provenances*,' he forced out. 'And it's not always clear how these relate. Your parents maybe went too deep from time to time, and not everyone liked that.' The log was heaved into the air with a roar, and the brass band struck up again.

'Who didn't like it?' I asked, but the mayor had become engrossed with unusual fervour in shaking hands with a passer-by wearing a sash. When he turned back to me, the question had become obsolete.

'You work for the Countess?' he now asked, as if to change the subject. 'Very hardworking.'

'Yes, I do. Why? You get on with the Countess, don't you?' I said.

'You get along with those you have to get along with. Whereby the getting along is also always a question of letting things go.' This answer also confused me.

'So there are points of friction? Is it difficult to be involved in political activities when you have the nobility next to you in a parallel system?' I was in full flow, suddenly daring enough to ask everything. But he had his nose deep in his glass again.

'The nobility, well,' he finally began, slurring. 'I wouldn't say we were talking about nobility in the classical sense.' With these words he looked around like a persecuted man. 'Your parents knew that. I'll only say this much: you shouldn't believe everything that the Countess tells you. Fifty years ago,' then he corrected himself, 'maybe eighty years ago, the castle belonged to someone else. Then there were certain changes that everyone in Greater Einland agreed not to talk about, because a lot of good came out of them.'

'The Countess's family were originally the owners of the mines, right?'

'Some say a direct descendent of Pergerhannes. But that can't be true of course, because Pergerhannes is a mythical figure,' babbled the mayor. 'But what isn't a myth is this: someone wanted to, so to speak, rise up to the nobility. The Countess belonged to the first generation in which social change had been implemented with violence. Out with everything to do with mining, in with having more land. She grew up in great hardship, that has to be said. My father told me that the Weidenheims sometimes didn't heat the children's bedroom for the whole of the winter. To encourage self-discipline. Had her taught by a French general, only the best education. Never went to school with other children, all private. I'm saying nothing. I'm just saying you have to respect that,' he said. 'Anyway, when old Weidenheim died, the nobility was already fully developed. From then on, the mines were no longer a decisive factor for the family's prosperity, but the daughter has administrated the town excellently. Of course, some estates only came about by dubious means, if you know what I mean.'

'No, I don't know what you mean,' I said.

He took another breath, put his hat back on, sighed three times into the Rákóczi March currently being played and then leaned over towards me. 'It has to do with what your parents were interested in. There were omissions, I'll say that much, the house, the one you're living in,' he cleared his throat, then started up again in a different place, 'because the mine was controlled by forces from the town which were not unrelated to the Countess. And quite a bit had been accumulated through the predicaments that arose at the time.' I needed a few moments to process the chaotic mess he had created.

'Have I understood correctly that the Countess isn't a noblewoman at all?'

'Listen, that I'm telling you this is, to be honest, no accident. Everyone in the town knows that you're sniffing around. I advise you not to draw attention to yourself.'

This directness appealed to me; for the first time, I had the feeling that someone was really talking to me.

'Mayor,' I said, leaning towards him, 'I know only too well that I am in a grey zone. But it's like this: I believe that my parents were onto something, and maybe …' — I considered for a final time, whether I should touch on it, and decided to give it a try — 'You see, the night before my parents' accident, they were at the castle. Isn't that a strange coincidence?' Now the mayor looked as if he had suddenly sobered up; he sat up and was breathing heavily.

'What unspeakable things are you suggesting about our

Countess?' he whispered, even though he had just been talking in the same vein. 'You've got a nerve saying that while I'm sitting next to you in public? You must have misunderstood me.'

Then he straightened the cord tie inside his jacket, as if he had said too much. The conversation was over. In fact, he got up and we shook hands, as if saying farewell; neither of us would leave the party, though. Instead, he stepped towards the steeply towering May Pole.

In 1801, Thomas Young carried out the double-slit experiment for the very first time: an electron emitter was placed in front of a barrier with two slits and was used to shoot particles at it. The surprising thing was that not only were impact points able to be seen behind the two slits, but also next to them — in the form of a fringed interference pattern. This was a strong indication of wave-particle duality: electrons behave both like individual particles and like periodic oscillations. Furthermore, even a single particle could apparently take both paths at once — bilocation, the breaking of time, was a reality on the micro level. A modification of the detectors revealed even more astonishing things. If one affixes an apparatus that records the gap through which a particle flies, the particles only take one path and the interference pattern disappears. It was only when the electrons were given the freedom to break the laws of nature without being seen that they would do it.

15

At the beginning of September, an area of low pressure drew in over the Hochwechsel and brought with it the longest-lasting drizzle that had been recorded in the last sixty years. After an unbearably hot summer, where one had fevered with the earth and the panting plants, it was a relief for us all. For about two weeks, a besprinkling set in over the landscape, which was further eroded by blasting wind against the stone ridges. Which is why the people in the community hardly noticed anything of it: only that on seemingly clear days, one still had to turn on the windscreen wipers, and walk a little more carefully on the asphalt in their patent-leather shoes because the puddles no longer evaporated. The fact that one could barely see the Hochkarner ridge only unsettled a few people. The scattered light got lost in the oversaturated air and never emerged from the haze. This was the autumn weather longed for during the long, hot summer — local weather conditions, they said, normality.

But the surface of the ground, the meadows, the forests, the machine-tamped soil beneath the buildings — all of them, meanwhile, sucked the moisture out of the air in thirsty gulps, faster than had ever happened in such a short period of time. Eighty kilometres away, the Schwarza had already powerfully

215

broken its banks and had flooded the cellars in the surrounding area, from which people hurriedly carried their preserves and table-tennis tables. But Greater Einland didn't know anything about it.

By the middle of the month, the ground beneath the town had drunk in excess of its capacity, so that when the onset of October showered the first plants, the herbaceous, tender ones began to drown under our feet.

The pressure of the water had to therefore escape downwards, a layer deeper, and it was, as was later reported, around 2 November, when, deep beneath the main square, south-east of the large shaft, one of the stone walls, which had been excavated too far during the era of mining, broke. It couldn't withstand the water any longer. The crack, which reached semi-diagonally from the cemetery to the main square, did not immediately lead to the collapse of the area, as the edges of the layers of rock still overlapped one another. This meant that the water could now finally run into this crack, and the rock itself was disturbed by an increase in pressure. The fibre connections, formed over the course of millennia, broke apart — the base of the mountain, which had been stabile since the Mesozoic Era, swelled up like an edema. This meant that, far below the surface, where we carelessly went about our daily work, shaking the inconvenient droplets from our raincoats, everything was swimming.

The events of 14 November began for me when I was awoken by a sharp banging sound around four in the morning. I sat upright and was for a moment in panic mode, before realising that the noise was coming from the window. The outer shutters had come loose in the stormy gusts of wind and were now knocking with a jumpy flightiness on their hinges, as if they were trying to gain entry to my house. I wiped the sleep from my eyes and opened the window in order to reattach the shutters once more. Outside there were hurricane-like conditions: for a moment I had the feeling that the wind, which drove sprays of droplets into my hair, would grab me, too, and tear me into the open. This moment of fear then sank in the fog, because I went back to bed and fell into such a deep sleep that when I woke up again, around eight, I wondered if I had only dreamt it. I hadn't: even now a strong storm was blowing down from the cloud-shrouded Brunnenkogel Mountain. I rushed to get dressed, as I was already running a little late.

At the exact same time I was climbing into my trousers, 8.30 to be precise, work began on the nearby construction site next to the church, as it did every day. I had been annoyed by their racket for the whole of August, yet in this cloud of ire, I had never looked at the renovations — so my entire knowledge about these works only consisted of stories from third parties. Every child knew that the church tower had been tilting bit by bit over the years. A wretched sight, *as if forsaken by God*, the people said, and there was no question that of all the buildings with this fate, the tower had to be the first to be straightened, if one wanted to obtain a blessing for the salvation of the rest of the town. It was to be unveiled again at the Easter Mass this coming year with a solemn procession, and would be therefore encased for its straightening out for the whole year.

A foreman from the local construction company went to work there every morning with fourteen temporary workers, who were always hired on a project basis. On site were four men from Kosovo, six from Slovenia, and another four from Bosnia. Even though they had worked together for the past nine weeks, they were still struggling to find a common language. They called to one another, from down below up to the tower and back again, in four different idioms, with German ultimately dominating. Around 9.45, six of the men were on the scaffolding, beginning to render the crumbling facade. The din of the building work masked the swelling sounds of the town, in which people in every part of the place began to leave for work. As was so often the case, today the doors slammed twice. Though the day looked sunny and clear from inside, almost cloudless, when people stepped outside they noticed the cold, damp weather that seemed to rise from the ground, and the drops hanging in the air, against which they were now pointlessly arming themselves with an umbrella or rubber boots.

I had started making my way to work around nine, the documents I was carrying with me encased in an additional plastic slip. In the last week the papers were constantly arriving in a terrible condition: damp, as if they had been steamed — and in some places a word had run into the one adjacent to it. I clearly remember that day — the feel of the plastic in my hand, my fingertips, which already felt waterlogged. Then I saw something unusual in my path: I could see, from a distance, that in the large square in East Town a group of people had gathered, which I now joined. The statue of Pergerhannes that was erected at this location, which had been in a conqueror pose, pointing at the ground with an outstretched hand, had fallen over in the night. Its base had pressed into the cobblestones, and the downward thrust had brought to the surface what was underneath: sludge. The sight of this clay, which was white with lime, particularly worried me. My worry was eclipsed only by the position of the statue: the arm that had pointed at the mountain for the last two hundred years, was now, due to the incline, pointing at the primary school. I walked on, as did the rest of the small crowd, who were just in the process of dispersing. We were used to daily collapses. This was also the reason, it can be said in retrospect, no storm warning was issued: because we had all become resilient to the incessant demolitions. As we would later learn from the newspaper, the wind had swelled so violently since the early hours of the morning, that by midday, fourteen windows had been broken. The homeowners secretly swept up the shards and attached the frames that had twisted in the rage to the hinges with tape, each in the belief that they were an isolated case and ignorant vis-à-vis the widespread destruction. A two-hundred-year-old oak came down on Beethovenstrasse and only just missed a parked sports car, which the owner perceived as cosmic luck.

The castle remained, as always, completely untouched. No storm could carry away the two-and-a-half-metre thick stone walls. Only the bushes were forcibly sloping, and an uprooted yucca tree from the garden blew past as I arrived for work. I worked undisturbed until around two o'clock, only temporarily interrupted by my own agenda. The remarkable thing was this: it was precisely this day, but probably already beforehand, on which I had resolved that I could no longer keep my suspicions to myself. While I was once again poring over papers for hours on end, I decided today was the day. For this I would have to stay longer for once. At five o'clock, when the Countess arrived at her work salon, I would go to her and ask her about it. From then on, I couldn't keep still; I got up and drank five cups of coffee over the next few hours to pass the time.

Nothing remarkable happened between one and four, apart from a meeting that took place on the building site. The output target for the day had almost been achieved, but only with great adversity: all day long the wind had torn away the tarpaulin under which they had been trowelling and chiselling, and the relentless rain had soon run under the shirts of the workmen. One or two had wanted to finish work early, but, as the commission would later establish, it had turned out quite the opposite.

Early that afternoon, sometime around three-thirty, the foreman of the church tower renovations, Karl Leitgeb, had called a break and had the four men in the scaffolding at that time fetched down. They had taken shelter in the crypt and discussed their next steps in whispered tones: the subject of the brief discussion was the fact that they were clearly behind schedule, due to various factors. Leitgeb therefore asked whether the men would be willing to work twelve instead of the usual eight hours for the next fourteen days in exchange for an advance payment. All the workers except one, who was commuting from Slovenia and could not spare the extra hours, accepted the offer, and went back to work after a short break. But this time they wore chest harnesses; the wind on the wooden platform sixteen metres up in the air made it too dangerous to stay unsecured.

When overtime began for the temporary workers, the bell rang, signalling the end of the day for the upper years at the nearby grammar school, whose students unburdened themselves with ease from their afternoon lessons. By now, a whirlwind had torn nine satellite dishes from the prefabricated building on Genossenschaftsstrasse, uprooted around twenty fir trees, and pushed a cat into a drainage shaft, which was subsequently rescued by ten volunteers from the fire brigade. When the same cat, which, according to the regional newspaper, was called Samira, was wrapped in a towel and handed over to its happy owners, the children gathered at the primary school meeting point to set off for the lantern procession.

What an exceptionally large number of the participants would remember was how, beforehand, they'd had to step into shoes that were already wet: it had rained for so many days now that no one owned a dry pair. Around forty middle-school students and their parents had gathered in front of the church at 5.15pm. The children nervously rocked back and forth; carrying their lanterns felt like an important, almost earth-shattering task, while their parents were clearly in significantly worse moods. Many of them had found damage to their houses only a few hours before, and no one yet knew that almost everyone had been affected the same way. So they kept furiously silent, and fretted about when to repair. A bright light shone on the street from the Pumpkin, where the usual suspects had taken refuge after work. The priest had had the rochet put over his cassock, which had become dewy from the fine water, and was shaking hands with the children in turn. The parade would last around an hour, and go from the parish church through the Brunnengasse, and, once past the old West Gate, through the entire town centre. It would be followed by a performance of the story of St Martin on the Perger Platz. For the first time in over one hundred and fifty years, the Market Square was in too bad a shape to display the saint's exploits. Everyone had to struggle to light their home-made lanterns in the windy conditions — if the wind didn't instantly blow out the lighters, it swung the lanterns away wildly. The children tensely held their sticks, which the gusts tried to wrench from their hands.

I appeared in the Countess's study at five-thirty sharp and found her, as expected, sitting at her desk in front of the wall of books. In contrast to my own office, which looked down onto the courtyard, the wind couldn't be heard in hers.

'If you please,' the Countess said. 'You're positively crashing around.' As always when she criticised the least essential aspect of my behaviour, my face flushed with shame.

'I have something I'd like to discuss with you,' I said as I entered, and pointed, as if as proof, at a pile of papers, which I only then identified as the wrong ones. It was a shopping list of delicacies for the next salon, and I quickly let my hand fall.

'I'd like to talk to you about two discrepancies that have preoccupied me for a long time,' I said, feeling rage in my solar plexus. 'It's about the number of concentration camp prisoners and their whereabouts.'

As if I'd said something of interest, yet at the same time strange, the Countess got up from her desk and came closer, all the time locked in on me.

'Here,' I said, pulling out a piece of paper. 'On Easter Monday 1945, eight hundred people were murdered and buried, and one thousand two hundred further people died on a death march. But only thirty-four were found and taken into account during the trials.'

'Wait a moment. It's a little noisy in here, don't you think?' the Countess said, and made a show of bringing out a small glass bearing the Melk monastery coat of arms from one of her desk drawers.

'And here,' I said, 'is a document that states another aeroplane fuselage left the factory four days later — after it had been supposedly evacuated. The question is what happened to the prisoners, and I thought' — heat rose to my head — 'that you ought to know, because the mine belonged to your father.' The Countess was calmly polishing the little glass with a cloth, as if it was an important piece of evidence in the subject being discussed, then she filled it to the brim with pine-cone schnapps. *Time and Eternity*, I read beneath the naked angel printed on it.

'In any case,' I said firmly, 'before I continue researching the filling agent, I would like to have certain things cleared up. I've been working for you for over a year, and I have a moral obligation to investigate. The measurement results don't match the official data. I would like to undertake a local inspection, in the structures, in the passageways, in short' — I coughed from speaking too quickly — 'in the hole.' Then we were both silent.

'Listen,' the Countess said finally, but so quietly that it was difficult to understand her. 'I have no idea what you're trying to achieve here. You haven't actually asked anything thus far, so how is one supposed to give an answer?' She raised the glass and emptied it in one. The light from the chandelier shimmered on her tilted-back forehead.

'I can only say so much about it. First of all, they were chaotic times, terrible times, of course, but above all, times in which no documents were prepared. Well, then it's just word against word, nothing can be done. Next topic.'

Nothing had been answered, and my anger at this disrespect spurred me on.

'I must insist,' I began shakily, 'because I have done a lot of research into the town and its ownership structure over the past few months, and I believe that my parents were pursuing exactly the same questions as I am. May I ask whether they had discussed anything like this with you?'

'What bound me and your parents was friendship.' Without asking, the Countess had pushed a second glass of schnapps across the desk.

'Why did the adjoining property to my house, the one belonging to my paternal grandparents, transfer into your possession?' Growing more courageous, I continued. 'This is a general query. Around 1930, most people still owned their own property themselves. How did Greater Einland become one single address?'

'What a stupid question. Each had their own reason, a different story. How can one respond to such a simplification?' She refilled her glass.

'I just noticed that —' She cut me off.

'What my family has invested in this town is immeasurable. You are slandering that which is dearest to us and from which you, young lady, benefit, namely from the effort of rebuilding it. Nonsense! Ungrateful talk.'

'No, I'm not slandering anything,' I said, but the Countess seemed to no longer be able to hear me.

'Or perhaps you're delusional from your drugs? Did you think the pharmacist wouldn't tell me about your little addiction? Who do you think he orders your oxycodone from?' For a moment, there was silence.

'I have an illness, I —' I whispered.

'Your parents talked about this problem and that for the last few years they could hardly talk to you. I can't blame them.'

'How dare you use my own parents against me?'

'Well, if you already have your answers!' she suddenly screamed. I was so close to her that her heavy-sweet perfume went up my nose as if it were a personal matter.

'Listen. You've come to me in order to have your own, long-held ideas approved. You have no idea of the complexity of the matter. And I'll ask you something: has anyone ever prevented you from finding out about it? Or did you just want to take the comfortable route? Get everything given to you?'

She started walking around the study. 'You don't want to know at all,' she said, pointing at my face. 'And to create a judgement based on this hodgepodge of trivialities in your mountain of papers, you fantasist, is a mistake. You must have noticed that everything is layered on top of each other? One can't simply fill two needs with one deed. Of course I know answers. Answers, answers.' She waved her hand through the air. 'But that won't satisfy you. It wouldn't be the exciting story that you so want. Do you think it wasn't brought to my attention that you've been sneaking confidential documents home with you? Not everything in life is black and white. Some people have to make decisions.'

She sat back down at the table as if deep in thought. I was delirious. 'You're wallowing in yesterday's news, while turning away from the problems we face today. Egoism! Typical of this generation.' Her words sounded almost scornful, like a provocation: 'But you see: if it's really so important to you, then no one will stop you. Just go to the old water tower under the Perger Platz and take a look for yourself. Then you'll certainly see if something's there. But you won't do it,' and she accompanied this closing flourish with a dismissive hand gesture. 'You are interested in something completely different. You are obsessed with your parents and their affairs. I'll tell you something you don't want to hear: your parents had a completely different set of goals from you — they were decent people. Whatever you suspect, your parents and I were on completely the same wavelength.' I wanted to respond, but I was stunned. 'Now, if you don't mind. I have to work — the salon's tomorrow.' And with that she sat back down at her desk and looked at her documents. As I went back to my office to get my coat, I saw, for a second time, a potted plant being flung upwards from the terrace below.

It was precisely this rubber plant, carried by an almost tornado-like vortex, that later landed on a car not far from the church where the workers noticed its crash landing. At exactly this time, they had eaten their dinner at the tower, three Leberkäse rolls each, and begun their night shift. But for a moment they leaned out of the cladding to watch the lanterns: some of them thought of their own children at home, others simply liked the spectacle — the way the mighty monstrance was carried out of the church.

The middle-school children, who were finally all there, made to set off, even though many of the parents had insisted it should be postponed due to the rain. The priest said no. As a result, there was a certain irritation among the participants: no one wanted to have sick children lying at home the next day. But they couldn't spoil the event for them either, and so the grumbling procession was put in motion, led by the Reverend and six altar boys. The gusts billowed mightily between the houses, which were gradually turning on their lights. The various layers of air of the storm carried the St Martin's song and *I go with my lantern* in every direction, making certain frequencies whiz as if swooping downtown and snatching others right from the mouths of the children. A dishevelled melody lay over the town at six o'clock, and because it was so frayed, people everywhere were wondering what kind of sound it was — what strange soundscape of children's voices and yowling weather was skimming around the house. Sister Elfriede, who was making her soup deliveries to the elderly townspeople, later said that it had sounded like a wrecked record, because the children were packed into plastic raincoats like shrink-wrapped vegetables. Impossible for the sounds to escape from the plastic bags: she had been surprised the students could even breathe.

The workers hanging from the scaffolding stopped their work for a moment and directed their headtorches towards the street to watch the brightly coloured children's train disappearing. Increasingly larger raindrops made it difficult to work on the facade, which is why the foreman ordered them to concentrate on the erosion for the next few hours.

I had, while all this was happening, slipped on my rubber boots at home and fetched a boltcutter from the garage, which I stowed with a torch in my dry bag, before I set off. At the Johannesgasse/Brunnengasse intersection, I came across the crowd of singers, who were turning into the East Town singing, and I walked downhill past the white horse that had been parked in a side street for the show taking place later on. I paid no attention to the expectant children's laughter, the windblown scenery, the people poking their heads out their houses to catch a glimpse of the performance. All I felt was annoyance at the delay in getting to the lower part of the city, and the miserable wetness that seemed to permeate the fabric of my clothes. When the voices became quieter again, and I arrived at the former entrance to the main shaft, it was already after six-thirty. Total darkness: the wooden doors with their iron mountings glistened damply in the cone of light from my torch. Although heavy chains lay in front of the hole, as I approached I was urged on by that heavy, dank-earth smell that I knew from the old lime cellars. Then I began to tamper with the barriers using the boltcutter.

At around the same time, the twenty-year-old butcher's apprentice, Hans Bretschneider, who, with his red cloak and metal leg guards, had been dressed up as St Martin, climbed onto the horse. The animal had to be held by the bridle by two people, it was so nervous on account of the storm, which lashed through the treetops, and at 18.45, just as the performance was about to begin, a row of roof tiles was swiped onto the street from the late baroque-style houses along the Silberzeile. The crowd flinched.

The report later revealed the following: far below the main square, in the hole, the sand had long since drained away. In other words, in three or four places in the town, the asphalt was nothing more than a thin crust over nothing, held in place only by the tension of the material itself. Like a sheet of paper which, when clamped to solid objects that are drifting apart, slowly loses its inner hold, the concrete between the church and the East Town crunched barely audibly in the rain, as the weight of the horse burdened it. Half of the population was bent over their festive meals in deep intoxication.

It was 19.02 when one of the workers saw a crack in the cladding of the church tower, which appeared so slowly and clearly before his eyes that he could trace the crack with his finger while it was splitting. He called down to the foreman, who had just started a phone call with the building firm's regional director, that he needed to come up. The foreman, however, couldn't hear him because of the wind, and turned away into a niche of the church building in order to finish his conversation. Without further ado, the worker filled the crack and continued plastering as normal.

Meanwhile the children had arrived at their destination, having made their way clockwise through the town centre, and the performance of St Martin's story began. Around 19.05, sixty middle-school children, and around two hundred parents, siblings, and residents, watched as Hans Bretschneider cut his cloak in two and threw half of it from his horse to an actor playing a beggar. Only a moment later, as St Martin was riding back to his station in Northern France, the horse bucked and interrupted the history of salvation: it stamped its hooves on the broken paving that a few minutes before had been lying straight, but now seemed to have sunk by a hand's breadth. Bretschneider dismounted to take a closer look at the ground, and immediately called for his associates: one by one, the stones had popped from their fortifications, as if a huge hand had pulled an underground zip that was just about still holding the town together.

This happened while I slipped several times on the wet grass, regained my composure, and finally got back on my feet. When touching the ground I'd become puzzled — I'd never felt such a consistency. It was neither wet nor firm, much more like a dense modelling clay that pulled on your arms if you reached into it. I finally reached the doors: I intended to wrestle the first chain to the ground, but the links bent under the slightest exertion like a crayon. It was so brittle that I could have broken it with my bare hand. I wiped the water from my forehead, pushed the wood aside, and came face to face with the hole for the first time.

The St Martin's show in town was cut short, and the priest had the church choir intone a final hallelujah. Master-Builder Keinermüller left the window of his inner-city palace for a moment to fetch a third quarter of wine. The rain bounced off the asphalt at an angle constantly being changed by the wind so that it briefly looked as though it was crosshatching the scene as much from below as from above. Even after several attempts, the horse could no longer be calmed, and was tied to a rain gutter.

For a few seconds it was so quiet that time seemed to stand still, people said in retrospect. This was around 19.20 — which means that only a few seconds passed before a cracking sound could suddenly be heard in the vicinity of the church, which was even discernible by the crowd on Perger Platz. Only a moment later there was a deafening bang, followed by a hissing sound that caused hundreds of people to startle at the same time. The children began to scream, as, out of nowhere, a dust cloud rolled over the heads of the terrified spectators. Several dozen tumbled over the cobblestones that had earlier breached from their entrenchment, and mass panic spread while the thundering wind propelled pieces of debris between the raindrops. Everyone in the dispersing crowd attempted to grab their own child by the hand and pull them from the epicentre. But no one knew where this boom had come from. Only a few people who had been standing at the gateway leading to Johannesstrasse ran straight to the place from where the commotion had originated.

It was the Church Square. Cries for help could be heard coming from there, rising in volume, much more pitiful than anyone had ever heard before. At 19:26, the first people arrived on the scene from downtown and saw what had happened. The church tower had been severed along an even groove that had sliced cleanly through the stone, and had fallen to the ground, dragging seven workmen into the depths. Those living in the immediate vicinity who had not attended the parade came from their houses, alarmed by the noise. Someone called the emergency services; chaos ensued. Some banded together to pull the injured out of the rubble, but their harnesses had become so deeply twisted in the stone that it was not possible to shift those calling for help even a centimetre. Two of the workmen had died on impact, three were critically injured, and the two who had landed on the upper side of the tower were still responsive. But this was discovered bit by bit, and everyone called out things in batches, which the wind immediately carried off again.

I myself did not notice the growing unrest. I paused at the entrance of the hole for a few minutes and saw my beam of light dissipate in the distance. Only ten metres through the gate to the tunnel, and already the storm outside could no longer be heard. I waited a moment — I had expected to hear a dripping sound or an echo of my own breathing. But there was nothing but silence. Almost a deadening of sound, a swallowing of it. The outline of a stone staircase led steeply downwards, sculpted out of the mountain in hurried blows. Above my head, the earth was held back by thick beams, on which the iron fittings still gleamed.

It wasn't difficult to climb down the steps, which were surprisingly dry: the contours of a small room stood out in the blackness. *The break room*, I thought, then I sat on the steps and stared into the darkness.

At exactly 19.30 the ambulance showed up, but concluded that without the fire brigade none of the victims would be rescued from beneath the rubble. Nevertheless, the emergency doctor present was able to determine the cause of death of two of the men on the spot. The clocktower was looming, unsettled, over the mountain of rubble and kept almost falling on the growing crowd of people, who would scatter screaming every time it moved. Soon every spectator from the St Martin's play had relocated to the Church Square, most of them foggy from alcohol and adrenaline, along with a shapeless growing anger. A group of a hundred had assembled, a bellowing, uncoordinated group at the edges of the rubble. The fire brigade arrived and the heavy equipment started up. People watched the yellow crane in the heavy downpour and observed ropes being lowered onto the pile of rubble. Then the skin broke.

What was later considered the most incomprehensible thing about all the events of that day, began with a blank. Nobody was able to recall the short but crucial period between 19.35 and 19.40. The collective memory resumed as Police Chief Matthias Gruber, who had been on duty in the gendarmerie, ran over to a small group of people who, it was said, had broken out into angry shouting for a second time.

At that moment a switch was thrown: without any cause, even before Gruber could prevent it, someone punched the foreman, who was trembling and cowering on the floor, in the face. As if all they had needed was a hole through which the long-standing pressure could escape, the crowd sighed, but disguised their sighs as screams, and they watched in relief as a second person fired a second blow in the face of the foreman. At the same time, however, this triggered a kind of suppressed panic, the crowd shrinking back from itself. Who had ever seen a man punched so hard in the face, and who hadn't, in fact, yearned for it? The fire brigade, who had arrived with two more fire engines, had a difficult job to get to the injured through the riled-up groups, and it was scarcely possible to contain the flow of people.

I had, in the meantime, shivering from the cold, lost all feeling in my body; it could have been ten hours or five minutes between my attempts to descend the steps. It was as if there was a physical obstacle preventing me. When I had taken three steps down, a strange combination of nausea and exhaustion forced me to sit down again, because I suddenly wondered what I was going to do with the information I was seeking here. What a hardship it would be to dig and understand more deeply — because I indeed only saw a mine looming ahead. But it was late, maybe I was just tired. I hadn't climbed down deep enough to be able to see more precisely what lay before me. On the other hand, however, I was already too deep: too deep to hear what had taken place so sonorously outside that half the town had peeled out of their houses; too deep to be able to imagine that whatever I would find might matter in the outside world. So I hovered in indecision.

By 20.01, the fire brigade had pulled all the injured men out of the rubble on the Church Square. One would die on the way to the hospital. Ferdinand, whose presence in this tumult with his oxygen bottle and his trailing foot I can't make sense of to this day, told me that he had seen rescuers grab the foreman and drag him into an ambulance, and that two or three more had jumped onto the loading bed after him.

It was unspeakable chaos. Later accounts came from three to four hundred people present, as more and more people were driven into the street by the noise and gathered, enraged by a sudden sense of collective injustice. Groups came together to rebel against the sinking hole: a few of them began throwing bricks through the windows of nearby houses in a total frenzy. Other bystanders pulled the rioters — who were local doctors and lawyers — away. (It's important to put into perspective that the investigation determined that it was a single brick that had been thrown. In reference to the prompt that at least six shop windows had been smashed, the assertion stood: all six were destroyed with a single brick). An outright mass hysteria descended — the demolished church tower acted like a drug on the population.

But perhaps this wasn't the complete truth: for one thing, there *were* isolated records that gave the impression of a collective rage. Perhaps ten people who were causing havoc, and five who had allowed themselves to be carried away into violent excesses. The majority were, so to speak, peacefully aggressive: they pulsated with suppressed hatred for the hole, which couldn't be hit because there was nothing there. At 8.30, around twenty fathers and young men had gathered in front of the demolished clock face. You could see them shaking with excitement — a quivering, standoffish group who had to bury their fists in their pockets because their hands didn't know what else to do. But nothing happened. It would later be summarised thus: as soon as the fire brigade and ambulance had driven off, and the town office began to transport away the rubble with four trucks, the crowd suddenly calmed. As suddenly as the uproar had spread, it now seemed rather absurd not to go home and discuss it further in private.

It was 21.00 when I left the entryway again, closed the door behind me, replaced the chain, admittedly without locking it — surplus to requirements. No one had ever touched it. No one would attempt to in the future. It was only now, as I was walking up the Schulgasse, that I noticed a certain disquiet, and was surprised for a moment that the whole town seemed to be up and about. Families were heading for their homes with purpose. I noticed their silence and that everyone was avoiding the gaze of others. Taking the eastern route out of the town, I arrived at the Brunnen Arch, and had to pause a moment to gather my impressions: a sea of glass shards and terrible desertedness. What had happened? The inns had turned out their lights, the pavements were empty, and there was a centimetre-thick film of dust and rubble over everything, so that I had to be careful not to fall over. Only two street sweepers, working alone, braced themselves against the mountains of rubble. In the midst of these impressions, I became aware of tinnitus wandering into my own ears, as if a sound that had been accompanying me for the longest time had been turned down. I finally pulled my hood from my head. The weeks of rain had stopped.

16

The festival would take place on a Sunday, as Sundays are the raw material for a contented look back on an accomplished work of godly scope. There will be a spring-like mood for the tourists (even if it is autumn), as if you can already feel the crocuses breaking through from beneath the lawn. In the event that the weather and/or landscape conditions do not comply with this maxim, help must be given to find another way to make it happen (as yet unspecified).

Generally, the festivities will take place in three phases, which will be carried out as follows:

1.) The arrival — the tourists will be brought from Vienna in chartered buses to the town entrance at nine in the morning. Hundreds of people from home and abroad, with a strong focus on China, Japan, and the United States. An arrival area will be set up in advance for this initial stop-off for the groups, which, in addition to four thousand carpark spaces, will also include a refreshment station for those waiting, where all kinds of typical Austrian fare will be offered, including Sachertorte, cheese-stuffed smoked sausage, crepes, and punch cake. Everything will be served as take-away.

Then the first highlight: a procession towards the town centre. The tourists will be escorted from the town gate by a four hundred–strong marching band. Eight drum majors and their battalions will each be responsible for one tourist section, and will lead them into the centre, playing 'Radetzky March' as they do. The first part comes to an end here with a spectacular beer brunch, where, in addition to the usual speeches and honours, the Greater Einland craftwork will be presented on stage in the manner of a circus performance: our machine embroidery and cutlery fabrication ought to be as monumental as Cirque de Soleil, a brewer's drayman should shoulder-carry his ten barrels of wine, and a master bronze-castor shall make a baptismal font in which the priest would immediately baptise the most recently born child.

2.) Station-hopping — the second part follows on from the first around midday. The whole event is intended to be a combination of art action and natural spectacle: in other words, an encounter between performance and natural purity, which must be closely interrelated. The crowd will be dispersed and, as is done at Dokumenta Festival in Kassel, visitors will be invited to roam around the town, which has itself been declared a sculpture. For the next few hours, events will be held at smaller sideshows — secured appendices and side branches of the hole. A depression (up at Auf den Haiden) will be consecrated as a chapel, a larger hall opened underground for weddings ('Weddings in the Hole', check availability). The afternoon will be shaped by a specialist in passion plays from Oberammergau: geological art and subsidence installations will lead to a massive re-evaluation of the population and public's mental conditioning. The hole ought to be presented as a mythical force of nature, with which people live in harmony. An underground wine trail is still being evaluated.

3.) Injection — the third part will begin in the evening hours, when there will be a romantic sunset. Brought back by stewards lurking for this very moment, the crowd will gather on the football pitch for the final act. This, of course, comprises the insertion of the filling agent into the mountain, bringing the subsidence to a standstill. The filling process, which will take the whole night, will be accompanied by a specially commissioned composition created solely for this purpose by a Greater Einland secondary school teacher. The aim is to create

an oratorio that tells the story of the local legend
Pergerhannes and will, ideally, be composed in
the style of Hayden, but contain elements that
will allow people to dance the cross polka. An
incomparable spectacle produced from the power
of Austrian industry, mechanical engineering as
well as down-to-earth folklore and high art is to
be offered to the tourists, before they are loaded
back in the buses in the late hours of the night
and transported back.

With a feeling of barely suppressed shame, I signed this agenda
of lunacy drawn up in the salon, and sent it to the councillors.
We had been working under inhumane pressure for the last few
months, and my thesis had been out of the picture for a very
long time. It was only during this period — when the festival
program was being re-sublimated and there was more and more
talk of its earning potential — that it become apparent that the
town wasn't as well positioned financially as it appeared from the
outside. No wonder — the stopings and support brackets that
we had to regularly attach went into the hundreds of thousands.
The ceremonial acts had long since turned from a prestige project
into a stopgap in order to be able to carry out the planned fillings.
Perhaps that had been its true purpose all along. Twenty-nine
September of next year. An unreal date. I could have sworn that
we had only just made the decision to have the festival, but when
I looked at the calendar it confirmed that it had already been a
year ago.

After lunch I packed up my things and headed for the secondary school. Scattered groups of students stood around on the schoolyard, talking with each other and laughing — it must have been their lunch break. I stood on the street in front of the premises and waited for the bell to ring. When the youths still didn't disperse, I had to walk past them. A deeply inscribed fear, which came from my own schooldays, briefly made me worry that they would turn to me, mock me, comment on my clothes — but nothing happened. I was an adult, I no longer existed for them. I walked to the upper floor and knocked on the door to the music room. A man with tousled hair and a shirt collar, an unknotted tie hanging pointlessly around it like a ragged ribbon, opened the door and gave me a damp handshake.

'Prof. Hausbrecht,' he said. 'Please, take a seat.' He sat down at his teaching desk, and I lowered myself into the chair offered to me. The man seemed nervous, under pressure, and what's more was badly shaven.

'Finally, a free period,' he said, sighing ostentatiously like a man convalescing. 'At moments like this I can devote myself a bit to my actual task — art.' He pointed at the piano, and then stood, as if I hadn't understood his gesture, and laid his fingers on the keys.

'Would you like to hear a bit of my new composition?' he asked, the end of his sentence already being drowned out by the first chord. 'I'll take the liberty of playing one of my works. I actually want the commissioned composition to be similar in form. It's an Austrian piece, but very different to what people already know. Much more contemporary.' I could have sworn that what he was playing on the piano was Strauss's Rosenkavalier Walzer. 'I've developed my very own sound language, which is shaped by our current problems with the hole,' he said. A couple of small secondary motifs might have been altered, but it sprang right back to the repartee between the Marschallin and Octavian.

'Lovely,' I said. No sooner had he finished his performance than he reknotted his tie and sat back down to continue sighing.

'Well, it's difficult to compose when one has to deal with the children all day, but one simply shifts one's creativity to other times of the day,' he said and then elaborated, as if he speaking to a complete ignoramus: '*Nights.*'

'I see,' I said. 'You don't have to rush in any case — I wanted to talk to you about something else. It's about the festivities, about the brass band.' While I said this, I blushed. While working on this event, I always thought that others would notice its ridiculousness as much I did and laugh at me for the pipedreams I was involved with. But to my surprise, no one did.

'We're actually planning' — I laughed a small, half-hearted laugh — 'four hundred marching musicians. And we need a layout from you as soon as possible.'

'That won't be a problem,' Hausbrecht replied archly. 'We're bringing together everyone from the region. It's no problem at all. But under *no* circumstances will we be going downtown. That would be a death trap in view of the circumstances, with so many people. And the farmers have to stop their cultivation two months beforehand.'

'How do you mean?' I asked, not understanding the relation.

'The farmers,' he said, and then more sharply: 'The peasantry.'

'What about the farmers?'

'Everyone knows what's going on with the farmers.' He began to polish his glasses with his sleeve, but pulled so hard on it that the bottom of his shirt pulled out of his trousers. 'You're trying to fix the subsidence. There,' and he pointed at the ceiling. A crack as thick as a fist that ran from the middle of the room to under the piano into the corner. 'It always upsets my piano in these temperatures, you understand? The taproots' — he formed a funnel with both hands — 'dig up the ground and loosen the soil. Carrots and radishes, for instance. It's called subsoiling. Why do you think the fire station over there keeps collapsing?'

'Because of the hole, I think.'

'Yes, yes, but the question is, how did the hole come about in the first place? Taproots,' he said again. 'The farmers earn themselves a pretty penny from these kinds of crops and think that a person of science won't see through it. It all comes from South America, from the pharmaceutical companies. This means that after poisoning the intellectual climate we now have to bear considerable costs for the town because of the farmers. Yes, yes, I'll sign it now.' He waved his hand when he saw the form I had to get everyone contributing to the festival to sign.

'It's completely irrelevant what the exact cause is. But we're certainly not walking four hundred people's worth of live weight over a hillside filled with root vegetables,' he concluded, thrusting a leaflet at me. It read: 'Secondary school teachers against taproots — a reckoning.' Below this, a stop sign was stamped over a weeping black salsify. I hoped that he was the only member of this group.

'Thank you,' I said, confused.

'Ah, you're not interested in ecological issues. Here's my signature, for my part,' he said, taking the form from my hand. 'We'll have to bring in a few less gifted people, of course, if we really need four hundred people. So I wouldn't get on the bad side of the farmers and their saplings, I mean offspring, too much. There we are — my free period is almost over. All the best. You don't have an easy job,' he said as he gave me his hand, but it sounded more like he was referring to himself.

Although the cold wind whistled through the streets, I sat on a park bench bathed in sweat, as if I had just climbed a difficult summit. What he had told me about the farmers didn't surprise me, because during the last few months new alliances, associations, and initiatives had been developing, merging, and once more dissolving, like a heat mirage on a hot day. What they all had in common was this: they refused to understand that we were dealing with an organic, natural phenomenon, albeit accelerated by the former mining.

For a few days we had been occupied with hundreds of phone calls all talking about the conviction that Slovenes were crossing the border at night and carrying off the bricks from the middle school. It was actually falling bit by bit into the hole, while the popular belief spread that the good imperial and royal Austrian bricks had long been transported to Maribor. In some respects, this was due to the fact that we within the castle were instructed not to tell anyone about the real dimensions of the hole — on the Countess's advice, so as not to cause unnecessary panic or even an outright exodus. However, our silence had laid the groundwork for this void to be filled with imaginary matter. Real problems were adamantly suppressed: the church remained bare and unrenovated, without it having been discussed, because no one wanted to touch the building and with it the events of November. I was amazed at how much the building itself was redefined as a result of the destruction — a church without a steeple could not be recognised as such.

The way back to the castle led me down Langegasse, which was one of the most desolate areas in the town, and which I had to climb through. Like when you start to cut pieces from a carefully iced cake, and the middle emerges from underneath it, the jagged edges on both sides of the pavement led craggily into bare earth. On some of the properties bordering it, you could see funnel-shaped pits, in which the water that had been forced upwards, already frozen solid on the surface, was now a metre high. One might have thought that the town council was trying to dig a small dredging pond in front of each house in preparation for the next summer, and had withdrawn after only finishing half the job.

That I took this route in spite of this was like a walk of penance: with my head bowed, I passed Sister Elfriede's property and stood for a moment in front of the fence, where I always saw with horror, as if for the first time, the progress of her house's collapse. Two months ago it had been, though riddled with cracks, at least level. Then an incredible metamorphosis had unfolded, and now one could watch the right side of her beautiful half-timbered house sinking into the mud. This corner, hanging at a fifty-degree angle in one of the ponds, had long since begun to suck up the moisture, and now the mould was feasting higher with every passing day. It was a hazard — especially for its resident, but in the meantime also for passers-by, because the wooden beams that held the roof were dangling out of the facade.

I had stood in this exact spot three months ago, with Philipp, who was once more trying to urge me to visit him again.

'I've got a tiramisu in the fridge,' he had said with a wink, while I said nothing. 'You can come over to mine, I won't be able to eat it all by myself.' I shook my head and said I had to finish an article. He insisted. 'That's alright, we could watch DVDs instead if you're watching your figure.' He was still laughing at this, his non-joke, when we rang Sister Elfriede's doorbell.

'The beams won't be able to carry the traversal loads for much longer,' Philipp said, looking at the house. That a person could be socially uncouth to such an extent and yet so assured in his expertise amazed me time and time again. Sister Elfriede opened the door to us, and it was uncomfortable to see how difficult it was for her to climb over the shattered threshold with her stiff legs. She herself seemed to have come to terms with things, however, because she asked us to come into the house without the slightest word of explanation — an invitation we declined.

'It's actually too dangerous to even get close to the house,' Philipp said, when we finally sat down on a bench in the garden. 'To be frank, we're here on the instructions of the Countess to request that you move out.'

'Oh come, it's just a passing phase, the subsidence will be over at some point,' Sister Elfriede replied. 'Excuse the way the place looks, children. I can't afford to have it pushed back up at the moment, but I'm saving for it. It's annoying, of course, that it rains in my bedroom, but I'm sleeping on the sofa for the time being.' Even though she tried to give a positive front, I could tell that she knew exactly what was happening to her house.

'We have a resettlement program,' I ventured. 'Lovely new apartments down on the Koloniestrasse. It's paid for by the town — you could move in right away.'

'Come off it, the Koloniestrasse,' she said. 'Ruth, save your breath, I already know. I know, but I'm not going. I've lived here since I was four years old. In the town centre and nowhere else. I still have the soup kitchen after all. Back there, next to the house, that's where I used to play with my brothers. It's survived through two world wars.' She patted herself on the breastbone, as if she were accomplishing a part of this survival herself. 'And my father repaired every bit of damage himself. I still remember when we concreted the garage together. My goodness, what a mess.'

I saw that far back in the garden, almost against the neighbour's wall, a section of decking had been put down — a common sight in Greater Einland where a branch of the tunnels broke through onto someone's plot. *So that's where*, I thought to myself. That's where Sister Elfriede's parents had thrown the bodies underground. That's where someone's dog had gone berserk, and the police had pulled two half-decomposed corpses out of the ground. They were portrayed as victims of an accident in a speedily conducted trial: 'Maybe burglars, climbed over the wall at dusk, fell into the shaft,' it said in the court record, which I had only recently found in an old file. Had Sister Elfriede known? She must have known about it, she had to have been at least school-age by then. And although it was clear to me that precisely *because* of cases such as these the filler should never be developed, I could feel nothing but sympathy for Sister Elfriede and her childhood home.

'You should get yourself to safety until the subsidence is under control,' I tried again. 'Do you remember Stokke's equation? We talked about it at the Pumpkin that time. The sedimentation speed of the mud isn't that fast yet, but three or four downpours could be enough to reduce the viscosity significantly.'

'There are always good and bad times. One minute things are down, then they're back up again.' I was irritated by this cliché — until I saw that the hand in which she was holding her glass of water was trembling.

'The house won't remain standing, there's no way of saving it,' Philipp said with an admirably realistic coolness. I felt queasy.

'There's always a way.'

'Not in this case, unfortunately.'

'I can't leave my parents' house,' Sister Elfriede said. Or maybe she said something else, but I knew that was exactly what she meant. I could understand how she was feeling, and stared blankly at a red bucket standing next to the bare plaster. She wouldn't leave until the very end, even though she knew exactly what was going on. So Philipp discussed with her the same measures one would with someone who lived in an earthquake zone — that she had to crawl under the table if she felt vibrations, and the windows should be open at all times of the day and night.

I was glad that he'd brought the conversation to an end. I couldn't do it anymore. During this get-together I was overwhelmed by feelings of guilt the like of which I'd never felt before. I could save the foundations of this house that meant so much to her, but I didn't, and the longer I remained in this situation, the more I lost my reasons for neglecting to do so. As I lay in bed that evening, eyes closed, the situation compelled me out of the dark into a waking state. Time and again I had to sit up for a few minutes and explain to myself that I was not responsible for the others, and that dozens of people shared the same fate. There was no reason to focus on Sister Elfriede as a victim, I kept telling myself until I sank back in exhaustion. After only a few hours, I awoke in the morning in sweated-through bedsheets, and felt like I was walking on clouds. The following evening I resorted to Valium.

At the end of 2012, while attempting to once more take up the strange history of my house, I had discovered the history of Johann Kienagl in the town archive. It was a chance find, and yet I soon became obsessed.

Johann Kienagl was a boy from Vienna who, between the years 1942 and 1946, travelled to his uncle's place in Greater Einland for summer retreats on account of his health. He was a high-school student, had a passionate desire to become a biologist, and every day would undertake extensive excursions in the surrounding countryside, where he gathered objects for his microscoping. That he was suffering from a lung disease almost seemed to suit him, because he was excused from his Hitler Youth duties during the holiday months. (I also researched what kind of illness he might have had — although the descriptions were at times imprecise, it had to have been tuberculosis.)

Three full diaries, which were later brought to the town archive, reported on his stays on the land that were available to him because of it. Kienagl unfortunately succumbed to his infection in 1950 at the age of only twenty, and the matured forest belonging to his childless uncle was auctioned off after the war. I read the notebooks, which he had written like adventure novels, only occasionally getting up from my armchair to verify details of his descriptions in other works.

The writings of Kienagl, who did not sympathise with the regime, but did not especially oppose it either, testified from their first moment of his extraordinary sensibility and sensitivity for nature, which he feared might fall victim to a cruel slaughter for the war. In contrast to the Viennese woods he lived near during the year, widespread logging was conducted in Greater Einland. The quick transportation of wood was needed for trenches and ramparts, but also for local aircraft production, which was carried out underground. Five times in these five years he spent July and August in Greater Einland and depicted snapshots of local life in his diaries.

He was always alone. From the first to the last summer that he recorded, it was very difficult for Johann to establish relationships with other young people, whom he described as distant and hateful towards him. He was teased for his accent, for his, as he put it, effeminate demeanour, for his interest in taxonomy and his weak constitution. Apart from his sister, who unfortunately died even earlier than he did, in her adolescence, he never had friends. The most heart-wrenching thing for me as the reader of his diaries was that although he was able to occupy himself very well and for long periods of time, he still seemed to feel a strong longing for human company.

For many hours of the day, Kienagl roamed the slopes of the town, and sat with a book about wild plants in the branches of any tree his constitution would allow him to climb. But he would also always observe the residents on their nearby properties, describing scenes with a hard-to-ignore focus on what he saw, which under normal circumstances would be regarded as everyday occurrences: what time a farmer's wife started milking the cows or pulling the weeds; how families gathered in the garden in the evenings and picked berries for dessert together; how the newspaper seller, after a night of excessive drinking, fell off his bike on Saturdays when he threw the weekend edition of *Der Stürmer* over the fences. On every page I had a renewed hope that he would meet a kindred spirit, but it never happened.

As far as I could infer from his descriptions, Greater Einland had barely changed topographically — I recognised each of the places he mentioned. As he sat in a treetop and wrote alternately about songbirds and people, whose behaviour he examined with the same scrutinising thoroughness, he became aware of the property that was right next to his uncle's house, the Villa Helene.

This was where my grandparents had lived — it was the building in which I was now sitting. As I recognised it in his writings for the first time, I was surprised and suspicious simultaneously, because throughout the diaries there appeared to be a certain attentiveness on Joseph and Petra Schalla, the parents of my as-yet-unborn mother. Their daily routines were described in meticulous detail. Based on the descriptions it seemed Johann Kienagl, whom I pictured standing on a tree stump in knickerbockers and lace-up shoes, seemed to have felt a particularly tender fondness for my grandfather. In none of the years did he miss describing how he set off early in the morning, and how he wore his tight woodcutter boots and a plaid shirt. Kienagl also described how he came home in the evenings and chopped branches, shirtless and with his hair shaved high up his neck. The most moving thing for me was what followed this. His wife often called over the fence to the neighbouring house, where my second grandmother, Gerda Schwarz, responded.

What an extraordinary account: that all four grandparents sat together and talked, drank wine and made music with one another until late into the night. Once, and probably only a single time, something happened that Johann Kienagl described as one of the happiest moments of his stays: while he was sitting in the long grass observing one of these tableaus, he rustled too loudly while getting up, and he was noticed. Joseph, whom he so admired, turned, smiled, and invited him to his table. A piece of cake was placed in front of him. Only the Schwarzs weren't eating yet, and as it got dark, they began, as Kienagl described it, to sing in another language. Very quietly, Kienagl wrote, who couldn't explain this behaviour and reported of it as if a little perturbed. Then they also ate.

I learned, through the eyes and ears of a thirteen-year-old boy, something I had never heard talked about: that my father's parents, or at least one of them, must have been Jewish.

(With this entry in particular, however, I asked myself whether it could have been just a fantasy — food was strictly rationed back then; fat in particular, which would have been necessary to bake a cake, was practically unattainable.)

In the third year of his visit, the Schwarzs were no longer there, but the handsome, sinewy woodcutter was. The little girl of the family had been born a few months earlier. It was only when the second child appeared at the Schallas', the child who had to have been my father, did my introspection start again, because the boy was about two years old when he first appeared. But that in itself wasn't necessarily unusual; a young family with a second child who, perhaps like Kienagl himself, had had to spend their first few years inside. Kienagl's resolution for next year, when he hoped he would feel old enough, was to finally speak to Joseph Schalla and invite him for a beer. But this would never come to pass.

17

As spring drew to a close, there was no longer any doubt that my house had been badly affected by the subsidence. The crack that had started beneath my threshold, a delicate serration through the flawless wall, was now wildly overgrown. Filling in the cracks was a lot more work that I had imagined: I often sweated through a clean shirt when I decided to renovate the walls that had cracked overnight before going to work. I also had to spend more and more time on repair work, the curing time of which was longer than it took for the water particles to reach the edges again.

We had experienced a winter full of collapses, the menacing fluctuations of which hovered over us: one midday at the start of December, a rumbling sound could be heard in the distance, and people looked up at the sky in amazement — it took a few seconds to process that it was a cloudless blue before then realising that it was a thunderstorm from the depths that was threatening us. Like many others, I had slipped on my shoes and intuitively found the exact place from where the rumble had unfurled: terrace houses whose steel posts had been forced sideways, starting with the one furthest to the right, had knocked over all the others in a domino effect. No one had been injured, because the residents, surprised by the force that had gripped their houses, had left just in time. Suddenly everyone standing in front of the carcasses of these buildings was overcome by a certain embarrassment. These days one encountered a strange kind of savoir faire: just as when a jaw tumour appears on someone, we look at the face neither particularly conspicuously, nor too little, and after a while one simply looks away. I subsequently came to cherish this form of tactfulness when it concerned my affairs, and the fact that no one spoke to me about my own ailments gave me a certain kind of reassurance. Until the day my flagstones cracked, of course.

Months had passed since the first crack had appeared in my walls, and I had almost come to terms with these circumstances, when a heatwave rolled over us at the beginning of July, which particularly tormented us because the swimming pool was completely unusable for the season. Above my cellar, at the back entrance to the house, there was a place where white marble tiles were laid, and where a kind of cooling pad would form on hot days. Last year, I had developed the habit of putting the heavy armchair, in which I so liked to read, on the tiles and spending the harshest hours of the day there. When, on the first day of this heatwave, I wanted to carry down my chair to align it in the right position, my legs locked: right where it had always stood, the tiles had fractured. I fetched the stone adhesive and tried to put the shards back together, but it was always either too few or too many — either a piece was missing or there was inexplicably a surplus. That was the moment I lost my composure.

I fell to my knees and cried like I'd rarely cried before. A feeling of injustice, of defilement, held me down; at the same time, it was just a house. But all the frustration that had built up over the past few months broke out of me, until I ended up crying on the stairs. As suddenly as my crying fit came, it passed again, and then I felt a restlessness that drove me out the door. No, at least no one could see it from the outside, that was a calming thought. I ran to the cellar, to the spot exactly underneath the cracked tiles, and my head spun: as I stepped down onto the dirt floor, I was in ankle-high water. And that wasn't the worst of it: the whole room, which I hadn't entered for a week at most, had in this time collapsed downwards. Skewed corners wedged up against one another; from the ceiling, a single wooden post protruded from the brickwork. Trembling with horror, I went back up to the ground floor.

A crying fit shook me once more — I dragged myself into the empty living room and huddled on the couch. A hideous thought that I kept fighting to suppress just couldn't be shaken off: *the house was the last thing that remained of my parents.* It had been entrusted to me and I had failed. I cried torrents. In the blink of an eye, it was evening. No one could be allowed to see anything, indeed — as long as no one saw anything, I could do what I wanted. It was all there. I rubbed the incoming sleep from my eyes, then went into the garage. From this moment onwards, my memories are porous.

In any case, I soon found myself on the cold bathroom floor, the formula for the filling agent spread out in front of me for the second time. My inheritance was not going to sink, I thought defiantly, this was why I had become a physicist, a physicist of time: to lend things eternity. I began giddily repeating this nonsense to myself while I put all the materials I had left in my bathtub and stirred the mixture with a wooden plank from the toolshed. Sixteen times in total I filled and emptied this volume. This meant that I had to go once or even several more times to the hardware store to buy myriad further materials. With a dreamlike certainty — and the decades-long practice of tablet-taking — I grounded myself every time I became aware of an impending episode: when I saw something moving in the corners, I looked away; when I itched, I refrained from scratching; when I poured substances in the bathtub I managed, despite my intoxication, to review the formula. Then, bathed in sweat, I carried mixture into the garden, two buckets in each hand, where I began to pour it into the small hole that led underneath the house. Naturally, half of it sloshed either side of it.

Again more stirring. The ground tipped away beneath my feet and I fell on top of the earth, fetched more mixture, kept plugging. As the height of the filler got closer to ground level, I improvised injection tubes for hard to reach places. I used a garden hose and water pipes, an electric ball pump, and a plastic tank designed for rain water. I was able to test out the pump in the cellar, relieved that I could flounder to and fro between my attempts in there, out of reach of possible glances. I inserted the hose into the deepest of the cracks, which was exactly under the broken tiles, then activated the motor for the pump and heard liquid flowing in the direction of the hollow room. (I marvelled in retrospect that I had possessed so much care and technical skill in my haziness — before I later found, on my desk, a plan for the apparatus, with precise instructions, that I'd been given by Philipp.)

My construction was not perfect, not in the slightest, and when I tried it for the first time in the cellar, half of the filling agent was forced back up. But enough of it stayed down, which — given the small volume of the cavity under my house in comparison to the mountain — gave cause for hope. I undertook a second and a third round, lost all sense of time, pulled the hose out of the cavity, stuck it in another crack, and at this point it had become another ten, maybe twenty, no, more like thirty bucketsful that I had pumped in without knowing whether it would be enough. The cellar had become boundless to me; it took me an hour to climb the stairs and fall into a deep sleep in my bed. It wouldn't be until the following day that I would comprehend the fatal consequences of my weakness.

Before long, respiratory depression of the soil caused by the artificial material would set in: the plants would suffocate over a matter of weeks, and simultaneously the microorganisms, trapped in the top layer of soil, could no longer submerge. Once the balance of my soil had been disturbed, the animals living there — squirrels, birds, rodents — would no longer have the chance to find nourishment. My garden would die, and the only way I could hide it would be to cover it inadequately with potted plants. It had been murder, or at least involuntary manslaughter, that I had committed. I looked fearfully out of the window: everything was still green.

Mathematicians interpret the structure of a Reissner–Nordström-type black hole as follows: at the outer limit of one is the so-called Cauchy horizon — a boundary beyond which gravity becomes so strong that the general theory of relativity and thus determinism no longer apply. After crossing this barrier, all physical causality is abolished; the past no longer dominates the future. While time slows down more and more as you approach the black hole, this changes when the border is crossed into the exact opposite. An infinite time lapse forms, and the entire history of the universe collapses into a single instant. If a person should ever enter this sphere, he would be unable to tell anyone about his observations, because at the same moment he passed the Cauchy horizon, he would be destroyed by a powerful beam of energy.

On 13 June, a Thursday, we were in the middle of a meeting when we received a call. Anita picked up the phone, and her expression deteriorated as she nodded repeatedly. Without knowing the content of the call, we had all automatically put down our documents and surrendered ourselves to its ominous momentum. There were four of us in the room: myself; Manfred, the head of the building yard; Karin, who was responsible for financing; and Anita, who put down the receiver and told us that a child had gone missing.

It was an eight-year-old girl, Valerie Spitz, who hadn't shown up for class that morning after having walked the mere eight hundred metres from her house to school. The family lived on the Burggraben, said Anita, and we all suspected, without anyone having to say it, what hideous thing had happened. Out from the Burggraben, behind the middle-school building, there was a short piece of dirt road, no more than fifty metres long. But on the left side of this path, which the girl must have taken, there was a hole. Not an official entry, but rather a shaft that was first created by the collapses, which we had incidentally, and without any special urgency, been trying to get under control for weeks. 'We should go take a look,' Manfred said.

A commotion could be seen from afar, and the fact that it was so quiet made it all the more disconcerting. Behind the school building was a fire engine from the volunteer fire brigade, who had fortified the small hollow with steel cranks. I pushed my way through the crowd to the firefighters, as if I had something to contribute. They were standing, looking into the hole, with climbing harnesses attached to ropes. Now I saw the entry for the first time in an unsecured condition: the canal was narrow at the top — an adult could barely fit through it — but became wider and wider towards the bottom. The fire chief, a lawyer who had pulled rubber boots on over his suit trousers, explained to me that it would take hours, if not days, to reach the bottom of the hole. A machine, which first needed to be procured from a neighbouring town, would broaden then mill the hole until an adult rescuer could pass through it. And even if they did manage to do this — he said in a whisper, and for a moment I wondered why he was telling me, of all people — the girl would have hurtled uninhibited a hundred and twenty metres into the depths. Indeed, the railings had been pushed to one side, probably by the storms of the past few weeks, and yes, there had been traces of slipping, but they didn't want to plunge the parents into total despair just yet. Fear that the town had been at fault wavered in his voice: The hole had not been adequately secured. Behind us, near the middle-school building, I heard the girl's name being called. The heat of the cloudless summer's day, which had been growing more and more merciless during the course of our conversation, shimmered over the dirt roads.

The rest of the children were being picked up by their parents, someone explained. Within the last hour, a group of volunteers had come together to look for the girl in the forest. We all knew that this measure would only delay the pain, and yet we were determined to help.

I walked like a sleepwalker, confused and seized by a sudden sense of guilt, to the place where the noise signalled a group. We walked in silence along the road to the protected forest, where we rolled ourselves out into a long line. I was integrated into the chain and went along the forest paths, shouting the girl's name over and over again. The light broke through the treetops; there was no sound apart from the cracking of the twigs and the repeated calling of the name, which lost all meaning. *Valerie* — *Valerie* — *Valerie* — *Val-erie* — *Va-lerie* — *Valer-ie*. There was an aggressiveness in the voices of the others, as if they wanted to direct it at somebody. The forest wasn't so much asked about the child's whereabouts but rather what had caused her disappearance. Someone pressed a flyer into my hand that depicted the girl's face. It was a portrait, like a school photo — those ones where the child's head remains frozen for all eternity, the word *cheese* or *spaghetti* still in their mouth. Valerie had a ponytail and there, where her front teeth should be, a gaping hole.

Frozen, I thought, and imagined how in a few weeks the filling agent might be led down all channels and lie thickly over Valerie's body. Not only Valerie's body, but also the bodies of those who were otherwise stuck there. Hundreds of bodies taken by the mine, bodies that time had washed up there, and all those who had been murdered and forcibly driven into the mud. And on top of all these now the child, set to remain forever petrified in the violent grip of the filler. A shiver came over me despite the stifling heat.

I sidled out of the formation, stumbled through the undergrowth towards a hiking trail, and ran out of the forest to my house. I wanted to go to bed as quickly as possible, darken the room and revive myself. But as I came down Johannesstrasse, something was different: a surprising number of people were standing in groups on the street and smoking. There was something unsettling about it — all huddled together in groups of four and four, seven and nine, although none of them said a word. I looked around furtively, expecting one of them to ask me something. As I turned right into Mondweg, I passed a couple of young men in blue overalls and wondered about it, seeing as the garage was so far away. Then I heard the name of my neighbour Glottersaat fall from someone's lips for the first time.

In my house the numbness of the street fell from me abruptly. I drank a beer, which I never did in the middle of the day, to cool myself down, and while I watched a mindless tabloid talk show on TV with the blinds closed, and a chubby-cheeked teenage delinquent found out the results of his paternity test, I dozed off.

I woke up when the sun was already going down behind the house. After the few seconds needed to wipe the sleep from my eyes, I opened the window. From a few streets away, a noise carried over to me as if from afar. Louder and louder calls, which seemed to be coming from the Römerstrasse, were soon ringing against my still-closed blinds. I pried apart the leaves of the blinds with my fingers, and peered out my living-room window. Coming from the left, less than a hundred metres from my house, I saw a person turning the corner, then two, then four, then ten people. Some were dragging a heavy burlap sack on four ropes behind them. Instinctively, I got down on my knees and ducked under the windowsill. But I had to know what was going on. Just before they reached my house, I emerged from cover and watched them go by. I remember how pure dread had overwhelmed me, because in those few seconds it took for the procession to pass by my house, I had seen pure, undisguised hatred in their body language. No one tried to disguise it; a few of them had wooden staffs in their hands, which they dragged along the asphalt behind them. One of them held a flat cap away from him, as if he had accidently besmirched it.

I felt dizzy. What I had taken to be a sack from a distance, left a mark on the concrete. *Blood*, I thought, and felt sick, *blood that must have flowed from a body*. I was trying so desperately to catch my breath that I wasn't sure how much time passed. But I thought I had seen a checked shirt and a heavy, large body. On the other hand, I *was* slightly drunk, and could no longer clearly recall the image. When I later went out into the street, because I could no longer bear wallowing in my own thoughts, there was nothing to see on the asphalt.

18

When we worked out that we had seventy days before the date of the festival, we were all, as we sat around the table, without hope that the town would survive this brief three months. And even if it did, nothing would be gained: since I had made everyone believe that I had made no progress, we still didn't have a filler. There was, however, one exception: the Countess seemed to be in a good mood. There were chocolates on the table — expensive ones that I knew the Countess bought in half-kilo portions and always ate alone. The rest of us drank filter coffee.

'I've spoken with an engineer who will construct this for us,' she said, rolling out a plan. 'A rollercoaster train for this *omission*.' The Countess would describe the hole euphemistically as an omission, as if someone had deliberately left out the earth so it could be supplemented with her inventions.

'He would be able to build this for around three million euros. Is that still within the budget, Philipp?'

The Countess had already put this question to me, as she often did, at three in the morning, briefly tearing me from my sleep before I dozed off again, annoyed at not having pulled the landline out of the wall as usual.

'I don't think so,' said Philipp carefully. Everyone else was silent.

'I think it's possible,' the Countess insisted, and pointed at the plan as if it were proof of what she had said. According to this, a vertical track with steel girders was to be bolted into the ground. The diagram showed people shrieking with delight while corkscrewing through the damp tunnels. We could make out their hands sticking exuberantly in the air only a few metres away from the shaft wall.

'We can make savings elsewhere. I'm not very knowledgeable about power lines, but it looks like we need to put one in — can you arrange that as soon as possible, Herr Loreth? We should start everything immediately.'

Again there was an embarrassed silence.

'Lady Countess, that's impossible,' Manfred Loreth said finally. 'We would neither receive the safety certification, nor do we have the financial means, and here and here' — he pointed at the positioning of the steel girders — 'the subsidence is particularly extreme. The rollercoaster would sink within a matter of days.'

'Fine, then we'll have to come up with a solution,' the Countess concluded, as if what had been said had simply been a reinforcement of her plans.

The town, in the meantime, had become a single field of rubble. A regular road network could no longer be maintained: the ridges caused by the road rising and splitting were so high and insurmountable that no one could make it to the supermarket without four-wheel drive. Some drivers were taken unawares by the transformation in the town centre especially, so that they would drive into a dip that they could no longer get out of — and would leave behind their cars, which remained, as if frozen in time, in the middle of the road. The community's ability to suppress was remarkable: if from one day to the next a pavement was missing or one was still there but hanging a metre below street level, the next day you would find a rope running parallel to it tied between two lampposts, which everyone held onto on their daily journeys, as if it were the most normal thing in the world to lead your life as if at the base camp of Mount Everest.

The taverns, which were all grouped around the main square, were considered to be in danger of collapse, which did not put off anyone from continuing to frequent them. In the back rooms, the plasterboard was supported with billiard cues, and every establishment had suddenly acquired an increasing number of poker machines to lucratively cover up the cracks in the walls. In the mornings, a police officer went around the wretched buildings and drove people out for safety reasons — by noon they were once more full to bursting. When large piles of rubble formed, which was inevitable, the town council poured a huge amount of earth on these mounds and formed pyramidal flower beds, on which dahlias would later be planted.

Parallel to these collapses I can especially remember the little things: the time I spat my toothpaste into my wash basin one evening, and the vortex, which, according to the laws of nature, should form in the middle, was broken like a torn circle. And as the liquid disappeared down the drain, at some point I felt my socks become wet, because a crack had appeared in my sink overnight.

On another occasion, I was walking through the town one evening, and suddenly heard a grinding sound, as if someone were crowbarring the world. I stopped and stood in the dark, convinced I'd only imagined it, then, as if touched by an invisible hand, the iron garden gates were forced from their latches and swung open. First one, then fifty metres down a second, then three or four down the street, until the air was filled with the clanking of metal.

The greatest horror, however, was the only thing not affected by the subsidence: my own garden. No one had noticed yet, but starting from the entry point on the house facade, into which I'd injected the filling agent, the grass had become an ever paler green; the blossoms I had planted over it in despair were already drooping, and the large fir was in the process of dying. I prayed that no one would notice it, and watered everything four times a day.

'Good,' said the Countess. 'Then there's only one thing we're waiting for,' and she pulled back the elasticated band of her calfskin-bound notebook, as if to fire a starting pistol. The elastic snapped; I flinched. Of course she was looking to me; every day she looked to me, and so did everyone else, when they nervously crept by my desk with suppressed rage while I carried out my covert work.

'Yes, Frau Schwarz, how is it looking?' asked Site Manager Stocker, striking his palm several times with a rolled-up plan. 'It would indeed be prudent to make progress in the matter of the filling agent.'

'I'm nearly at a breakthrough,' I said, perturbed.

'That's all very well, Frau Schwarz, but could you hurry up and get there. Perhaps you're not fully aware of the cost of this delay,' Stocker replied with undisguised anger.

'I'll have a prototype a week from today.'

'We have to,' he began again, 'order the filling vehicles, train the workers, which will most likely take half a year —'

'Yes, yes, Frau Schwarz will do it,' interrupted the Countess — she would defend me in the most peculiar situations. 'The money will pour back in through tourism. The hotels are getting ready. Is it not true, Frau Raich, that if we reach full capacity we could earn a profit?'

'Well yes, *if*,' said Frau Raich, who represented the tourist office in our group.

The meeting was over, and we were panting like we had run a marathon. There was no longer any doubt that all of us, with the exception of the Countess, had reached our limit. We had installed a potent administration for the disintegration, and led the regiment with our eyes respectfully closed.

As I did every day after work, I loaded up a shoulder bag I'd brought with me with documents, which I intended to work through in front of the TV, and which I'd lug back up the steep path to the castle again in the morning. Although I had been transporting everything that seemed crucial for my own research out of the castle in this manner for months, I was still nervous when I passed the butler, and as a precaution I had hidden every piece of paper in a folder of work-relevant papers.

It was a blissfully wonderful early summer's evening; the shouts of the teenagers, spending their whole day on the football field, overwhelmed with happiness about their holidays, were carried up the mountain. It was at these moments that I was most often overcome by an excruciating feeling of isolation, as if the mild weather were trying to persuade me of a level of contentedness that I was incapable of reaching. But what did that change? I would be gone soon anyway, I thought, unlocking my front door. Once inside I had to push my way past stacks of boxes, like a hoarder dwelling in an ever-narrowing system of aisles. In the living room, on the other hand, everything had been cleared out a long time ago. As of around three months ago, it had been like living in a compartment of a warehouse. I had crammed packed bags along the walls of the entrance hall, as if I would at any moment have to jump into a waiting getaway vehicle that would stop with a screech in front of my house. But there was no chance of that happening: this perpetual state of readiness for an imaginary move was, in reality, as I know now, a kind of substitute for the fact that I hadn't done anything for far too long.

I had tried in vain the last weeks to get back my car, which had been in the workshop for two and a half years, waiting to be repaired. This had never struck me as strange. But when I had gone into the garage the previous week and found my car in the exact same condition I'd left it in, I knew that it couldn't have been a coincidence. I had to call out three times before Mario marched in, a pockmarked man whom I also knew as a petrol station attendant. For a moment, I was at a loss for the words to even ask for my car, after I'd let the matter slide for almost three whole years. As I turned around while Mario was still mining awkwardly at the computer, I noticed that my car was the only one in the whole garage — and that it was still positioned on the lifting ramp, just as I had left it. An air pressure gauge was stuck in the tire — nothing had happened. The moment I touched the fender a spanner fell to the floor. I spun around and looked at Mario, whose fingers were pretending to be typing on the keyboard — it was like a photo shoot for a pianist. In order not to break the farce, Mario finally said: 'Maybe in two weeks.' I nodded.

I had started packing my things after I got home from the visit to the garage. Having them standing in the hallway gave me the assurance that if I decided to go, I wouldn't need more than twenty minutes to leave it all behind. Whether it had been the Countess who had intervened so my car wouldn't be repaired, or whether it was a common custom that no one ever considered moving away, I no longer cared. My life couldn't take another mystery. I sat at my virtually overflowing desk, which was so full it had incapacitated me for the longest time already. For years I had done nothing but the work of a crypto-analyst: finding patterns, clusters in the files, so that with the intuition of a detective I could immediately doubt them again. I had found a total of seventy-one 'cases', as I called them. Twenty-five cases of land purchases by the Count's family in 1950, and forty-six transactions made in 1962, after the Schlaf trial. There was hardly any unsold property left. All seventy-one instances were in order, and had been prepared with the relevant material ready for handover. But to whom were they handed?

Then on some days, everything once more collapsed over my head: in the darkest moments, I wondered what difference it made — thirty-four dead or two hundred or two thousand? What was the point of finding the place where they lay, and the names and identities of those who had buried them?

What difference did it make to know about the Countess, whom I had long since found out was *not* a Countess, and whose family had simply made a career as industrialists seventy years ago and risen to the monarchy through an improbable bureaucratic act? What would it mean to be a real Countess anyway? Wasn't all noble blood essentially imaginary?

The history was maddening. I knew intuitively what had happened, and yet I still couldn't prove it — not even to myself. This was my daily struggle. It was so obvious: ten men alone would never have been able to kill eight hundred forced labourers, and it couldn't be purely coincidental that the bodies would later end up in people's gardens.

The ironic thing was: all the documents that I needed in order to be able to prove what had happened and when, my parents had borrowed and carried off to Vienna. I was firmly convinced that the two of them had been researching the exact same thing that I was, and I needed their findings. After a lengthy struggle, I had finally decided to write to my aunt. I had been waiting for the materials for many weeks now, and she had still not been in touch.

Nothing fit together at the edges; the transitions remained frayed. If the rubble was cleared away a little too quickly or if one were to skip a few weeks in an otherwise completely chronological story … if the words became permeable and imprecise, I copied the documents and began to brood over them. I wildly desired an accusation, but it was clearly nothing — almost always nothing. Instead there was a too-little, a vanishing. I had to be able to prove things in order to pass them on to the media; inconsistencies alone wouldn't be enough. After ten minutes of digging through piles of papers, I was completely beside myself. I wanted to hand over the material to journalists, yet feared the consequences. I wanted to get away, yet was hopelessly matted together with this town. I took every precaution, but life after leaving Greater Einland seemed to me like a cloud of fog, within which I couldn't envisage anything.

I looked at the time and realised that I had been fussing around for two hours without having done the slightest thing. There wasn't actually anything more to do; everything had been put away in boxes and emptied out. Although I wasn't really looking forward to it, I was to a certain extent relieved when I set off around 7pm for some social distraction.

19

The doorbell ringing surprised me the following morning while I was showering. When the bell rang a second and third time, I finally wrapped myself in a towel and went to the door with my hair still dripping. It was only Philipp, probably wanting to admonish me to do some work.

'For God's sake, I was still in the shower,' I said, and wanted to slam the door right there and then, but he put his foot in the way.

'It's important,' he said. His expression was deadly serious.

'No sermons, it's my day off. Did the Countess complain about it?'

'You got your car back, I see.'

'Oh, yes, now that the roads will be passable again soon, I thought it couldn't hurt,' I said, avoiding his gaze. 'What's up?'

Suddenly, and against all expectations, my car had appeared in front of my house one morning, and every day when I returned home, I made sure that it was still there. I still couldn't believe that it was on my property, and that the keys to my departure were jangling around in my handbag. Furthermore: I'd been rehearsing, as I called it in my head, in that I sat behind the steering wheel for a few minutes every day. I stayed there, tensed, my hand on the clutch as if the car were about to lift off from my garage and leave the atmosphere. Fortunately, Philipp didn't seem further interested in my car.

'I don't want anything special, I was just on my way to work and wanted to ask you something.' He shifted from one foot to the other and cleared his throat. 'Your garden,' he said at last and then broke off again.

'What about my garden?' In one fell swoop, the volume of the surrounding area powered down.

'All of us up at the office — it doesn't matter. I mean, that's the best place to see it. And I wanted to ask you personally. To be honest, I was shocked when I realised.'

Like two hundred-metre runners who are only a hare's breadth apart, no one had noticed at first how the general landscape, frantically racing towards the finishing line of summer, was being lapped in aridity by my garden. But at the end of July, when the orange stripes reached into every field to gently force them out of this year's lifecycle, my plot was already parched. I had sprayed and sprayed, sprinkling the plants with atomised water to cool them from above, but it was hopeless. A whitish-yellow stain had appeared in the green of the town, as if someone had stubbed out a huge cigarette and dead tissue had remained. Ashamed, I had dismissed my neighbours' inquiries by claiming to have used the wrong fertiliser, but the consequences quickly became too severe to sustain my excuses. Suspicion around my property grew in silence. When I awoke one morning, I found that the linden tree in my garden had shaken off all its leaves in a single, final exhale, and I hastily shoved them into rubbish bags before someone saw what I was doing. There was a dogged stench of rot, but who would notice that in a town being swallowed by a huge hole? I was embarrassed about the filler, but there was nothing to be done about it now.

The most horrific thing had been a moment, one day after work, when I took the long-avoided way through the backyard: it was a windless late summer, and yet there was an odd movement on the lawn. The long dried-out grass swayed to and fro. As I bent down to see what was causing this waving motion, I saw that the whole of the yellow lawn was teeming with worms: worms that had escaped from the airless earth and were writhing, lost between sky and ground.

I had lain down on the couch as if in shock: I had poisoned nature to save a house that could by no means be saved. From then on I was haunted by horror — when I was sitting at work, when I ate, when I outwardly appeared to be having fun, but especially when I planned to go for a walk, as I had so often done in the past. It was then that the betrayal was most palpable to me. Had I once really loved this land? Yes, of course I had. The most important thing was that I hadn't handed over the filler. It was only a tiny little patch that had been affected by the poison. Yet my treachery haunted me, a relentless indebtedness to every little shrub. When I walked passed a tree, I looked around furtively, as if we shouldn't be seen together.

'I thought we were on good terms.' It was the first time Philipp had spoken to me this way. His jovial flirtatiousness was as if blown away, and I said nothing — the time for denial was long past.

'I want to be honest with you,' he said. 'I don't know why you're doing this, but it is deeply selfish of you.'

'I don't follow,' I said, and could hear for myself how ridiculous that sounded.

'We all know that you've found a filler.'

I trapped Anita in the office with my arm, just like when someone catches a ball they've seen racing towards them out of the corner of their eye. It happened almost reflexively, so that I didn't know how to even explain the gesture. 'Was there something?' she asked. I nodded first, and then agitatedly shook my head.

'I wanted to ask if you'd maybe like to go for a beer with me, now for instance.'

'We're not finished yet,' she said, even though she already had her coat over her arm, ready to go.

After it had come out that I had kept the filler a secret from everyone, the atmosphere in the office, after the expected explosion, was markedly frosty. Strangely enough, the Countess had been the first to forgive me, even though my story of how I'd wanted to test the substance myself was completely implausible and full of holes. Nevertheless, she had, after a few stern words about my misconduct, let it go. More than anything, she seemed glad that things were now getting underway. My colleagues, on the other hand, let me know that they didn't believe a word I said. Having said that, the now necessary overtime was done in silence, and for the first time, the dogged listlessness of the people of Greater Einland that made them shy away from any and all conflict suited me fine. My relationship with Anita, however, had remained distant, and although we came in at eight in the morning, and sometimes did not leave the office before ten, we hadn't really spoken for weeks.

'Come on, one beer,' I insisted. 'We won't get anything else productive done today anyway.'

It was shortly before nine. 'Just one,' Anita said, shaking her head despite this affirmation. We walked into town in silence for ten oppressive minutes, whereby I kept clearing my throat and breathing heavily in order to commence with an explanation, but kept refraining from doing so at the last moment and only asked whenever we turned 'Left?' or 'It's a right now, isn't it?' even though I knew the way. It was only once we'd arrived downtown that I plucked up the courage.

'It's been very difficult,' I said at last.

'The calculations this afternoon?' Anita asked, and I nodded, even though I meant the matter about the filler.

'There are so many fiscal obligations to consider, that's why — I'm sorry I didn't tell you about the filler sooner,' I finally said, incoherently. We were both silent for a while.

'Do you remember, when we were cooking at my house, two months ago? You claimed to have made no progress whatsoever.'

Of course, she was right. I walked silently beside her as if superfluous.

'Now that I come to think of it,' she said, drawing a breath to elaborate, 'you actually put on a right farce that evening. *I feel incapable of being a physicist*, you said. I comforted you.'

'It was a Friday,' I said, even though that didn't explain in the slightest.

'You downed a glass of wine and stared at the wall, Ruth. It was Oscar-worthy. Maybe you even cried? I think you cried.'

'No, I didn't,' I replied quietly, because we were already near the main square.

'Absolute torrents were running from your eyes. I gave you serviettes because there weren't any tissues left, do you remember?'

'No.'

'Whatever. The properties and homes of dozens of people are in danger of collapsing, because you kept it to yourself. It doesn't matter to you — you safeguarded *your* house in good time.' I was stunned at the anger that Anita, usually so soft and shy, could suddenly manage.

'It's not as simple as that,' I said. 'Didn't you see what happened to my garden?' I was slowly regaining my composure.

'That's beside the point! What good is a garden if it's a hundred and fifty metres deep in the mountain?' She was right, of course. Still, I struggled for an answer.

'I loved the nature here, Anita, and what has come out of this bloody filler? Must we either have no landscape at all or only a dead one? No home or a rotting one?' While I had been saying this, we had taken our seats in Café Français.

'I could have handled the work that you've saddled us with,' Anita said. 'But that you lied to me as a friend is unforgiveable,' and then she turned to the waiter, smiling politely. This made me explode.

'Everyone here lies all the time! No one is honest, everyone does what they like!' I said, swiping the toothpicks from the table while doing so. The cup they had been standing in broke with a clatter, and for a moment the whole restaurant looked over at our table.

'Well then, please,' she whispered. 'Explain it to me.'

'Excuse me, there's something on the floor here!' I quickly called into the room.

'I'm listening,' Anita said impatiently.

I laughed to show how unwilling I was to reveal my motives. 'You should trust me more. You might not even believe it anyway. There were certain things I needed to evaluate,' I raved aimlessly, while a waitress kneeled on the floor to clear up the broken pieces.

'This is pointless, I'm leaving,' she said, picking up her jacket. I dithered helplessly between options. This was Anita, my friend. And yet: she was a Greater Einlander, raised in awe of the Countess and the mountain.

'Okay, let's go over there around the corner,' I said finally, and we sat at a secluded table. I thought over for a long time how I should begin.

'It might sound weird now, but over the past year I've been conducting research,' I said, detecting a glass splinter in the sole of my shoe.

'Everybody knows that you take documents home for your memorial service.'

I looked around. 'I have collated certain incidents in Greater Einland that are not directly related to my parents. From the National Socialist era.'

'Incidents, regarding whom?'

'The hole. It's to do with crimes.'

'Crimes in the hole?' Anita asked, confused.

'Of course in the hole. Unsolved murders,' I hissed. The glass splinter fell with a tinkle from my sole to the floor.

'How do you mean, inside? The main shaft is vertical, how could someone murder someone in there?'

I tried to stay calm. 'The exact location doesn't matter. The hole was just a cover-up. Listen —' I was suddenly so nervous that I had to drink half my beer in one gulp. It was the first time I'd spoken these thoughts out loud, and they sounded strange even to me. 'You know that concentration camp prisoners were stationed here, right? At its peak almost two thousand of them.'

'Everyone knows that. It's even in the local chronicle,' Anita said.

'One thousand two hundred of them left for Mauthausen — so far, so good. The rest were said to have been killed by the guards. But in the mass grave on Johannesstrasse only about fifty were found.'

'But everyone knows that, it's in the local chronicle,' she repeated, as if our conversation had slipped into a time loop. 'None of that's new.'

'Where did the other seven hundred and fifty go? I've been researching this for a long time.' I was sweating like I was in a sauna.

'Since when have you been interested in local history?' Anita laughed, as if to break the tension, and then fidgeted with her hands. 'Maybe they ran away? Who could possibly find that out now?'

I wanted to respond, but in that moment two schnitzels were brought over, which I couldn't remember having ordered. Bemused, I waved my hand to call over the waitress. That I was silent for a moment seemed to calm Anita.

'Ruth, please let's stop arguing. You won't be here forever, why reheat these old stories? Other people have to take care of Greater Einland.' When the waitress had still not reappeared, I bit into the schnitzel, which I hadn't wanted in the slightest.

'There are enough other things going on in the world. More important, more current things. Can't you devote yourself to them for a change? I would care more about the rest of the world and its abysses if I were you.'

'Since I've known you, you haven't left Greater Einland for a single day to take care of the so-called rest of the world,' I said.

'Well, how can I? I have a family!' she replied snappishly. 'What I mean to say it: everyone in this town — every single one — has brooded over the hole for long enough.' She ate her schnitzel too, as if there was nothing strange about it — it had probably been served to us due to our changing tables, I thought.

'Be that as it may,' I began once more. 'Certain things need to be discussed. And now, before the damn filling in.'

'You can't force anyone to do anything. Freedom is humanity's most valuable possession,' she said in her usual mild tone — a mildness to which I didn't intend to respond.

'Do you remember Hat-Maker Schlaf's parents? Bodies were found in their garden in the sixties. After that, the police wanted to check more properties, but they were all bought up by the countdom.'

'Help ought only to be given to those who ask,' Anita interrupted me again. What was she trying to say to me with these meaningless verbal castlings? I was becoming more irate by the minute.

'All the public land, including the private houses. If the authorities sent a letter stating they wanted to investigate somewhere, the place in question was bought by the Count's family two months later. If the documents I've found match up, there is a total of seventy-one instances of such cases. Seventy-one!'

While listening, Anita had become distant again.

'You're completely paranoid,' she said at last. Since I had mentioned the countdom she had shifted about restlessly in her seat. 'And you have to make up all of this right before the festival?'

'These seventy-one plots were bought exactly where branches of the hole are located. And I can't allow the filling to begin until it's clear why exactly that is. It's not a fantasy.'

'And why now?'

'What do you mean why now?'

'You digging up these old stories. What do you expect to come of it? You want the attention, is that it? Why didn't you say anything at the time?' she spoke so forcefully that a piece of loganberry sprayed from her lips over the table onto my jumper.

'Because it was thirty-five years before I was born,' I said.

'Well, that's easy for you to say. You know what? I think you were right earlier. Nature can't help it. Just as little as the people here can, your neighbours and friends.'

'That's not what I meant at all,' I replied.

'Yes exactly,' she concluded incongruously.

I took a deep breath, shoved the rest of the greasy schnitzel in my mouth, and carried on talking. 'Have you been listening to me at all? The point is that bodies were highly likely thrown into the hole. On private land,' I whispered, because I assumed that she simply hadn't understood. 'By everyone.'

'By everyone! Right, so my grandfather, for instance, who was in the resistance.' She wiggled a bone that had strangely been in the schnitzel out of her mouth. 'And even if that were true. What is that supposed to change? In all the talk about the dead, don't we often forget about the living?' Anita had suddenly become a stranger to me.

'Murder doesn't come under the statute of limitations,' I said defiantly. Anita took her mobile phone out of her pocket and looked at the display for minutes on end

'Do you not understand me at all? My parents were researching this matter, too, and then they were suddenly dead. A mysterious car accident. Sound as a bell beforehand. What are the chances of that just happening?'

'I beg your pardon?' Anita asked, startled. Now she had pushed herself back from the table.

'You know what I'm talking about. It's obvious. They spoke with the Countess on the eve of their death. Maybe even about this.'

'I'm leaving,' Anita said, looking around the room almost hysterically. 'I won't go down with you. What you're claiming is unspeakable. Your parents had an accident. If you weren't so much of a coward, you would have looked at the pathological report a long time ago. Good night.' And with that she left me sitting alone at the table.

The next morning I woke up hungover, even though I'd only had two beers. I had no desire to go to work, and furthermore it now dawned on me that I had lost my best friend. But I had at least made a resolution overnight, and I stumbled over to the telephone before I'd had my first coffee. I telephoned the Vienna state police, had my call forwarded by overworked and unresponsive officers, and finally got through to the Scheibbs State Hospital, where someone checked my details, incredulous that it had taken me this long to get in touch. I was put through to pathology.

'I requested a report from you two and a half years ago,' I said, clearing my throat three times in this short sentence. 'But then I never followed up.'

'Your parents, is that correct?' The doctor rummaged through paperwork for a few minutes. 'Yes, here we go, almost three years ago. My colleagues came to their conclusion very quickly at the time: your parents died in the collision. Due to a blunt trauma that wasn't seen at first, because their bruising wasn't visible until much later. In both their cases their spleen was torn. They had very poor seatbelts, in the opinion of the expert. The report concluded that they had died in a car accident.'

'How did the accident happen? Have you — I mean, were they examined for other causes of death?'

'Came off wet motorway with summer tyres, says here.'

'It definitely wasn't — did you find poison? Damage to the vehicle? I mean, I'm sorry for asking.'

'As far as damage was concerned, the car was pretty much intact. We naturally also checked for intoxication, so no, it was actually just a wet motorway. Well, not just — I didn't mean it like that — I wanted to say: my condolences again.'

In the middle of the preparations for the festival, a phenomenon of vanishings unfolded within the whole community, and, strangely enough, it was the Countess who drew my attention to it. Only a month before the festival, she wrote me a message that had got lost in all the chaos of the strange tasks she served up to me on a daily basis. I ought to take a look at a folder that she had put on my desk for me and tell her what I made of it. Floating right at the top of the pool of my unfinished business was the binder the Countess was referring to. On the first sheet was a post-it on which she had written in her playfully disciplined handwriting: 'Please look into this, best wishes, Ursula.' Momentarily stunned, as I always was whenever she was informal with me, I looked through the papers. They were gendarmerie documents that described incidents on different days, between which I initially found it difficult to make a connection. Almost all of them were regarding an officer having been placed in front of someone's house, and spending the night in his vehicle without anything of note happening. The papers always ended with the police officers leaving at seven in the morning.

It was only then that I saw that some of these otherwise uneventful reports had printouts stapled to them. They were, for the most part, anonymous emails, and always described the same thing. The first, for instance, went like this:

> I am a resident of Parkstrasse and would like to draw your attention to something I've noticed happening on my neighbour's property over the last few weeks. Around two or three times a week, under cover of darkness, they transport a cart bursting full of objects to the entrance of the mines on the corner of Hauptstrasse. They unscrew the ten or so safety slats and then start throwing the objects they've brought into the shaft, which you can hear banging right up to my roof terrace.

Incidents like this seemed to keep happening: with increasing frequency, complaints were being directed against strangers, whereby it was evident that the accused were almost always their own neighbours. The stories were about someone throwing all kinds of things in the hole, mostly at night, and taking every precaution to ensure that no one saw them. Generally speaking, this wasn't a surprise. In a few weeks, so everyone thought, the cavity would be pumped with a filling agent that would forever make it impossible to access anything in the hole. Everyone had something to dispose of that in previous years they might not have known where to put. But as I flicked through the mountain of uniform accusations, I felt strange; in unbelievable synchrony, the population had begun throwing things into the hole.

It amazed me that the Countess was interested in knowing more about it at all — these weren't usually the incidents she sought to explore. I called her once I'd read through all of the documents, and she briefed me further: one can certainly overlook certain things, but with other things one certainly needed to know more. 'It always depends on who it's regarding,' she said cryptically, and I understood that this was actually less about potential crimes, and a lot more about keeping the public calm so shortly before the festival. 'Maybe just take a look if and when you have time, Frau Schwarz. Alongside your speech.' The speech, it hit me. I had allowed myself to be talked into giving a speech at the opening of the festival; *speak about the metaphysical aspect, the philosophical aspect*, the Countess had instructed me. I had been wrestling with how to formulate it for weeks and had only got as far as the title: *The Liquid Land*.

The speech can wait, I thought, and buried myself in the official documents, entering the listed persons in a spreadsheet. The most astounding thing was that almost everyone had something to *discard*. But at the same time, it was often the people who had themselves allegedly thrown something into the hole, who would send us condemning information about their neighbours the next day. I thought of it as a kind of redress for a guilty conscience that plagued them, and which demanded that they implicate another perpetrator as compensation.

No matter how explicable these things might seem, I had the feeling that in some cases there might be more to it, and I soon developed the fantasy of catching someone in the act. One account stuck in my mind: someone had accused three different families of throwing things into the hole together, of cooperating on their nightly excursions, which for some reason intrigued me. However, after one of these families befriended the Countess, she wanted me to not investigate this particular case any further, and instead choose a different incident to take a closer look at.

Although I had to get up early the next morning, I decided to take a detour to a house that had been reported to the police the day before. It was a detached house on Korngasse — three children, a dog, was written in the file — and on my way there I imagined what such people could have thrown in the hole at night. So around 9pm I sat down in a blind spot, unable to be seen by the house in question, a few hundred metres down the street, on the still warm asphalt, and waited for something to happen. I had observed the family in their sheer harmlessness behind the illuminated terrace door: the pleasant married couple who gave one another faithful kisses, the baby, who had gone to sleep as if of its own accord in the arms of the mother, the little boy lifted up by the waist by his father and thrown into the air.

The light finally went out, and I lit a cigarette. I could rely on smoking as an easy way to regulate my emotions. I stared in the persistence of the dark and thought in circles. Out of all these people who were undoubtedly involved in throwing things they wanted and needed to rid themselves of into the hole, in this groundless abyss, the bottom of which not even a sensor had been able to reach — out of all these people, it was practically impossible to catch even one committing the deed. More than that: the population of Greater Einland had probably always done this, for decades, if not centuries, and that I was lying in wait here was nothing more than a diversion.

I startled as day once again broke. With a sore neck and full bladder, I noticed that there was a burn hole in my shirt, and I sat upright. I must have fallen into a deep, almost comatose sleep from which even the pain hadn't jolted me awake, because on my stomach I could see a tiny burn. In the morning light I looked back one more time: the lights were out.

Although I could have left it at that, I was occupied with this matter for the next week: there had to be a reason for this secrecy. On Saturday I went to the side entrance to the hole that was in the vicinity of my house and, while holding onto tree branches, examined the shallow part of the entryway. In fact there was a lot of junk here, too, and just about too deep in the shaft for it to be impossible to get to it. So I went home and made myself a fishing rod out of a stick and a paperclip: a box was wedged in right at the top that was almost completely eaten away by the damp, but after several attempts I managed to manoeuvre it out. A cloth bag had got caught on my miserable hook. First I opened the little bag and found two gold rings — wedding rings, there was no doubt about it, because engraved on the inside of one was 'Oliver and Julia' and on the other 'Julia and Oliver'. *Julia and Oliver Heidenreich*, I thought, a young couple that had divorced a few months ago. Still moved by the intimacy of the first objects, I opened the box: the picture of a young man with Down's Syndrome, laughing, holding up a drawing in his hand.

I knew him, too: This was Fritz, the son of Lilly Rank, the head of the Grocery Shop Association. More photographs and finally the drawing that he had been holding in his hand in the first picture. This was a purely personal confession of guilt: I knew from Sister Elfriede that Lilly Rank had had her son put in a care home in the nineties and since then had barely spoken about him — he had died there a couple of years ago. I felt embarrassed: what was being thrown in the hole were things people felt guilty about. No wonder the Greater Einlanders had an almost mystical relationship to the underground, I thought to myself, and threw the box and the bag back into the hole in frustration. And so the trail was lost.

20

In his later years, Johann Kienagl's notebook entries became increasingly fragmentary. My explanation for this was the following: the undiagnosed tuberculosis that had formed encapsulated cysts in his organs, and had left the healthy tissue more and more perforated, had had a similar effect on the continuity of his thoughts. He was often bedbound for days with fever; periods that swamped his impressions in a mess of bodily fluids, sweat-drenched delirium, and bursting abscesses, before returning with admirable optimism to remarks about the sighting of a rare bird. Knowing that his life would end in an early death, I read these accounts with the feeling that I was connected to the fate of someone who was unsaved.

In 1944, during his penultimate stay in Greater Einland, Kienagl relayed an episode that gave me a serious headache. He had over the previous years reported several times about house searches by the SS, which was nothing unusual in the whole of the German Reich, and would have been observed every now and then by anyone looking out of their window. But the tone and detail of this particular entry were very different from what he had previously recounted.

> When I came home yesterday evening (Trude had
> asked me to be on time because she had got the
> meat fresh from Gloggnitz), I could already see from
> Johannesstrasse that around twenty SS men were
> standing outside the old Schwarz place shouting
> commands. Heinrich was standing with my uncle,
> and there was a wild commotion. A desk, like the
> ones used in school, was in the middle of the street,
> and I half-jokingly asked whether I had detention,
> but my uncle was very stern and immediately sent
> me to my room.

The officer leading the searches was also a Viennese who spent the summer in Greater Einland, where a large number of villas had been built for SS functionaries in recent years. His name was Karl Heinrich. He was a friend of Kienagl's uncle, and a frequent guest in their home. Johann had up to that point described him with the same combination of awe and aversion that he showed for anyone in uniform: whenever he sat with him at the dining table, he answered all questions duteously and comprehensively, but would go to his room as soon as possible to read a book.

It was around seven in the evening when Kienagl was sent into the house by his uncle.

From his bedroom window he continued to watch the happenings going on down below and composed his diary entry. He described how the Schwarzs' house, which had been vacant for over a year and had even been boarded up, was now being searched by the SS. How furniture and books were thrown from windows that had been broken open with crow bars — that the men broke windows and wooden floor panels with the butts of their rifles, and emptied the contents of jewellery boxes. After a good hour it came to an end. Nothing noteworthy appeared to have been found; an SS man stroked the head of my one-year-old mother, who was standing on shaky legs beside the fence, in view of my grandmother, who was joking with the men. My grandfather led the officer into the living room — to the exact spot where I was sitting while reading these lines. Kienagl was called back down soon afterwards, and dinner was served as if nothing had happened. Only there were still rumbling and crashing sounds coming from outside, because all the neighbouring homes were combed through; things were thrown into the street and burst open on the asphalt. Above all, however, a legion of people was involved in throwing the resulting detritus, and everything that no longer seemed to be needed, into the hole, as Kienagl put it.

Over the next few days he himself kept a special eye on my grandfather, who had been excessively harried since the night nothing really happened. Instead of going to work, he stayed at home the next day and the day after — and if he did leave the house, he came back immediately, as if he wanted to make sure no one had stepped foot on his property in the meantime. I didn't attach much weight to these descriptions. A few days later, however, Kienagl described a nocturnal episode that caught my attention.

Probably due to his frequent nocturnal hot flushes during this time, he hadn't been able to sleep, and had rolled over on his sweaty covers in order to *cough up* into a vessel, as he put it. At that moment he heard a noise and went to the window. Below, in the yard in front of the house, he saw my grandfather Joseph Schalla standing there, exuding a great tenseness. *He was kitted out in his full woodcutter gear and smoking a pipe, as if waiting for something. This went on for over an hour — he refilled his pipe three or four times, and, because I was not able to sleep, I simply watched him.* While reading, I had the feeling that Kienagl had been initially delighted to see my grandfather — that the sick boy's loneliness had perhaps been alleviated by the wakefulness of another person.

Soon afterwards, however, he described something that I read through dozens of times without having an explanation for it: how Schalla disappeared into the house, after having finished smoking his pipe several times, and reappeared after a few minutes, *as if struggling*, Kienagl wrote. He carried a heavy sack on his back, and now set off to carry it to the edge of the forest, where the asphalt ended in boggy morass back then. It was the side towards the mine, and Kienagl made a special point of mentioning this, as it was strictly forbidden to be closer than five hundred metres to the entrance. A fence had been erected, as I confirmed when looking it up on old maps — and on the other side of it were the barracks housing the concentration camp prisoners. Around an hour later, it says in the diary, Joseph Schalla returned without the sack. Johann Kienagl was convinced that a person had been inside it.

For a long time I thought about whether this could have taken place. Had Schalla hidden someone in his house, beneath the parquet under the floor, and could this someone have been my other grandfather? More importantly: what exactly had happened after the raid? Had my grandfather been afraid and if so, had he actually made as grave a decision as Kienagl's account suggested?

Of course, there were several ways to put this story into perspective: For one, Kienagl's report, as earnest and as naïve it might be, was full of logical errors, overlooked facts, and the overinterpretation of even the smallest details. Because the composer of these lines was a lonely, sixteen-year-old boy hungry for experiences, who yearned for any kind of occurrence in his ivory tower. In addition to this, he already had serious health problems at this point, and severe attacks of fever, which could have compromised his ability to make judgements. Secondly, even if it were a factual account, the scope of the implications would be enormous. Perhaps he just wanted to see something in it. And this ferocity of interpretation applied equally to me: the findings that I absolutely had to acquire, made them, as it were, worthless.

I remember the last forty-eight hours before the festival as a single expanse.

The first thing that is still present for me is the music, and how the brass band paraded in front of my house — an implausibly, eternally long, almost continuous procession that would not stop playing 'Radetzky March' until the following day. I awoke early in the morning and spent an hour or two lying on my back in bed, as if my bedroom ceiling held the answers to all the unasked questions I would have to confront myself with that day. The whole town resounded with hundreds of musicians rehearsing their marching formations at the last moment. The curtains fluttered, and I was sweating from the first coffee of this final day in Greater Einland, while I got dressed and carried some things to the car.

There was a spirit of optimism outside that soon gripped me, too: the atmosphere was brimming with enthusiastic energy, so I decided to take a short walk.

Apparently every resident was already up and about at this time, and supporting one another on their many paths to get things done. Housewives were setting out coffee and cake on the street with a sign that said 'Free', and people who were busy tying garlands to the streetlamps in their dozens helped themselves. Others carried an entire living room's worth of furniture out into the street: sofas, side tables, and winged chairs, so that the theatre groups could sit down between rehearsals in the middle of the road, where they had conversations with the dogsbodies over a beer. Everyone was slightly drunk and softly beclouded, the conversations wadded, faces blurry. The children ran across the squares in their freshly tailored lederhosen and dirndl and played with footballs, especially in places where no one had ever been allowed to play football before, and it seemed as if all prohibitions had been swept away. I hurried to get back inside before anyone spoke to me.

What I had to do upon waking was to bring my highly efficient preparations to an end. I had everything I would need for my departure in two travel bags and a box, which fit in the boot of my car. I said goodbye to everything else inwardly — I'd done laps around the house yesterday before cutting myself off from every single thing individually, mostly wistfully, yet finally sure of my decision. I had memorised the route I would drive out of the town tomorrow: Johannesstrasse — Auf der Haiden — Gmeingrubenweg — Schlossstrasse, and then the well-preserved forest road behind the castle. All the other roads were either too decrepit to be used, or guarded, like the two fresh access roads that had been built for the tourist coaches. In the last few weeks, I had settled my so-called affairs: the house had become, as I had declared in a legally binding manner and had confirmed by a notary in Vienna, the property of Sister Elfriede, who had finally entered emergency housing two weeks ago. The plan to say goodbye to my acquaintances and friends here by letter, on the other hand, I had ultimately quashed after the first few fruitless attempts — all connections would have to be severed. I kept getting the peculiar feeling that someone would hold me back, that I wouldn't be allowed to leave this place after spending three years here. No one had ever done anything like this before. Nevertheless, I now locked the hard copies in the armoire upstairs, and put the key in my pocket to take it with me.

Tomorrow at eight, when I was supposed to give my speech, I would, naturally, not give it. Instead, as soon as all the journalists and guests were in position, I planned to announce, loudly and clearly, what I knew no one wanted to hear. My report was patchy, but shocking. Was it shocking? The gaps wouldn't matter, if everything went according to plan. The printouts I had prepared for the journalists now lay on my otherwise empty desk.

At the same time, I still had no idea how I was supposed to hand them over without being noticed. That wasn't the only unknown. Whether I would be forced away from the microphone or whether I would finish what I wanted to say, time would tell, but one thing was certain: at the first opportunity after that, come what may, I would have to get into the car and flee. I would push my way through the crowd, maybe have to run — but why would anyone chase me anyway? I wasn't doing anything illegal. A snack station was being set up at an intersection not far from my house; a great number of beer barrels were being hung on hooks. I greeted a couple of women whom I knew by sight, and received as thanks a piece of cake along with a cold mug of Zwickl, which I hastily and gratefully guzzled. Then I went up to the castle and made a couple of phone calls, just to reassure myself that no one would forget what to do tomorrow, before I walked back down to the town at noon. Strange: everything was ready, and yet there were still a thousand things that needed to be done. Everything had been resolved, and at the same time nothing was.

'Hey Ruth, I'm looking forward to your appearance tomorrow!' someone yelled my way, and I raised my hand before I could see who it was. Laughter in the distance. And then there was this atmosphere again —

It felt like we were experiencing the busiest hour of the year and the most significant public holiday at the same time: no one went about their business, unless it was of importance to the progress of the whole thing. This atmosphere spread over everything like a velour carpet, with a softness that seemed to be redrawing everything anew.

Whereas the truth was, of course, that many of the questions we'd been asking ourselves for months were still unanswered; we did not know whether the safety of the visitors was guaranteed or whether the moment all the heralded tourists marched through the town gate, the asphalt would break. Yet precisely because nothing was certain, we walked towards the coming day with somnambulistic self-confidence.

With a weak dose of lithium, I prepared myself for another wave of social interactions: I trembled as I shook hands with the politicians, trembled as I handed out the coupons for the market stalls, and trembled as the filling trucks rolled in and parked on the football pitch for the next day. I was extremely nervous about the following day, and not only on account of my revelatory intentions. I felt responsible for everything that could go awry — and the fact that I might already be over all seven mountains by then didn't change that. Or was I trembling at the thought of my own flight, and the possible catastrophes didn't change anything? Would the inhabitants be shocked by what I said, or rip me to shreds as the harbinger of doom? Lately, instead of becoming more familiar, the Greater Einlanders had become an impenetrable riddle. How they would react could never be anticipated.

Now, for example, while I was walking through the town, I only saw smiling faces: two weeks ago the public's anger at a local council meeting had escalated to such a degree that this joviality seemed practically uncanny. To our great surprise, the meeting had been attended by a large number of Greater Einlanders.

Even when the mayor cleared his throat four or five times, the heated crowd hadn't wanted to shut up. This is why he hit the microphone several times with the palm of his hand — a gesture that has stuck in my memory. What kept the crowd in verbal motion was a polyphonic 'broken windows' effect: whenever anyone intended to be quiet, the others continued to speak for a moment, and the person who had actually wanted to stay quiet imagined that they could respond to what had just been said without any harm being done. When the mayor had finally yelled authoritatively into the microphone, after many minutes of trying to tame them, there was silence for a moment.

'We have gathered here today to discuss the festival taking place two weeks from now,' he said, thrown off by the silence. 'As you all know, after we had too few volunteers to organise this great and also difficult hour for our town, we issued a binding decree according to which every resident of Greater Einland must do their part. Not many have refused, but it's still a few too many. Failure to comply will now result in a penalty.' A murmur had already been simmering underneath the mayor's speech, which now sparked from one person to the next, like small spreading fires.

'So we ask,' continued the mayor, sweating profusely, 'that you don't hold it against us if you're assigned an unpleasant job or put to work clearing or brightening the place up. These are tasks that no one signed up for, and, in the name of community cleanliness, we must devote ourselves to them. Most urgently.' Whistling ensued — and at the same time a couple of people stood up and signed up on the lists provided.

'For example, there's still a strong so-called surplus in the area of …' but then it was over, and the first member of the public interrupted his speech.

'And what about the danger to our children? And to anyone who works?' someone shouted, and I had been compelled to stand up and see who had spoken, as remarks such as these had never been heard in this narcoleptic community until now. But whoever it had been — he had already fallen back into the collectively surging ocean of anger, from which it had started to froth.

'I don't know what you mean. We are acting to the best of our knowledge and belief. We aren't able, as some people believe, to do the filling first and then have the festival, because then all of our planning would be redundant,' the mayor said.

'The town looks like a pile of rubble. And what are you going to do if someone dies? What about Himmelgründen?'

A predictable question — yet the inevitable collapse of the mayor had begun. The accident on the Himmelgründen, south of the primary school, would have been almost comedic if it had not led to serious injuries for some of the children: a group of pupils, who were supposed to be practising a ribbon dance to a medley of works by Gustav Mahler in a daring array of styles, were rehearsing their repertoire there when the unexpected had happened. The girls had on gold tassel hats, which were tied with red ribbons to a May Pole. In the course of the performance, these were to become braided with the boys' white ribbons — in other words, all the children were more or less fixed to the pole and were animated to dance to the sounds of 'I Walked Across the Fields This Morning' when the stone material suddenly loosened, causing the concrete plinth to collapse.

The wooden post to which the child dancers were chained plummeted downwards into the ground. Within a second, the girls were launched into one another by the hats firmly attached to their scalps. The boys, instructed not to let the ribbons slip out of their hands, were caught in the middle of going through the motions of their shoe-slapping. Although the May Pole was sucked downwards and disappeared into a hole barely twenty-five centimetres wide, none of the children had suffered the same fate, because the gap was too small for a human body. It had only resulted in minor injuries and concussion, but the incident had, for the first time, caused severe irritation.

'That was down to bad planning and won't happen again,' the mayor said, and waved towards the first row, where Philipp had risen. 'Our structural engineer,' he said, but the people were shouting across one another like naughty schoolchildren. To my astonishment, even Sister Elfriede had got up, raised her hand at a right angle, and pointed at the stage.

'I am greatly worried about how the public will see our town if things don't change. What will people say about us if the journalists come and Greater Einland is hanging lopsided? We're actually a clean town, upright and beautiful, always have been. The fact that everything's crooked now doesn't suit us at all,' she repeated. Isolated clapping. Upright, I thought, looking around at the assembled community.

'You have to think of it as a habitus, a kind of brand. We're not, so to speak, hanging wonkily, it's going to be highly stylised when we're done. You will all understand that afterwards. Yes?' Like a high school teacher among chaos, the mayor pointed to someone right at the back with their hand up, as a reward for their civilised behaviour.

'I see it the same way,' said the man, whom I recognised by sight. 'Nobody should be able to judge us from the outside, no one can do that.' And then he added, as if it didn't contradict what had just been said: 'And if someone from outside does judge us, then it can only be the way we want it to be.' Hoots of agreement. Now even the less courageous among them felt compelled to shout things out. Although the mood was so turbulent that to an inexperienced observer it would have appeared as if it was threatening to deteriorate, I got up and left. I was dead tired and knew that nothing would really escalate here; knew that the Greater Einlanders turned away before the actual act, and everything fell in on itself like a pan of overboiling milk taken off the hob. The same thing happened a day later.

As much as it simmered below the surface, on the surface it was wonderfully languid and festive, where there was a mutual lulling effect. I, too, succumbed to this magic: what had seemed a sure sign of decay for all the previous months and years suddenly turned into historical scenery before my eyes as I walked through downtown.

The filling trucks were already parked next to the stadium. There were ten vehicles, each with a capacity of thirty-two thousand litres, and a compressor, along with a twelve-metre-long hose that could be connected to the hole at special docking points. In the middle of the football pitch, a gigantic area had been set up for the ceremonial speeches. A thick pipe was connected to the main chasm underneath the Market Square to attract the public — and, like tapping a beer keg, a kind of bolt would be driven in and turned to set the pumping in motion.

The presentation space of this folly was a one thousand and fifty square metre stage, which covered a good third of the playing field and was deliberately exactly a hundred square metres larger than the one at the Vienna Municipal Hall. A good dozen technicians had disappeared behind the pompous machinery and were in the process of setting it up.

Stocker, the head of the builder's yard, jumped out of a truck and came over to me. When I was standing opposite him, I saw that he looked at least as worn out as I felt myself, marked by the sleepless nights. Indeed, he needed a moment before he even realised who I was. 'Everything's ready, Ruth, we checked the docking points yesterday. The trucks deliver,' he said, pushing back his cap. The Countess had financed the vehicles personally, which was an absurd investment, especially since they would never be needed again. 'Are you going to go over later? To the mixing factory? It's meant to be an impressive sight, I've heard.' I shook my head. At that moment, the filling agent was being mixed together in ten converted barns throughout the whole of the town, ready to be collected by the trucks that night.

'Who can I give my speech for tomorrow?' I asked.

'Tomorrow,' he said and screwed up his eyes, as if he first had to force a double image to overlay itself. 'About tomorrow, yes, that's right. We'll do it in this order: First the mayor will speak, then the Countess, then me, then you. That means you're on at eight.'

'Eight,' I repeated nervously, handing him a piece of paper. 'Here's my speech.'

'Very nice,' he said, scanning the text I had no intention of reading aloud. 'A speech about Greater Einland and its nature, I like it. Certainly better than what I've come up with. We'll set up the microphone tomorrow morning, alright? Headset?' I nodded and patted him on the shoulder, before I climbed back up the stadium steps.

After I'd arrived home, I checked three times that the doors and windows were tightly shut, and went through all the rooms to make sure that no one had got in while I'd been away. Nothing conspicuous, of course — then I sat on the sofa and waited. She would call me at three, she said, but now the minutes were dragging on, and when the phone finally rang, it was as if it had happened out of nowhere.

'Hello,' I said. 'Thank you for calling.'

'Not at all, Ruth,' my aunt answered gently, as if not to spook a small animal. 'Thank you for your patience. Will we really be seeing each other in Vienna next week?'

I looked around one last time, fearing for a moment that someone might overhear my answer. 'Yes. Did you have a look?'

'I have,' she said, audibly relieved by my confirmation. 'Listen, Ruth, how should I put this? Your parents did actually bring all these loaned documents back to Vienna, and we found the folders in the jumble of what they left behind.'

'And? Where are they?' My aunt didn't say anything for a moment.

'It was a very long time ago, all of this. I had to look at the estate list first, and you may not know, but at the time there were some ambiguities regarding the inheritance. Especially since we couldn't find you. So much happens in six years.'

'Three,' I said. Silence on the other end.

'Six, Ruth. You've been gone for six years.'

'Nonsense,' I said exasperatedly, and began counting the years on my fingers, but nothing fitted together anymore, then my aunt was already speaking again, as if to resolve this conflict before it had even arisen.

'It's not important,' she said. 'In any case, we actually found the folders, even if we had to rummage through all the boxes at the storage depot.'

'So, can you send them to me?' I clung on tightly to the edge of the coffee table, still dizzy from the lithium.

'Ruth, that won't help you much. That is to say, they were empty. It was very strange.'

'What do you mean empty? What did they have empty folders for?'

'I don't know, Ruth. I don't even know what was in them originally, but it wasn't the original documents, and instead there were blank sheets of paper. I fear that your parents threw away the documents before they died.'

21

The town did not wake early that fifteenth of September. It didn't wake up at all, for it had never slept. By the time the brass band started marching at five in the morning to announce the start of the festivities, everyone was already awake: filter coffee accelerated the processes, which from above would have looked like a chaotic, fragmentary flickering — caffeine kept everything on track before cognition could keep up. Everyone was punctual, everyone outwardly full of enthusiasm, but that couldn't belie the real state of things.

The town had bags under its eyes and the inertia of the bleary-eyed, a delay in reactions that made one's walk drag. If one had looked down with a bird's perspective between the treetops, one would have seen the band's hats, the way they swayed restlessly on their heads, because everyone was impatiently stepping from one foot to the other. At seven o'clock, the town had double vision from exhaustion, as buses packed with tourists drove in on the freshly levelled roads from the north and the west. People were freed from the aluminium pods, and by eight o'clock, thousands had gathered on the specially excavated forecourt outside of the town walls. Diverted by small delicacies and much good will, they were kept under control by a troop of stewards. Meanwhile, in the town, hundreds of heads, filled with hundreds of tasks, were inside keen to tackle that very thing, and get a motor going that had been oiled for such a long time — and hundreds of watch faces, on hundreds of wrists, became illegible with nervousness. In the sky there was that strange hum, familiar from marathon events, as if there were a helicopter in the air that was nowhere to be seen. The conversations from a thousand mouths and the tension of zillions of tiny muscle fibres made everything oscillate. Then, on the stroke of nine, a shot was fired from a starting pistol, and everything erupted.

The four-hundred-strong marching choir, led by choirmaster Hausbrecht, climbed out of the forest, and the crowd, who didn't seem to have been expecting it, broke into loud cries of *oh* and *ah*. Now they marched from the Mühlgasse towards the town centre, dutifully drawing in the more than four thousand tourists behind the brass band. On the way through the rows of houses, sweets and little doughnuts wrapped in cellophane were thrown out of the upper floors by families. Everyone, including the children, had something to do.

Little by little, the human particles dispersed urgently into the town and fitted into every nook, every street, every recess, until everything was filled, just as the hole soon would be. The crowd split along the aisle of main attractions as if on hydrophobic surfaces. Blocks of hundreds washed up because the vortices pulled them in their direction: they streamed to the underground bumper cars, where they could collide with one another in complete darkness, while the muddy earth dripped on their heads. Or they ended up at the demolition station to the south, where you could hire a sledgehammer to smash a building destroyed in the subsidence with your own hands, and spend five minutes hammering the furniture, the windows, the splintering bricks.

In the north was what ultimately attracted most people in the sloshing human basin: a healing spring in a small St Mary's grotto, in which three priests blessed endless streams of tourists with the assistance of about twenty acolytes. The blessing time per person was around five seconds, and the people were led back out of the underground tube in a loop.

On the other hand, if you were to peer out of the lookout hole of the old fire station at midday, you could observe how individual families moved in this multi-layered social quake. Mothers wanted to go to the naming office: an institution where one could have small side branches of the tunnels named after oneself or one's family, in order to proudly carry home a certificate showing the fresh nomenclature of the tunnel. Fathers, who hitched their sons over their shoulders, strove to join the machinery display together with their appendages, where hoses, complete with masculine purr, were shown detonating into the ground at a pressure of fifty tonnes a second and two hundred and fifty-nine kilometres an hour. The children steered their parents to prospect for gold, where they feverishly looked forward to the exciting prospect of a tremendous find. Everyone bowed to the movements of others and held each other's hands, so as not to, as they say, *lose one another*.

But if you stood at eye height, or on a gallery raised about a metre off the ground, like I was at that very moment, you finally saw how the individual person fared in this swilling about. Let's say: a woman from the not too distant surrounding area, maybe fifty, who was sceptically swaying between the options, even though none of them really suited her; perhaps she was already exhausted by the far too dense impressions, just as I was, for that matter. For a moment she seemed to reject each of them, but then looked around and could only see people screeching enthusiastically. A jolt went through her body: she spun in circles for a moment, and the first thing her eyes found were the signposts pointing in the direction of the artisan village.

'Excuse me, can you make things there yourself?' she asked me, while I was waiting on the small platform from where I was to conduct the approaching parade. I had to briefly concentrate until my eyes had refocused on what was near to me.

'Yes, you can,' I answered. 'You have to sign up on site, thirty-minute waiting time.' I had been expecting all morning for the sheer mass of people to lead to the collapse of the long-overused ground. But nothing had happened.

Then the so-called 'small parade' was approaching: a procession of children's brass music, and supposed artists who were dressed up as folklore figures (Danube maidens, Rumpelstiltskin, a dragon). Some of them tried, as they had been instructed, to ride unicycles in their costumes, but kept falling off them and making others coming up behind them fall off, too. What's more, the children were playing badly. It was a miserable sight, out of which now suddenly fell Ferdinand, dripping with sweat and with his face painted white. In spite of his oxygen mask, which today he had tied to his back, he jumped up to me and threw his arms around my neck, and the curve of his belly almost knocked me off the platform.

'Ruth, isn't it all great? I've lived here my whole life, and I've never experienced anything so amazing,' he said, panting and looking at me with wide eyes, as if he had been holding off crying for a long time. I nodded and tried to encourage him with a movement of my head to get back in formation. I just wanted to wait for the parade and then, when I was allowed to take a lunchbreak, steal home unnoticed. But Ferdinand hung off me like an embedded thistle.

'I'm so looking forward to your speech this evening. Are you excited?'

'No, not at all,' I said, wiping his hands from my shoulders. I had a guilty conscience: it was childish, and I knew that I had to wrest myself from this feeling.

'We'll have a beer after, okay? And for the first time we won't have to be afraid that something will collapse while doing so, under our bellies,' Ferdinand said, laughing.

'Yeah, I'll see you later. I think I might still be nervous about the speech.' I really was an appalling liar, I thought to myself, and jumped from the platform to signal my departure.

'Ruth, wait!' I heard Ferdinand shouting after me, as I began to dig my way through the crowd, my face turned away and my hand raised for nothing more than an abandoned farewell.

I arrived home sweating from the exertion. The car, hidden from view in the backyard, now seemed to me to be a vehicle like the hot air balloons used to flee East Germany: an incredibly illegal mode of transport that no one was allowed to see. Only here and now the escape part wasn't the most problematic thing. I went through the house a final time, but I had long since said goodbye. All the melancholy, leaving the only place that had ever felt like home, lay far behind me.

The printouts for the journalists drilled painfully into the flesh underneath my ribcage, and at that moment, still in the doorway, my heart suddenly burst. The last Xanax, but it didn't soothe me, so two Valium, then I left the house, for the last time, locked the door, and threw the key through the letterbox. This was the final farewell.

I sat on the steps and took a deep breath. Up to this point everything had been so easy, and what was to come hardly seemed more complex: I would wait until the evening event began, and, shortly before, I'd go along the rows of journalists to give each of them a file. From these, as incomplete as the data was without my parents' books, they would learn about the facts that I had gathered: about the seven hundred and fifty vanished people and the ownership of the mine, about the thwarted searches and complicity of the town, of the nobility, the Countess and Glottersaat. When it was eight, I would take the stage, ask the journalists to look at the top page in their pack, and then begin to give my real speech. It seemed so simple.

I walked up the steep Johannesstrasse — the only direction from which no tourists came towards me — and now I actually hoped to be able to rest in nature for one or two hours; to disappear before my greatest task approached. Now it began to pursue me after all: I winced at the thought of how my acquaintances would look at me, surprised at first, then disgusted, then horrified as I ruined the celebration that everyone had been toiling over for years. The celebration that everyone viewed as a new beginning after half a decade marred by personal catastrophes, and, ultimately, the celebration that should have adjusted the image of the town to the public. As if something were gripping my neck with cold hands, I quickly shook myself, and finally dropped, exhausted, into a meadow at the topmost point of the hill. The sun on my face, the buzzing down in the valley felt like white noise. Insignificant — soporific, almost consoling.

I had just closed my eyes a few moments when someone sat down next to me. A nuisance — robbed of the last moment of happy loneliness I would have for an unforeseeably long time. I turned my head to the side and jumped in fright. It was the mask dealer, sitting in the meadow with knees raised and looking down at the town below.

'I was thinking of you today,' he said, and waited until I'd sat up before continuing. 'Do you remember how we met back then? In the Thousand-Year-Old Oak Tavern?'

'I remember,' I said heavily, sitting up. 'It has to be around here, but I never went back there again.'

'No, it's over a hundred kilometres away.'

'That can't be,' I said, and pulled a tuft of grass out of the ground. The damp, interwoven stems dangled before my eyes. 'My father always told me that when he was a child he spent the summers there, and that it was walking distance from his house.'

'You must have misunderstood,' the mask dealer said, leaning back. We were silent for a while, looking down at the town, which was covered by a multitude of whirring heads and scraps of colourful disguises that spread a pointillistic sea over the broken surface.

'I hear you're the saviour of the town,' the mask dealer said, pointing into the valley. 'Soon we'll be all in one piece again.'

'Yes, maybe. You know, sometimes I wonder whether I should have refused the Countess's offer of work.'

'What's that supposed to mean? You did a great job.'

'The good for the one side comes from the exploitation of the other,' I said, noting inwardly that it sounded like a cheap aphorism.

'Correct,' agreed the mask dealer. 'But tell me: you're a theoretical physicist, if I remember rightly. It must have taken some effort to develop a filling material.'

'Yeah, you know what,' I laughed, 'at first, I had no intention of taking this seriously. It was more of a fluke really.' I blushed, looking at the ground, and for a few minutes we listened to the brass band. 'I thought of our conversation often,' I said at some point. 'Do you remember telling me about your excursions in Arnhem Land? About the ancestors and their movements in the Dreaming? Sometimes I have the impression that in the last five years I haven't spoken to a single real person made of flesh and blood.'

I tore the greenery from the ground with a slow regularity and threw it, lost in thought, while I wondered what I was saying. 'But only with ancestors. Always with ancestors. And when I could not bear this losing myself in time, I had to think of you. Of your stories from Australia. Spiritual and physical world combining in an eternally created present, the Dreaming, to a place where we can come into contact with our forefathers, isn't that what you said?' Now that my departure was imminent, I was beset by sadness. I struggled to hold back the tears.

'All these years I had the feeling that the landscape wanted to convey something to me, this allegedly unconscious nature, that it could tell me about my own rootlessness. I wrestled with it — my God, that sounds crazy — and felt that this place was my fate. And then I just stayed here.' I took a deep breath. 'Isn't it ironic that I so quickly found a home right where it's threatening to sink into the ground?'

'The best place to put down roots is where much of what is in the soil is rotten,' the mask dealer said, and chuckled. The children screamed in enjoyment on the Kirtag machines that were closest to us, a sort of whisk to which they and their parents were strapped, and that now buffeted in a rapid circular motion.

'Or time, do you still remember what you said back then? That for Aboriginal Australians everything becomes a metaphor, and chronologies taper to a single point? I have long believed that I was acting as an individual in the present and that I could be completely independent of everyone else. But you're right: we can't take a single step without colliding with our past.'

The mask dealer burst out laughing. 'Did I tell you that? You caught me on an extremely wretched day. I don't know, I see it more as philosophical folklore that I tell to persuade people to buy my masks. Authenticity, that's the buzzword that interests customers. I'll let you in on something. I've never been to Arnhem Land. I have a mask shop in Mistelbach and make them myself there. But don't tell anyone.'

I dropped a buttercup stalk mid-throw, and now it dangled from my knee. 'The masks aren't real?' I whispered, pointing at the rucksack lying behind us in the meadow.

'What's real?' he said and laughed again, and now I saw that he wasn't in the least bit mythical or mysterious, just elderly and provincial. His face was bashful and pudgy, with crow's feet and a double chin in spite of his wiry stature: all over his face, I now saw in the glaring sunlight, was a layer of cheap make-up. I was overcome by an unfathomable dismay at how banal he and everything else around him suddenly seemed. I saw the wooden faces dangling in the wind — the African masks and the Black Forest carnival larvae — the artificially aged witch carvings that I had thought dated back a hundred years, while a fraudster had manufactured them in Mistelbach. Just in Mistelbach. This got me on my feet, as if I had finally seen through an optical illusion.

'Going already? Do you still have to prepare your speech for this evening?'

I ran down the hill without answering, re-joined the street and entered the Market Square, was carried by the euphoric crowd, who couldn't see why they were cheering, onto Margaretenstrasse, and stumbled around between the streams of people. I could hardly free myself from one group, a huge maelstrom-like delegation, and was dragged to the corner of the Church Square, where I backed into the May Pole. I pulled myself away from the crowd, using all my strength, and escaped to the Schulstrasse. My whole body shaking, I saw how people were breaking away from the fixation on the town centre and were being driven, as individual particles, in the direction of the sports field. This signified that the evening event would begin soon. I asked someone for the time: six-thirty. I felt the tablets were slowly starting to wear off in my warming bloodstream, and I reached in my trouser pocket — but I'd left my medication in my car.

Then I heard the mixer trucks rolling in in the distance, and ran off in the direction of the school as if they were chasing me, as if they wanted to fill me up instead of the hole. I caught my breath behind the school building, but then it gripped me anew: in front of me I saw the tunnel, sealed off with red and white tape, into which the little girl had fallen a year ago. She was never found — in a few hours her body would be enveloped by the filler. The thought caused me unspeakable claustrophobia, but in this confinement a decision finally grew. I pried away one of the slats, which had been spread over this duct like a pot lid, and looked down into the depths. Even after I'd wiped away my tears, I couldn't discern anything. I took the cloth bag that was hanging over my shoulder, and once more checked its contents: the original documents, the copies, my speech. Then I tossed it, and with it everything that had been my nightwork for the last three years, into the hole. The folders that I'd prepared for the public opened and their white contents disappeared into the darkness. All the folders that I'd filled with evidence of all the uncoiled corpse findings — that is, the last thing that could have made the uncoiling possible — was gone in a matter of seconds. I thought I heard a crash, and was shocked at myself for a moment, but this sensation disappeared as soon as it came. I felt freed from an oppressive nightmare and stood back up.

The people marching to the sports field no longer bothered me as I went back to the town centre. Someone shouted my name; I couldn't tell who, but managed to turn while walking and reply: 'Yeah, I'll be right there, let the others know I have to get changed quickly.' I pierced the cushions of noise from the various instrumental groups, and before they could stop me, I was already home and had jumped into my car. I started the engine and rolled along the streets in first gear, just as I'd learned off by heart: Johannesstrasse — Auf der Haiden — Gmeingrubenweg — Schlossstrasse. The impassability of the terrain knocked off my bumper as I turned onto the first forest road, just like years ago when I arrived. And like then, I still managed to make the crossover back to the forest road and drive infinitely slowly back up it.

'[…] past times are just as real as the present time. Thus they believe that just as you are sitting in the present reading this paper, so — for example — Nero is sitting in the past watching a gladiator bout. And just as you think to yourself, "I am sitting here at the present time", so Nero thinks to himself, "I am sitting here at the present time."'

(Trenton Merricks, *Oxford Studies in Metaphysics*, vol. 2)

The illusion of the present disguises the fact that every person just swims at any arbitrary point in the landscape of all possibilities and, in his egocentrism, imagines himself at the Archimedean point. You think you have a view on things from your own plateau, while it's your position on the plateau that prevents you from having an overview. And yet it is inevitable to look into the landscape — together with everyone who comes after you and was before you — together with everyone who is this landscape.

Only now, desperate on the steep slope, did I reflect on the fact that I was actually about to leave Greater Einland. Yes, this was also an act of resistance, I thought, that right now, down below, Philipp would be announcing me, and that I wouldn't emerge from the audience to take account of his announcement. The soil seemed to want to counteract my plans one last time and, covered by the early autumn leaves, spilled towards me. From down in the valley, the commissioned composition was already beginning to reach me. This meant that my disappearance had been noticed and things had carried on — it amused me to imagine the Countess wondering why I wasn't there, and especially how she would later realise that I would never return. Silence, the refusal to speak, I thought again, taking the first switchback, was the highest and most far-reaching act of rebellion. I would simply withdraw from Greater Einland, turn my back on my so-called home, and then nothing would remain of me — that is, except the tonnes of filler that were currently being pumped into the ground. If one didn't approve of the actions of a group, then one simply had to find a new group in order to eliminate this problem — yes: problems didn't demand a solution, but a complete volitisation, an obliteration.

The sun had gone down by the time I reached the top of the hill, and the liquid land suddenly became firmer. *The filler*, I thought in awe, and even though it was not at all possible, I thought I felt a solidification. I imagined that in this moment, the forest so intimately familiar to me had been killed through a weakening of its nerve function, without anyone noticing. The network of roots would be gripped by this substance, right now, as I drove the final few metres of this slope, over which I had crashed into the valley basin three years previously. I felt against my tyres, as if they were my own skin, that granular solids were already floating in the dank, liquid surface of the moss floor. The crawling motion of my car gripped better and better as the atoms seemed to unite, and the crust of the world, which had been drifting since the Hadean, hardened.

The wave motion of the Alps smoothed out, my engine did its job and propelled me onwards without any impediment. Everything that had swirled in the ground, this never-ending process of creation and decay, was stopped in a single blow. I had almost penetrated the protected area of forest, left the castle far behind me, and had to already be near a country road. The hardening filler gripped the grasses, the microorganisms, the delicate and the coarse joints of the world from below, and screwed them tightly into an eternal present, a display case in which Greater Einland and all its inhabitants would be banished forevermore. I thought that if I looked back, everything would be killed and the grass would be nothing more than a tangle of yellow lines, weathered threads.

But as I drove over the last ridge that had kept me from the concrete road, I turned around and saw: nothing. The festival was a long way off in the distance — too far to be able to still hear the Kirtag music floating on the layers of air. The treetops in the evening light looked as if they had been painted on canvas, right at that moment, as I climbed out of the car. I searched for a reason to look back and to look further again, to turn one last time in the direction of the town that had given me a home, but there wasn't one. The landscape had become like any other; there was nothing to find in it other than another postcard design. On top of that, my tremors had stopped: I felt, for the first time in years, complete clarity. I climbed back into my car, which was less damaged than I had feared, and, still wary, shifted into third gear. You'd have thought I was driving down a highway for the first time in my life. Turning on the radio was so unfamiliar to me — I did so clumsily like a child — and as soon as I had finally done it, amazed that it still worked, a gravelly voiced Schlager musician blared unbearably from the speakers.

I sing a song for you, and then you ask me, will you go dancing with me, I think I like you — I turned it off again on the spot. I took the road where I had it left years ago, and an irrepressible desire for the city overwhelmed me. I would, that same evening, I thought, sit on the Danube Canal, on this dead straight concrete border of the river, and people from all nations would walk past me with loudspeakers and cans of beer in their hands. Greater Einland would be nothing more than a strange dream, if I seized the thread where I had lost it.

While I gently accelerated my car to a hundred km/h, I sensed the immovable asphalt. The earth on which I was moving was no longer a barrier to my progress. Everything proffered stability.

As if to make sure that no one was approaching from behind, I looked one last time in my rear-view mirror: nothing fluctuated, everything in its place, and me finally in mine. The forest, behind which I had lived for so long, parted either side, thinned out, and made way for a large, clearly cultivated area of arable land, behind which I could see Vienna.

Nothing that would remain unclear.